Memphis Blues

CHERYL MATTOX BERRY

Memphis Blues
© 2017 Cheryl Mattox Berry
LaBelle Publishing

ISBN: 978–0–692–88245–0

First LaBelle Publishing trade printing

Manufactured and Printed in the United States of America

For James, Josephine, and Lucile
(The Winds Beneath My Wings)

Chapter One

$\sim$

Memphis, Tennessee, 1967

The green shotgun house that stood at the edge of the sidewalk on Alma Street was quiet for a change. No crying babies. No loud, scratchy-sounding radio. No arguments. Just the whirring of the window fan, stirring up hot air. Carrie checked on her twin infants, Vicki and Victor, to make sure neither had awakened while she was on the back porch hunched over the big tin tub scrubbing diapers.

A few feet away, Nee Mama lay on her back in the middle of the big bed snoring like one of the drunk, nasty bums in downtown Court Square. Her crusty feet were tangled in a pile of clean clothes at the foot of the bed.

Carrie shook her head. How was she supposed to get in the bed when her grandmother was spread-eagle in the middle? She walked through the cluttered living room and out onto the front porch where she plopped down in the rusted, green and white glider.

She stared at the overgrown, empty lot across the street. A family of lightning bugs danced above the weeds and the carcasses of dead cats and dogs. The air smelled of burning wood. When the teenage boys down the street played cards on the front porch, they always lit a smoke pot to drive away the mosquitoes. Carrie had no smoke pot. She swatted mosquitoes and fanned herself with a piece of folded newspaper.

The swing squeaked as she moved back and forth in slow motion. She hadn't slept more than three hours at a time since the babies came two months ago. Everything was jumbled up in her head. What day was it? What time was it?

Carrie felt like she was losing her mind, and she looked like a woman on the verge of a nervous breakdown. The golden sunflowers on her soiled housecoat had long faded to the color of weak vinegar. She was musty as a goat but too tired to wash herself. Besides, there was nothing to wear because she had gained thirty pounds since she had the twins. Even her shoes were too tight. Her jet-black hair was nappy around the edges and braided into a long, fat plait that hung down her back. It had been a long time since a straightening comb passed through her hair.

Her looks didn't matter. She stopped rocking, hoping that the Almighty would give her a sign that things would get better. They certainly couldn't get worse. Here she sat, nineteen years old, with twins, down to her last few dollars, living in a shotgun house with a sickly, drunken grandmother.

Carrie rubbed her forehead, disgusted with herself for getting in this predicament. She had big plans when she left the country and came to Memphis. She was going to finish high school and then go to nursing school or beauty culture school. She got her diploma and took a job cleaning office buildings to earn money for tuition. Then, things fell apart.

She wrapped her arms around herself and rocked in despair. Carrie had broken a promise to Mama and couldn't bear the thought of seeing the look of disappointment on her face. She begged Nee Mama not to write home about the babies because she wanted to tell Mama when she got up the nerve. The little speech Mama gave the night before Carrie left home echoed in her head.

Ruth called fifteen-year-old Carrie into the kitchen and told her it was time they had the talk. Carrie's baby sister, Cleotha, followed her, but Ruth sent Cleotha back into the living room to watch TV.

"What is it, Mama?"

"Sit down, I need to tell you something." Ruth looked like somebody had died.

"What's wrong?"

"Carrie, I know you don't want to leave, but there's no future for you here. Look at your older brother, in and out of jail every time you look around. And your sister, the only thing she after is a good time. She so drunk off of that grain alcohol that half the time she don't know her name. You're a smart, pretty girl, and if I don't get you way from here, some nigga be done filled your head with all kind of foolishness so he can get 'tween your legs. The next thing you know, you got a house full of babies, and that nigga ain't no where in sight."

"Mama, that ain't gonna happen to me."

"Just look at me. I'm a living witness. I got four of y'all, and I wouldn't give you back for nothing in the world, but it sho ain't been easy. When I was coming along didn't nobody tell me to get my education. I started out good, but when Nee Mama needed help washing, I had to put down the books. Next thing I knew I was grown and on my own, trying to figure out how I was gonna eat. And once I started having babies, I had to keep doing what I was doing to feed y'all. It was too late to change. What happened to me don't have to happen to you."

"Mama, what things was you doing?"

"Ain't no need to go into all that. What's done is ancient history. Even if you get yourself in a family way, there's a way to fix it. I didn't learn nothing 'bout this 'til after I had my last one." She pulled a piece of tin foil from the pocket of her dress, opened it slowly, and showed Carrie a beige powder. "Mix a tablespoon of this in some hot water, like a tea. Drink it straight, no sugar, *hot as you can stand it before you go to bed. I guarantee your period will come down before morning. Now promise me you'll use this if it come to that."*

"I ain't thinking 'bout no boys, Mama."

"You saying that now, but you just wait. One will come along you like. Do as I say and take this."

"Okay, but I won't need it," Carrie said, staring at the crinkled foil.

"I pray you right. Just keep in mind that babies is fine if you ready for them. Once they get here, you can't send them back. Remember that."

By the time Cyrus came along, Carrie had forgotten Ruth's advice and had lost the little packet. She was so smitten by the tall, light-skin doctor with wavy black hair, a thin mustache, and pretty white teeth that she didn't think about protecting herself.

Cyrus, who was an obstetrician/gynecologist, offered to give Carrie an abortion when she told him she was pregnant, but that was out of the question. Ruth always told her babies were a gift from God, and she truly believed that.

Now, Carrie wasn't so sure. She wished that she could start all over, go back to being that big-boned, pretty country girl with the golden brown skin. The one that all the boys liked. Right now, she didn't like herself very much.

A car pulled up a few houses down the street. She sat up to see who was visiting at this hour. She recognized the turquoise Thunderbird.

"Humph," she uttered.

Cyrus hopped out of the car and walked quickly, head down, occasionally glancing right and left, and over his shoulder.

Carrie's breathing quickened as he approached. He stopped on the sidewalk, a few feet away from her, and removed his hat. For a few seconds, they locked eyes, neither spoke. She was so overcome with emotion that she couldn't speak the angry words that were on the tip of her tongue.

"Hi, Carrie," he said hesitating. "How've you been?" He ran his finger around the brim of his hat.

"Wh...where you been, Cyrus? I ain't seen you in three weeks," she said, her voice quivering. "You ain't called or nothing. I thought you forgot about us."

"No, no," he said, shaking his head. "I've been busy. Seems like everybody's having babies all at once. How're the babies?"

"You mean *your* babies? They doing just fine," she replied, trying to keep from breaking down in front of him. She didn't want to come across as a desperate woman though she wanted Cyrus to take her in his arms and tell her everything was going to be okay. She straightened up, tucked the housecoat under her thighs, and crossed her legs at the ankles the way Miz Salisbury taught her in charm school at the YWCA.

He smiled nervously. "You take them for their first checkup?"

"Who else is going to take them?" she snapped. "I'm the only one here doing for them."

"Carrie, under the circumstances there's not a lot more that I can do," he said. "I can't come to Klondike every day. Somebody might see me and—"

Before he could finish, Carrie interrupted him. "That ain't what you told me before these babies come. You said, 'Carrie, I'll be there for you. I'll take care of everything.' But you ain't been nowhere in sight, just like Mama said."

"What did your mother say about me? Is she up here?" he asked, looking at the front door, like he expected Ruth to appear. "I hope she's not going around telling people I'm the daddy."

"Is that all you worried about, somebody saying something about you? I wonder what your precious wife would say if she knew you had two more babies."

Cyrus took out a handkerchief and wiped his face. "Are you threatening to tell my wife? What exactly would that accomplish?"

"If I was her, I'd want to know what my husband was doing behind my back," Carrie said. "You done played both of us for a fool."

"Carrie, that's not true. I really care about you. I can see how you might be a little upset, but I know you don't mean all these things you're saying right now."

"Damn right I'm upset," she said, raising her voice. "While y'all going to your fancy parties and dinners, I'm stuck in this house with two babies and can't work or do nothing."

Cyrus jerked his head from left to right, looking for nosy neighbors who might have heard Carrie yelling. He motioned with his hands for Carrie to lower her voice. "Can't your grandmother keep the babies while you work?"

"How, Cyrus?" she said. "Nee Mama either drunk or complaining about something hurting her. You know she sick in the head, be talking crazy half the time."

"Carrie, I'm sorry. I can give you some extra money, and maybe you can find somebody to babysit."

"Is that all you're planning to do? If so, just go back to your life and forget we exist," Carrie said.

He raised his hands in frustration. "What do you want me to say? I'm doing the best I can. I have a family and a medical practice." Cyrus shifted his weight, loosened his tie, and unbuttoned his collar.

"Have you thought about going back home?"

"No," she shot back.

"That might be the best thing. At least you'll have help with the babies."

"That was supposed to be *your* job," she said.

He looked exasperated. "Carrie, I can't be here playing house with you. I told you two babies would be a lot of work, but you said you could handle it. I figured you would have everything under control by now."

Carrie felt like whipping her own butt for being so stupid. She had been living in a dream world, thinking they would be one, big happy family.

"Go on 'bout your business, Cyrus. Me and the babies will be just fine."

Cyrus sighed. "Well, let me know if you decide to go home. I want your address so I can send you some money. I've got to run. I have an early day tomorrow." Cyrus reached out to touch Carrie's shoulder, but she drew back.

"You ain't even gonna look at them?"

"I was about to ask if it was okay."

"Yeah, you can go in. Nee Mama won't wake up."

Carrie watched Cyrus as he walked up the three front steps. The screen door creaked when he opened it. She fought the urge to follow him so that she could see his expression when he laid eyes on their babies.

Slowly, she pushed herself in the glider, praying that he would come out of the house with a solution that would solve all her problems. After about five minutes, the door opened and Cyrus walked onto the front porch. Carrie stopped the glider. Through fluttering lashes, she looked at him like a lost, frightened child.

"Uh, they're getting bigger," he said, smiling like a proud father.

Carrie chewed on her lower lip.

Cyrus stared at her, but she had nothing else to say. "I better be going," he said, reaching for his wallet. "Here's a little something to help out." He handed her fifty dollars.

She took the money and put it in her bosom. Carrie was mad at Cyrus, but she wasn't a fool. That money would come in handy.

"Let me know what you decide," he said, trying to make eye contact. Carrie didn't look his way. "Good night, Carrie. Take care of yourself."

As he turned, she muttered, "Lying bastard."

"You say something?"

Carrie glared at him.

He looked at her, started to speak but changed his mind. He descended the steps and walked hurriedly to his car. Carrie's tears came before Cyrus turned on the ignition. She sobbed until nothing was left. Then, she curled up in the glider with sheets of newspaper spread over her body to keep from getting eaten by the mosquitoes. Carrie stayed that way until one of the babies started crying. She wiped her face with the tail of her housecoat and got up to see which twin was hungry. At least now she had money to buy them some milk.

Chapter Two

~

Nadine stood on her tiptoes, pushed aside the heavy blankets, and felt around the top shelf of the hall closet. She found the crumpled brown paper bag against the wall and carefully dragged it toward her.

She stuck the bag inside her bathrobe, went into the bedroom, and locked the door. Nadine sat on the edge of the bed with the sack in her lap, pondering what she was about to do.

At the moment, she couldn't think of any other option. She was tired of being abused, called bad names, and worked like a slave. Cyrus and his mama, Miz Esther, had made her life miserable since she moved into their house on her wedding day – fifteen years ago. She was barely eighteen.

Her father and Miz Esther made her marry Cyrus when she got pregnant. She would never forget how he got her drunk and forced himself on her. After they got married, Cyrus insisted that she stay with Miz Esther while he was away at Meharry Medical College in Nashville.

Miz Esther's two-story, white frame house with windows flanked by black shutters stood on Edith Avenue, one of the prettiest streets in South Memphis. Mighty oaks lined the median, and crepe myrtle trees hugged houses and shaded patios, providing a brilliant burst of color in the summer and fall.

As a child, Nadine dreamed of living in a big house like Miz Esther's one day, but it turned out to be smaller than it looked from the outside.

She and the girls were cooped up in two bedrooms and a bathroom upstairs. She felt like a prisoner instead of a princess in Miz Esther's house.

Nadine grew angry as she remembered how long the Mitchells had mistreated her. Last night, she saw a sadistic side of Cyrus that made her feel subhuman. He came home drunk, demanding sex in the middle of the night. When Nadine rebuffed him, he forced her onto her stomach, hiked up her butt, and wedged himself between her legs.

"No, Cyrus," she pleaded. "Don't stick it in my butt."

"Hold still. It won't hurt if you relax," he growled.

"Stop! It hurts!" she whimpered, trying to throw him off.

Cyrus ignored her pleas and kept trying to push himself inside Nadine. He eventually gave up and took her the normal way. After Cyrus finished, he stood over Nadine and berated her.

"You're a piss poor partner in bed," he said. "After all these years, you still don't know how to please me. I get more satisfaction from a hand job."

She lay awake in pain for the rest of the night, feeling like a rape victim held captive by her rapist. By daylight, she had figured out a way to end Cyrus's cruelty and her misery.

Nadine put the incident out of her mind and brushed off the dust that had settled on top of the bag. As she removed two rubber bands, one snapped, startling her. She steadied herself, slowly opened the bag, and removed an orange shammy towel.

When Nadine unwrapped it, she smiled as if she were seeing an old friend. Her daddy's revolver. The smooth, wooden grip fit comfortably in her hand. When she was in high school, her daddy let her shoot at cans when they went to the country.

Nadine inspected the gun like her daddy had taught her. It was fully loaded and ready to be fired. But could she pull the trigger?

She walked over to the chest of drawers and placed the gun on top of the blue lacquered jewelry box that Cyrus brought her from a trip to San

Francisco. She walked in circles around the room, hands clasped under her chin in the praying position.

"I'm tired of living like this," she mumbled. "One of us is leaving this Earth tonight."

Nadine looked at the clock on the nightstand. It was close to midnight. She had no clue when Cyrus would be home. Occasionally, he called to say he would be late, but most of the time he didn't bother. He would be surprised to find Nadine awake because she never waited up for him.

She picked up the revolver and sat in a chair next to the window. The gun rested on her lap. Nadine could see half a block from this vantage point and would know when Cyrus pulled up to the house.

An hour passed, and Cyrus was still not home. Nadine went to the bathroom and washed her face with cold water, hoping it would keep her awake. She took up her post again. This time, she dozed off.

"Mama! Mama!"

Nadine jumped and the gun fell to the floor. She shoved it under the mattress and ran down the hall to her daughters' bedroom. Seven-year-old Salena was wide-eyed, sitting straight up in bed.

"What is it, sweetie?" Nadine asked.

Salena clutched her mother and said, "Vampires were after me."

"I didn't see anybody when I came in here. That was just a bad dream." She playfully pulled Salena's pug nose. "You need to stop watching those scary movies."

"What's wrong?" asked Jocelyn from her bed across the room.

"Salena had a nightmare," Nadine replied. "Go back to sleep."

"She's such a baby," said Jocelyn, who at fourteen was annoyed with her little sister and everyone else. She placed the spread over her head and turned to face the wall.

"Mama, will you stay with me, please?" Salena begged.

"Sure," she said, pecking her on the forehead. "Now, lie down and close your eyes. I'll be here all night if you need me."

Nadine lay on top of the spread and stroked Salena's frizzy hair. She welcomed these tender moments with Salena. She was Nadine's surprise baby but gave her the greatest joy because she looked more like Nadine than Jocelyn, who was the spitting image of Cyrus.

Salena's skin color was the perfect blend of Nadine's mocha and Cyrus's Creole yellow. Short for her age, Nadine guessed that Salena would be petite and shapely, too. Her exotic looks would someday have men trailing behind her.

As Salena drifted off, Nadine grew despondent. She wanted to be free of Cyrus but didn't want to ruin her daughters' lives. Nor did she want them to feel the loneliness she felt growing up without a mother, who passed away when Nadine was five. Salena's nightmare was over, but Nadine's would continue until she found a better solution.

Chapter Three

~

Cyrus didn't feel like going home to a dark house. He made a right turn on Jackson Avenue and headed downtown to Sonny's Bar and Grill on Beale Street. Arguing with Carrie had gotten him all worked up. A stiff drink, some blues, and talking trash with Sonny would help him unwind.

As Cyrus cruised through North Memphis, he thought about the twins lying toe-to-toe in their crib. They resembled Jocelyn when she was their age - fair-skin with rosy cheeks and fine light brown hair.

He envisioned a bright future for them. Victor, of course, would be a doctor and ladies' man. Vicki would be a stunning woman with her choice of suitors. He would always provide for them but couldn't be part of their lives right now.

Cyrus didn't understand why Carrie didn't see that he had a lot on his plate. He resented her for pressuring him to spend more time with them. "Damn it," Cyrus said, striking the dashboard. "I knew this would happen when those babies came."

He promised himself that what happened with Carrie would be the last time his johnson got him in trouble. From this point on, he would tell his lady friends up front that he didn't want any more kids and would never marry them.

Cyrus caught a yellow light at Danny Thomas Boulevard and made a sharp left turn. A few seconds later, the inside of his car was flooded with red, white, and blue lights. He glanced in the rearview mirror and saw a police car behind him. Cyrus steered his car into the right lane to let the cruiser pass, but it continued following him.

He pulled over to the curb, rolled down the window, and sat with both hands on the steering wheel, waiting for the officers. One of the cops walked to the driver's side. He banged on the top of Cyrus's car with his flashlight. Cyrus gritted his teeth, knowing the heavy object would leave a dent. The other officer walked around to the passenger's side.

The first cop shined the flashlight in Cyrus's face, and yelled, "Nigger, didn't you see my lights flashing?"

"Yes, officer, but I—"

"But nothing. Get out of the car," he ordered.

When Cyrus didn't move fast enough, the officer yanked him out by his lapels. "Officer, I'm Dr. Cyrus Mitchell. I'm on my way home from work," he said.

"I don't care who you are," said the policeman, slamming Cyrus across the hood. "You ran the red light and didn't stop when you saw my lights flashing." He jabbed Cyrus in the side with his nightstick. The pain brought tears to Cyrus's eyes. "Show me some identification. If you ain't got none, your monkey ass is going to jail."

"My ID is in my wallet, which is in my back pocket."

"Get it," he demanded. The officer turned to his partner while Cyrus fumbled in his wallet. "These niggers make me sick. They get a little education and think they better than us. Look at this car. He ain't got no fucking business with a nice car like this, and I'm riding to work every day in a piece of shit."

"Officer, here's my identification," Cyrus said, handing over his driver's license and hospital ID.

The policeman snatched it and put it under the flashlight. "Well, I guess you really are a doctor, but you're still getting a ticket for running the red light," he said. "Let this be a lesson to you. The next time you see the lights on a police car flashing behind your black ass, pull over."

"I will."

After Cyrus signed the ticket, the policeman threw it in his face. The cops sped away, leaving Cyrus on the side of the road clutching his side. He sat in his car for a few minutes trying to process what had just happened.

Cyrus knew other colored men who had been roughed up by the police, but this was the first time it had ever happened to him. He seethed as he thought about how they treated him like a common criminal.

He was in no mood for Sonny's. He turned around and drove home. Cyrus stayed below the speed limit during the thirty-minute ride, checking his mirror for cops every few minutes. The pain in his side was excruciating.

Inside his house, Cyrus felt safe again. He removed his hat and jacket, placing them neatly on the back of a beige French provincial chair in the living room. He tiptoed past Miz Esther's bedroom to the kitchen, where he filled an ice bag. After he poured himself a brandy in the den, he went back to the living room.

Cyrus sat on the gold French provincial sofa and placed the ice bag on his ribs. The cops humiliated him, but they would never break his spirit. He was the white man's worst enemy - an educated Negro. Cyrus raised his glass toward the framed college degrees on the wall and sipped his brandy.

***

"Cyrus, Cyrus, wake up!" Miz Esther shouted, shaking him.

"What? What is it, Mama?" said Cyrus with half-shut eyes.

"This chair is not for sleeping. You're thirty-seven years old. You should know that by now," she said, hands on her hips. "You're going to mess up the furniture. And why is this ice bag in here?"

Before he could answer, she spotted the glass on an end table. "Oh, my God!" she shrieked. "You put a glass on my table and didn't use a coaster. Boy, have you lost your mind?"

Cyrus sat up and stretched until the pain in his side reminded him that his ribs took a blow last night. "Forgive me, Madame Esther. I didn't mean to disrespect your precious furniture," Cyrus said in a French accent. "Are you going to send me to the principal's office for being a bad boy?"

Miz Esther inspected the table, ignoring his dig at the punishment she handed out for disruptive students in her English class.

"What time is it?" Cyrus asked.

"Almost six-thirty. What time did you get in last night?" Miz Esther asked, looking down at him. "I hope you didn't forget that Lillian is cooking dinner today."

"No, I didn't forget." When he stood and stretched, he grabbed his side.

Miz Esther caught his pained expression. "What's wrong with you?"

He started to lie because he was embarrassed by the incident but decided to tell the truth. "I got a love lick from a cop last night."

Miz Esther stopped straightening up the room and turned to Cyrus. "What do you mean?"

"The cops stopped me, claiming I was speeding, but I wasn't," Cyrus said as he eased into a chair. "And one of them poked me with his stick."

"Lord Jesus, are you all right?" Miz Esther said as she rushed over to him and raised his shirt. She winced when she saw the bluish bruise. "Son, you better go see a doctor."

Cyrus pressed the area with his fingers. "It looks bad but doesn't feel

20

like anything is broken. It's just really sore."

Miz Esther was outraged. "Didn't you tell them you were a doctor?"

Cyrus gave her a sideways glance. "Mama, they don't care about that," he said, yanking down his shirt. "All they see is a colored man. I'm never going to get any respect down here. That's why I want to leave this god-forsaken town."

"Don't start that foolish talk again," Miz Esther said, waving him off. "It's too early in the morning." She walked over to the window and opened the drapes.

"You know I'm telling the truth," Cyrus retorted. "The white doctors down here act like they don't want to work with colored doctors. Opportunities are much better for me up North. Everything is – the schools, stores, housing, you name it."

Miz Esther turned to Cyrus. "I know you're upset, but I don't think moving is the answer. Colored people got problems everywhere. Things are changing. Just be patient." She patted him on the cheek.

Cyrus threw up his hands. "Life is too short to be waiting around for something that might happen. The sooner I leave the better."

"I need to get breakfast started so we won't be late for Sunday school," Miz Esther said. "Are you going to eat with us or lie down for a while?"

Cyrus ran his hand through his hair. After a few seconds, he said, "I'll eat breakfast if you make some biscuits."

He couldn't stay angry with Miz Esther very long. He also hated when she was upset or disappointed in him, which is why he hadn't told her about the twins.

While Miz Esther was plumping the pillows, Cyrus slipped behind her and gave her a bear hug. There was nothing she could do but enjoy the moment because Cyrus's six-foot frame swallowed her five-foot-two-inch body. He was the male version of Miz Esther from her complexion to her haughty attitude.

"Go ahead and bathe before everybody starts stirring," Miz Esther said on her way to the kitchen with the empty glass.

"I'm going to eat a hole in that pan so you better make a lot of biscuits," he said.

Cyrus slowly climbed the stairs. When he reached the second floor, he peeped inside the girls' room, where he found Nadine in bed with Salena. He woke her. "What are you doing in here?"

"Salena had a nightmare," Nadine said. She slipped out of bed and followed Cyrus to their bedroom.

"How is she going to learn how to sleep by herself if you're always jumping in bed with her?" he fussed.

Nadine picked up the brown paper bag on the floor and tossed it in the trash can. "I don't do it every night."

"You shouldn't do it at all," Cyrus said. He removed his shirt but kept on his undershirt so that Nadine wouldn't see the bruise. "Did you drop off that envelope at Judge Jacobs's house like I told you?"

"Uh-huh," she said. She eyeballed the mattress to make sure the gun wasn't sticking out.

"Who did you give it to?"

"Mrs. Jacobs, like you told me."

"Did she say anything?"

Nadine shook her head. "What was in the envelope?"

"Nothing that concerns you."

Cyrus sat in the chair and removed his shoes and socks. "We should head over to Aunt Lillian's house around two-thirty. I asked her to make me a peach cobbler. Make sure you don't forget to bring it home."

After last night's plan went awry, Nadine was emotionally spent and didn't feel like socializing with Cyrus's family, though she genuinely liked Aunt Lillian, who was Miz Esther's older sister. She needed time alone to figure things out. "I'm not feeling well," Nadine said softly. "I'd like to stay home today."

Cyrus stared her up and down. "You don't look sick to me."

"But I am," Nadine said in a weak voice. "I need some rest."

"You'll be fine," he said. "Aunt Lillian has been up since daybreak cooking. All of us are going."

"Cyrus, please," she begged. "Let me stay home just this one time."

He got in Nadine's face. "Why do you always have to ruin things? You know how much these Sunday dinners mean to Mama and Aunt Lillian. I'm not going to let you spoil it. Go take an aspirin or Pepto-Bismol," he said, walking out of the room.

Furious, Nadine sat on the bed. "Ouch," she cried, touching her mouth. She had accidentally bitten her tongue when she clenched her jaw. The metallic taste of blood filled her mouth. She embraced the pain. It made her temporarily forget how much she loathed Cyrus.

While she was deep in thought, she felt a tiny arm around her neck. She looked over to find Salena sitting on the bed. "Did you stay with me all night?" she asked, jumping into Nadine's lap.

"Yes, ma'am," she said, hugging Salena. "Just like I promised."

Chapter Four

~

The Greyhound bus was only half full headed down to Hattiesburg, Mississippi. Carrie decided to travel on a Wednesday to avoid the weekend crowds. There was plenty of room to spread out. She lay Vicki on the seat next to her and held Victor. Carrie hoped the seat across from her would stay empty so that she could spread out her stuff, but a stout, dark-skin woman wearing a wide straw hat took the seat.

As the bus left the station, Carrie grew sad. She thought about her trip to Memphis and how excited she had been to come to the big city four years ago. So many dreams, and now nothing but heartache.

Victor, who had been wide-eyed and smiling all morning, started whining. "Don't cry, lil' man. We'll be all right," Carrie said right before her own tears flowed. She grabbed Vicki and held the babies tightly.

"Baby, you all right?" asked the plump woman.

Carrie glanced in her direction but quickly turned away from the woman, who had a shiny, gold front tooth. "Yes, ma'am, I'm fine," she said embarrassed.

The woman smiled. "Those some fat, pretty babies."

"Thank you," Carrie said, searching her pocketbook for a tissue.

The woman scooted closer to the aisle. "How old?"

Carrie held them forward so she could get a good look. "Nine weeks."

"They look like little dolls," she said, making a funny face at them.

"What names you give them?"

"Vicki and Victor."

"They're gonna break some hearts when they grow up. I'm telling you the truth." She let out a hearty laugh that carried throughout the bus.

Carrie laughed, too, though she didn't know why because what the woman said wasn't that funny. It was the first time she had laughed in weeks, and it felt good. Victor started fussing again. Carrie put Vicki on the seat and placed Victor in her right arm. Seconds later, Vicki began screaming.

"Let me have her," the woman said. "I've taken care of many a child in my day for colored and white people. Babies just love me. Come here, sugar. I ain't got no tittie for you, but I can rock you to sleep," she said, reaching for Vicki.

Before Carrie could decline the offer, the woman picked up Vicki and held the baby to her bosom, which Carrie guessed was about a size forty-eight, triple D. "You got any milk? I think she hungry."

Carrie reached for a bottle in the brown grocery bag she had filled with fried chicken, light bread, and potato chips.

Vicki gobbled up the milk and fell asleep. The woman held her close while she slept.

"By the way, my name is Ida Mae Higgins."

"Nice to meet you, Miz Ida Mae. I'm Carrie Boyd. Thanks for helping out."

As the babies slept, Carrie and Miz Ida Mae got acquainted. She told Carrie that she was the live-in help for a white lady in Memphis five days a week and stayed with a friend on weekends. She and her husband, who died five years ago, had a son, who lived in Jackson, Mississippi. Miz Ida Mae was headed home to visit her younger sister.

"How long you staying in Hattiesburg?" Miz Ida Mae asked.

"I don't know," Carrie said, looking forlorn as she pressed her face against the window.

Miz Ida Mae stretched out her stubby legs on the seat and placed Vicki across her lap. "You raising these babies by yourself?"

"I ain't got no choice."

"What about their daddy?"

"We ain't together no more," she said. "He don't even know I'm gone."

"Raising younguns is hard, but you got your family to help out," she said.

Carrie hoped her mother would be as easy to talk to as Miz Ida Mae. She didn't know what to expect from Ruth. Coming home with two children and no husband would anger her for sure.

She tried not to dwell on that during the six-hour ride home. When the bus finally arrived in Hattiesburg, both women ran to the restroom. The stench overpowered them when they opened the door. They relieved themselves and changed the babies' diapers.

"I'm glad this is the last stinky restroom we have to pee in," Miz Ida Mae said. "It's a shame we got to do our business in a nasty place like this, and white folks got clean, good-smelling restrooms." She took Vicki and waddled outside to the wooden bench. "How you planning to get out to your mama's house?"

"I don't know," Carrie said. "I'll have to call around and see who can come get me."

"My nephew is picking me up. My sister doesn't live too far from your mama. He'll be glad to drop you off."

"You sure, Miz Ida Mae. I don't want to be no bother. You've already done more than enough helping me with the babies."

"Ain't no trouble at all," she said, reaching for Vicki again. "Albert a little older than you. He probably know your brother or sister."

The women waited for about twenty minutes before Albert arrived in a late model green Ford. He bore a strong resemblance to Miz Ida Mae in color and size. He had two gold teeth at the top, one on each side. "How you doing, Auntie?" he said, embracing Miz Ida Mae.

"Fine, baby." She stood between them and made introductions. "This is Albert Jones, and this is Carrie Boyd," she said, looking from one to the other.

Albert removed a toothpick from the corner of his mouth, smiling as he reached for Carrie's hand. "Nice to meet you."

"Hi," Carrie said, giving him a quick handshake. She didn't like the way Albert ogled her.

He put their belongings in the trunk and helped Carrie get Vicki and Victor settled in the backseat. Carrie caught him looking at her butt when she climbed into the car. She rolled her eyes at him. He grinned like a Cheshire cat.

While Albert and Miz Ida Mae chatted in the front seat, Carrie surveyed the town. Newly planted cotton fields soon replaced buildings. Carrie's heart sank. She never pictured herself picking cotton or cleaning houses, but that might be her only source of income now.

Carrie dismissed the thought and replaced it with something positive. She focused on how happy she would be surrounded by family again, especially her thirteen-year-old sister, Cleotha.

Before she realized it, Albert had turned onto the dirt road leading to her mama's house. An old refrigerator and stove had been dumped in the tall grass. Closer to the house, a black car with no windows and only one door sat on rims.

She got out and collected her babies. Albert put her sack and two suitcases on the porch. After Carrie thanked him and Miz Ida Mae, she walked up to the house. It was smaller than she remembered. Traces of white paint streaked the outside of the house, which had turned gray. The front steps had rotted, and the porch sagged. To the right of the front door sat a dirty, orange floral couch that had been her mother's pride and joy.

Carrie gripped the babies, walked up the rickety steps and knocked on the door. No answer. She trudged around the back, but nobody was there. It was after six o'clock in the evening. Ruth was probably on her way home from her job at the cleaners, but Cleotha should've been home from school.

She sat on the couch that she hadn't been allowed to touch when she was a child and fed the babies their last bottle. As Carrie rocked Vicki in her arms and patted Victor as he lay on the porch, she thought about Cyrus. No matter how much she tried, she couldn't hate the man who gave her such beautiful babies. She had experienced the pleasure and pain of being foolishly in love, and it had made her a lot wiser. Never again, she vowed.

Carrie breathed deeply and shook off the somber mood that came over her every time she thought about Cyrus. About forty-five minutes later, a thin figure walked slowly in her direction. Carrie squinted until her mother's nutty-brown face came into focus. When Ruth saw Carrie, she hastened her step.

"Is that you, Carrie?" she said with a big, gap-toothed grin.

Carrie lay Vicki next to her brother, stood, and waved. "Yeah, Mama, it's me."

Before Ruth reached Carrie, she spotted the babies lying on the blanket. Ruth approached the porch slowly and stopped a few feet from her daughter. "What's this?" she asked baffled.

"Mama, these my children," Carrie explained, scooping them up. Nervous, she swayed and patted their bottoms.

The shock of Carrie's news changed Ruth's expression from confusion to disgust. Carrie would remember that look for the rest of her life.

Ruth placed both hands over her heart. "Babies? Lord, have mercy, you got two children?"

"Yeah, Mama. They twins."

"You dropped your first babies and didn't even tell me," Ruth said. "Why didn't you write me? I would've come."

Carrie lowered her head. "Mama, I didn't want you to know. I was trying to work things out."

"What's there to work out?"

"It's kind of long and drawn out." Carrie was tired and didn't want to go into details.

"Where's their daddy?" Ruth asked, putting a hand on her hip.

"Uh, he back in Memphis."

"Why ain't you with him?"

"I just ain't, Mama," said Carrie, trying hard not to cry.

"That ain't no answer. Why ain't he with you?"

"'Cause he…" Carrie stopped, too choked up to explain what happened. She wiped her runny nose on the front of Victor's shirt.

"He got what he wanted, and now he don't want to be tied down with you and no babies. Am I right?"

"Mama, please, can we go inside?"

Ruth was livid. "How did you let yourself get in this fix, Carrie? I told you a long time ago how to take care of yourself when you been with a man. If you did like I said, you wouldn't be here like this."

Carrie stared at the ground, not wanting to see the disappointment in her mother's eyes. When she looked up, Ruth was crying. Carrie broke down, and the babies started wailing, too.

"I'm sorry, Mama. I know I made a mess of things. Just let me stay 'til I get on my feet. Please, Mama."

"Hush, girl," said Ruth, wiping her eyes with the cotton handkerchief she kept in her bra. "Stop talking crazy. I ain't gonna turn you and my grandbabies away. This is your home."

Ruth took Victor and unlocked the front door, still dabbing her eyes.

"Cleotha will be glad to see you. She'll be along directly. She's helping out at Ben's gas station. I ain't seen your sister in a while. Your brother got into some trouble at the prison, and he won't get out now 'til next summer. I'll have to write and tell him that he's an uncle."

They weren't in the house long before Cleotha came home. She screamed, ran, and jumped into Carrie's arms. "I'm glad you're back. Why didn't you write and tell me you were coming home?"

"I wanted to surprise you," she said, tucking Cleotha's braid behind her ear. "Come here, I got something to show you, but you have to be quiet." Carrie took Cleotha's hand and led her to Ruth's bedroom. She opened the door, tipped in and stood over the twins.

Cleotha looked down at the sleeping babies and back up at Carrie. "Whose babies are these?"

"They mine. A boy and a girl. Victor and Vicki."

Cleotha stared open-mouthed at the twins. Before she could say anything, Carrie pushed her out of the room.

"You got two babies?"

"That makes you an auntie," said Ruth, who was sitting at the kitchen table.

"Why didn't you tell us?" Cleotha asked.

"Y'all got plenty time to catch up," Ruth said. "Cleotha, come over here and peel some potatoes so I can whip up something to eat."

After dinner, Carrie showed Cleotha how to change and feed the babies.

"Can one of them sleep with me?" Cleotha asked.

"You'll mash 'em to death bad as you sleep," Carrie teased. "They'll be fine on the floor," she said, pointing to a pallet.

That night, Carrie fell into a deep slumber, sleeping through the night and her babies' cries. While she slept, Ruth fed and rocked the twins back to sleep. The next morning, Carrie woke up feeling like a new person.

As word spread that Carrie was back, everyone came over to see her children. The twins were passed around from cousin to neighbor, and everyone loved on them. No one said an unkind word or questioned Carrie about the children's father.

Aunt Maylene took Carrie aside and asked what she was planning to do about work. "You got two mouths to feed now, chile. You need to take up a trade or something," she said.

Ruth, who was standing by to quash prying questions, overheard the conversation. "Carrie been talking 'bout being a beautician. My friend, Tess, run a beauty culture school in town. I'm going to see 'bout getting her in the next class."

"Really?" Carrie asked.

"Yes, ma'am. I've got to get you back on track."

Chapter Five

~

"What's burning?" Miz Esther yelled the moment she walked into the house.

"Oh, my God!" Nadine turned away from Salena and ran downstairs into a smoky kitchen.

Miz Esther had removed the blackened pot from the flame and tossed it in the sink under running water. "Can't you do anything right?" she said.

Nadine glanced at her daughter before she said, "I'm sorry. Salena had a cut and—"

"So you were just going to let the rice burn?" She shook her head and clucked like she had never seen anything worse. "Get out of my kitchen," she ordered.

Nadine wanted to stand up to her mother-in-law, tell her that she couldn't talk to her that way, especially not in front of her daughter. But she said nothing, remembering Aunt Bessie Mae's words.

"That woman can be your ally or your enemy," Aunt Bessie Mae said as she helped Nadine pack the night before her wedding. "Truth be told, she don't want your kind for her son. She want one of them high yella college girls whose daddy is a lawyer or doctor. If it wasn't for that baby you carrying, ain't no way Esther would let you marry her boy. You got to kill her with kindness no matter what she do."

With that in mind, Nadine retreated to her bedroom. She retrieved a stack of romance magazines from under the bed, where she hid them from the girls. A few minutes into a *Sepia* story, Nadine tossed the magazine aside. She wasn't in a lustful mood. She was worried about what Cyrus would say when he came home.

Nadine lay in bed, wondering what her life would be like if she hadn't gone on a date with Cyrus. She chided herself for being naïve. A second-year med student going out with a high school senior meant he was after only one thing, but she didn't see it back then.

The jangle of keys in the front door brought her back to reality. Nadine's heart pounded as she walked over to the railing. She could hear Miz Esther's and Cyrus's muffled voices and could only imagine what Miz Esther was saying about her.

When she heard Cyrus walking down the hall, Nadine ran into the bedroom, grabbed a magazine, and got into bed. He came into the room and shut the door.

"Mama said you almost burned down the house today. Were you up here reading that garbage and forgot the food was on the stove?" he yelled, snatching the magazine out of her hand.

Nadine was determined to tell her side of the story before Cyrus flew into a rage. "No, that's not what happened. Salena fell while she was skating and hit her head. I was trying to stop the bleeding when the water boiled out of the rice. The house didn't almost burn up."

"Turn the food off the next time," he said without a trace of empathy.

"Next time, I'll let your child bleed to death because we don't want Miz Esther to go without having her rice cooked so perfect that every grain stands by itself," she said, mocking Miz Esther's cooking instructions. She regretted what she said soon as the last word passed her lips.

Cyrus walked around the bed and stood over Nadine. She recoiled as he got close to her face. "Listen, lamebrain, this is Mama's house. She's got a right to be concerned about how it's being kept."

Nadine took a deep breath. "I haven't forgotten whose house this is because Miz Esther reminds me every chance she gets. If we had our own house, we wouldn't have these problems."

"We don't have any now except your carelessness," he said, placing his cufflinks in the jewelry case.

"No, Cyrus, that ain't the problem," she said.

"Then, what is?" he asked, turning toward Nadine.

Nadine took another deep breath. "This little house. Being cramped up upstairs. We need a bigger house."

Cyrus didn't say anything as he undressed with his back to Nadine. She couldn't see his face and didn't know if he was angry. "A new house, huh? I hadn't thought about that in a while, but now that you mentioned it, this place is beginning to feel small. I definitely need a bigger closet."

Nadine didn't allow herself to rejoice just yet. Cyrus had a habit of changing his mind, especially after talking to Miz Esther.

"I'll give it some serious thought," he said as he looked for his casual slacks in the closet.

Nadine closed her eyes and mouthed, "Thank you, Jesus."

***

Several days passed before the subject of moving came up again. The girls were in bed. Nadine and Cyrus were in the den watching *Bewitched*, and Miz Esther was grading papers.

"Mama, do you know anybody who works in real estate?" Cyrus asked.

"A couple of people at church do that kind of work. Who's looking for a house?"

"I think it's time we moved," said Cyrus, rearing back with his hands behind his head.

"Really?" said Miz Esther, who cut her eyes at Nadine. "Whose idea was this?"

"Nadine and I discussed it, and I think the timing is right."

"When did you want to move?"

"I don't have a particular date in mind. We'll take our time until we find the right house."

Nadine waited for Miz Esther to get upset, but she remained calm. "I couldn't imagine living anywhere but this old shack," Miz Esther said as she gazed at the room. "Jesse was so proud when he moved us in here. Do you remember that day, Cyrus?"

"Uh-huh."

"You were five years old, and we had just gotten married. Poor Jesse only got to enjoy the house nine years before he passed away. He was a good man and a successful businessman. He took good care us. I still feel connected to him living in this house. It would be hard to leave."

"Mama, you wouldn't have to move. This is your house, and I wouldn't dream of taking you away from your friends and neighbors. Me, Nadine, and the girls would move."

When Miz Esther heard this, she was crestfallen. She sat in stunned silence and quickly stuffed the papers in a folder. "Well, I'm going to turn in," she said. "Good night."

Nadine knew that Miz Esther was merely pretending to go along with Cyrus. She would try to talk him out of moving the first chance she got. Nadine looked at the TV, and the credits were rolling. She was ready to watch another show, but Cyrus had other plans.

"Let's go to bed," he suggested.

Nadine tensed up at the thought of what was coming next. After he tried to penetrate her anally the last time, she was scared to have sex with him. She went to the bathroom and changed into her gown and bathrobe, staying so long that Cyrus knocked on the door.

"What are you doing?"

"Nothing," she replied, unlocking the door and following him back to the bedroom. She sat in the chair and fumbled with the belt on her bathrobe.

"Are you getting into bed or what? I don't have all night."

"I, uh…" Nadine paused.

"If you don't want to be bothered, just say so," he said, yanking off his pants. "I'm not going to beg."

"Cyrus, the last time we had relations you hurt me," she blurted out. Her voice trembled as she told him how degraded she felt. "We're not supposed to do it like that. Men do that to other men. Homosexuals."

"You don't know what you're talking about," he snickered. "Couples have sex all kinds of ways. You're just frigid."

"Cyrus, I can't—"

"Stop yapping and get in the bed," he said.

Reluctantly, Nadine took off her nightclothes. She was ready to fight if he tried to make her have anal sex again. However, Cyrus apparently just wanted quick sex. He humped fast for a few minutes, pushed hard into her, and grunted. He rolled off and lay on his back. Nadine waited until he was asleep before getting up to douche.

***

The fumes from the spray-on cleaner were so strong that Nadine started coughing. When she backed into the hallway to catch her breath, she didn't realize that she was standing in Miz Esther's way.

"Excuse me," Miz Esther said, breezing into the kitchen. "Don't drip oven cleaner all over *my* house."

"Sorry," Nadine said, checking the floor for grease that might have fallen from her rubber gloves. When she didn't see anything, Nadine went back to scrubbing the oven.

While Miz Esther filled a glass with water, she asked, "Have you and Cyrus talked anymore about moving?"

"Not really," said Nadine, who had her head inside the oven. "He was supposed to call those real estate people, but I don't think he has."

Miz Esther sat at the table, sipping water as Nadine moved from the oven to the sink, rinsing and wringing a greasy rag. "I take it you're in favor of this move."

"Yes, ma'am," Nadine said. "Cyrus needs an office at home, and it would be nice if Jocelyn had her own room, and we had a bigger den…"

Miz Esther pounded the table, causing Nadine to jump. "What do you know about furnishing and decorating a house, let alone paying the bills? You've never done that. You being a doctor's wife and all, there are certain expectations that you won't be able to meet on your own."

Nadine could feel her blood pressure rising as Miz Esther prattled on about her shortcomings. She told herself to remain calm as she tried to block out Miz Esther's voice. The quieter Nadine got, the louder and angrier Miz Esther became. Never before had she seen the blood vessels popping out on Miz Esther's forehead and neck.

"Cyrus has made up his mind," Nadine said firmly.

"Well, you can unmake it because he doesn't know what he's getting into, and Lord knows you don't have a clue."

"How hard can it be? I do just about everything around here now except pay bills. I helped my daddy run his store. I know how to manage things."

Miz Esther scoffed at Nadine's notion of skills. "Girl, helping your daddy sell a dime's worth of souse to some little nappy head, barefoot kids doesn't mean you know how to run a house," she said.

"I don't want to hear any more about what I can't do," Nadine said angrily. "I'll do fine not having you picking at me all the time." Nadine tossed the rag in the sink and walked toward the dining room.

As she walked by, Miz Esther continued to hurl insults. "About the only thing you know how to do is lie on your back and make babies. You ought to thank me for making Cyrus marry you when you got knocked up by *accident*," Miz Esther sneered. "You aren't fit to be married to my son. No education. No upbringing. No nothing. Just a common woman who used her pussy to trap my son."

Miz Esther's words were so vile that Nadine wanted to rip her tongue out. She took a deep breath, and in the sweetest voice, told her off. "I don't care what you think about me, but your son ain't no angel. Why don't you ask him what he did to me the night I got pregnant. I don't have to defend myself to you because I know the truth. You might as well accept the fact that I'm Cyrus's wife and the mother of his children, and there's nothing you can do about it."

With a smirk, Miz Esther inched closer to Nadine. "Are both of them his? He's not sure about the last one, and neither am I based on how she looks."

"You know good and well that I ain't had no other men. When he was away at school, I was locked up in this house with you breathing down my neck every minute. You're a dirty-minded old woman with nothing better to do but run our lives, but that's about to end," Nadine said.

Before she could reply, Nadine bolted out of the kitchen. Miz Esther mumbled something, and a few seconds later Nadine heard a thud, like Miz Esther had thrown something at the door. Nadine went to her room to cool off. She was changing her blouse when Jocelyn ran up the stairs.

"Mama! Mama!" she shouted.

"Jocelyn, why are you hollering?"

"Grandma fell, and I can't get her up."

Nadine ran downstairs and found Miz Esther lying on the kitchen floor, curled on her side. The right side of her face sagged, and she was drooling. Nadine knelt and touched her right arm. "Miz Esther, what's wrong? Can you get up?"

Her eyes were open. She tried to speak but a gurgling sound came out.

"Oh, my God. Jocelyn, go get the quilt on her bed." Nadine ran to call Cyrus.

As the phone rang, Nadine looked at the clock on the mantel. Four-thirty. It was too early for Cyrus to be gone. He saw patients until three o'clock on Saturdays but didn't leave the office until five. On the third ring, he picked up. "Cyrus, something is wrong with Miz Esther. She fell out on the floor, and she can't talk or move."

"When did this happen?"

"About five minutes ago."

"Don't move her. Keep her calm. I'll call Dixon Funeral Home and have them send an ambulance. Meet me at John Gaston Hospital."

It seemed like the ambulance took forever to come, but it was only about ten minutes. Miz Esther looked dead by the time the attendants loaded her on the gurney.

Nadine called Aunt Lillian and Uncle Mack before she and the girls piled into her green Newport and drove to the hospital. Cyrus came to the waiting room forty-five minutes after they arrived and told them that Miz Esther had suffered a stroke. Dr. Adams was waiting on test results to determine the severity.

"Nadine, what was sister doing when she had the stroke?" Aunt Lillian asked.

"We were in the kitchen talking," said Nadine. She was afraid they would blame her if they knew about the argument.

"Had she complained about feeling ill or anything?" Aunt Lillian inquired tearfully.

Nadine shook her head. "No, she was her normal self today."

"Lillian, something else could have been wrong, and she didn't know it," said Uncle Mack, placing an arm around his wife. "We'll know something soon."

Chapter Six

~

Cyrus stood in front of bathroom mirror, both hands on the sink, worried about how Miz Esther would cope with the daily struggles of being disabled. She was only sixty, too young to be incapacitated. Ten days had passed since Miz Esther suffered the stroke, which left her partially paralyzed on one side of her body. Her speech was slurred though it was expected to improve gradually.

Miz Esther would have to retire now, and Cyrus knew how tough that would be because she loved teaching. He anticipated that she would shed a lot of tears over not being able to work and probably sink into a depression. Cyrus also realized that his world was about to change, too. Taking care of his mother would cut down on his free time and any hope of a late night rendezvous.

Cyrus got dressed and went downstairs. Nadine hopped up from her chair to fix his breakfast. "What do you want to eat?"

He looked blank. "Uh, nothing. I'm not hungry." Cyrus stood behind Jocelyn and placed his hands on her shoulders as he stared out the window.

"Is Miz Esther okay?" Nadine asked.

"She's the same," he murmured. "She's trying hard to speak, but sometimes the words just don't come out right. She gets frustrated and starts crying."

"When is Grandma coming home?" Salena asked.

Cyrus pinched her cheek. "In a few days."

"I'll be glad," Jocelyn added. "I can't stand going to that hospital. The smell makes me want to gag."

Nadine gave Jocelyn a disapproving look. "Y'all better get going before you're late for school."

After the girls left the room, Cyrus said in a thick voice, "There's something else you need to know."

"What?" Nadine asked, bracing herself. She turned off the faucet and dried her hands on a dish towel.

"Mama can't finish out the school year. In fact, she won't be able to work anymore. I don't know how I'm going to tell her."

"I thought Dr. Adams said she was going to get better."

Cyrus became irritated. "Her condition will improve, but she'll never be the same."

Nadine threw the dish towel over her shoulder and sat at the table. "I'm sorry," she said. "I thought she would be back to normal in six months."

"Goddamn it, Nadine," he shouted, kicking a chair from under the table. "Are you retarded? You obviously don't understand how serious this is," he said, moving closer to her face. "I'm going to explain Mama's situation to you in plain, simple English. Maybe this time it will penetrate that thick skull of yours." Cyrus jabbed his finger on her forehead so hard that Nadine's head hit the wall. She yelped at the pain. "Mama won't be able to bathe or get dressed or do anything by herself. She'll be totally dependent on us for everything for the rest of her life. Now do you get it?" he asked.

"Yeah," she mumbled. "I know exactly what this means."

Her life was about to take yet another miserable turn. She would never get her own house, and Miz Esther had gotten the upper hand. It was times like these that Nadine longed for her family, but everyone had died. Her best friend, Frannie, had moved to Cleveland, leaving her to figure out things on her own.

***

After Miz Esther dozed off, Cyrus and Aunt Lillian stepped into the hallway. She took a handkerchief from her purse and dabbed at her eyes.

"Are you all right, Auntie?"

"I feel bad for Esther," she sniffled. "She's looking at a long recovery."

Cyrus led Aunt Lillian to the waiting room. "Auntie, you know how tough Mama is. She'll have to make some adjustments, but she'll be okay. I don't want you to worry yourself sick."

"I keep thinking about how Esther was always in the streets, going to sorority meetings and church functions. She won't be able to do any of that."

"Well, not for a while," Cyrus said, holding her hand. "We'll ease Mama back into her social life when she gets stronger."

Aunt Lillian still looked glum. She folded her handkerchief and put it back in her purse. "There's something I've been meaning to ask. Have you seen Carrie lately?"

Cyrus lowered his eyes. "I went by there a couple of days before Mama got sick, and she was gone."

"Where to?"

He shrugged. "Her grandmother wouldn't say, but I assumed that she went back home."

"Did you get an address?"

"No, I didn't get a chance to ask. The grandmother was drunk, cussed me out, and threatened to call the police if I didn't leave."

Aunt Lillian sat back in her chair. "That's too bad," she said, shaking her head. "I mean, it's good Carrie went back home to get some help with the babies, but it's sad that you don't know how to get in touch with her."

"I know," Cyrus sighed. "But I'm glad she's gone because in her frame of mind she might have shown up on my doorstep. You know that would've been ugly."

"When are you going to tell Esther? She needs to know that she has two more grandbabies."

"I'll get around to it," he said, avoiding the question.

Aunt Lillian, who doted on Cyrus because she didn't have children, got upset. "Stop procrastinating," she said. "I feel so guilty about keeping those babies a secret. I wish to God that I hadn't introduced you two and asked you to talk to her about nursing school. This is all my fault."

"Stop blaming yourself, Auntie," said Cyrus, leaning forward with his elbows on his knees. "We were two consenting adults. Right now, we've got to concentrate on helping Mama get well. The rest can wait."

"You're right," she agreed. "Esther needs us now. Well, I'm going to tell her goodbye. I'll talk to you later."

"Take care, Auntie," he said, hugging Miz Lillian.

Cyrus gazed at the wall like he was studying a patient's chart. He had no intention of telling Miz Esther about the twins unless there was a compelling reason. He didn't want her to know that he had been whoring around.

Besides, Cyrus doubted that Miz Esther would accept his illegitimate children. She thought marrying Nadine was beneath him. Fathering twins by a country girl would be far worse in her eyes.

Chapter Seven

To Carrie's surprise, she settled quickly into a routine at her mama's house and began feeling better. Ruth and Cleotha helped her take care of the babies day and night. Now it seemed as if she had only one child because one of them always had the other one.

Everyone Carrie knew offered to help, including Albert, who hauled produce throughout Mississippi, Tennessee, and Arkansas. He stopped by one day with several baskets of collard greens, cabbage, rutabagas, green beans, bananas, pears, and apples. After Albert unloaded the food, he hung around playing with the twins on the front porch.

Carrie eyed him suspiciously, knowing that he would want something in return at some point. She decided to be nice anyway. "You got any children?" she asked.

"No, not yet. I'm on the road so much that I ain't had time to settle down. I want me a house full when I get 'round to it." Albert stuck both thumbs in his ears and made a face at Victor.

"They more than just a notion, I tell you that," she said, reaching down to get Vicki. "Bring Victor in the house so I can change him."

He picked up Victor, who spit up on the front of his shirt. "That's what happens when you jostle them too much. Sit him in the baby seat, and go tell Mama to wipe off your shirt."

"You should've warned me," Albert said, turning his nose away from the smelly puke.

A few minutes later, Albert joined Carrie on the porch as she rocked Vicki. The wet spot covered half of his shirt. "She might as well took off your whole shirt and washed it," Carrie said.

"She got my chest raw from all that scrubbing. She was worried about me smelling sour for the rest of the day. That couldn't have been any worse than this," he said, holding the wet shirt from his body.

"I'm used to that smell now. Ain't that right, Vicki?" Carrie said, nuzzling her neck.

Albert leaned back in his chair with a toothpick hanging from his lips. "You glad to be back home?" he asked.

Carrie turned up her nose. "It's all right. I didn't have no choice."

"There's always choices," he said, glancing at her. "Sometimes, we don't choose right."

"You sound like an old man. How old are you?"

"I'll be twenty-five next month. How old are you?"

"Nineteen."

He flicked the toothpick in the yard, moved his chair closer to Carrie, and draped his arm across the back of her chair. "You seeing anybody 'round here?"

Carrie stared at his arm, then back at him, waiting for him to move it. When she kept looking at his arm, he finally got the message. "Thank you," she said.

"You didn't answer my question."

"Why do you want to know?"

Albert put on his sexy voice and burst into a wide smile. "I thought maybe I could keep company with you when I ain't on the road."

"Boy, I got two babies. That's plenty company," she joked. "I don't need no more."

Although Carrie laughed it off, she was repulsed by Albert's offer.

Everything about him turned her off. He had pink and black gums, soot-colored skin, and wide hips like a woman.

"I'm sure you can use a little help. Be good to me, and I be good to you," he said, winking.

"I ain't looking for no man, Albert," she barked. "If that's why you coming 'round here with food, you can take it all back."

Ruth called Carrie, and she went to see what her mother wanted. "Ask Albert if he can stay for dinner," she told Carrie.

Albert declined the invitation, saying he had to hit the road early in the morning. He went inside to say goodbye to Ruth, who was snapping beans. He strutted past Carrie and hopped off the porch.

"You heard of that old saying, 'Beggars can't be choosy?' You keep that in mind," he said before getting into his car.

"I ain't no beggar," Carrie yelled.

After Albert drove off, she went inside and lay the twins on a pallet in the kitchen.

"Albert seem nice," Ruth said.

Carrie rolled her eyes. "I guess, but he kinda cocky." She got a bowl from the cabinet for mixing cornbread.

"Ain't nothing wrong with that," Ruth said, rinsing her hands. "He single and working every day. That's the kind of man you need."

Carrie got milk and eggs from the refrigerator. She slammed the carton of eggs on the table so hard that the lid flew open, and one egg fell on the floor. "Mama, I ain't interested in Albert."

Ruth grabbed the dishrag and wiped the floor. "Chile, your problem is you don't know when a good thing come along. If I was you, I'd be switching 'round, smiling, and doing all I could to make sure Albert came back."

"Don't nobody do that stuff no more. That was back in the olden days."

"When it comes to men, believe me, that old stuff still work. You'll start listening to me one day," she said, pointing a finger at Carrie. "If you had listened to what I was saying before, you'd still be in Memphis."

That was the second time Ruth had said, 'I told you so,' and Carrie didn't like it. Ruth claimed she knew so much about men, but she couldn't hold on to any of her children's fathers.

Carrie was curious why she didn't stay with her daddy. Ruth told Carrie his name but never discussed him. The only thing Carrie knew about him was that he was a smart man because Ruth said she inherited his intelligence and skin color from him.

No matter what Ruth said, Carrie definitely wouldn't date Albert. If he came bearing gifts again, she vowed to turn him away. However, Carrie wasn't home the next time Albert stopped by the house. When she returned, she found him and Ruth sitting on the porch eating fried chicken.

"Albert brought us dinner," Ruth said, wiping her mouth with a napkin. "Wasn't that nice?"

Carrie spoke and went inside to get the twins. Albert grabbed Vicki from her arms when she brought them out and began cooing to her. She felt like knocking him down and siccing the old hound under the porch on him.

"I got things to do so I'm going inside," Ruth said. "Thank you again, Albert."

"You welcome, Miz Ruth." Albert turned to Carrie. "I hear you going to beauty school. When you start?"

"In a month," Carrie replied tersely, hoping he would get the hint that she didn't like him.

"If you need some supplies, let me know. I can get stuff real cheap."

"No, thank you."

Albert bounced Vicki on his knee and held her like an airplane, making engine sounds, dipping her low, and raising her over his head. After a while, he said, "Well, I need to go. I'll check on y'all when I get back."

"Uh-huh," Carrie said dryly.

Ruth came out on the front porch and stood next to Carrie. "He'll get away if you don't act right."

"Mama, I told you that I don't like Albert, but he ain't getting the message 'cause you keep encouraging him."

Ruth placed both hands on her hips and wagged her finger at Carrie. "You listen to me, Miss High and Mighty. If you had any sense, you'd keep your mouth shut so we'll have some food to put in our bellies. Get off your high horse and start thinking about somebody else for a change."

Carrie pouted. "I'll be nice, but that's about it. Bringing us a few apples don't give him no right to nothing else."

"Just hold your tongue, that's all I'm asking. Go get something to eat before it get cold."

Carrie went inside, but she was so angry with Ruth that she couldn't eat. She felt bad for bringing Ruth more worries, but she wasn't going to prostitute herself for food.

***

Before Carrie knew it, a week had gone by, and Albert was parked outside their house again. Last time he was there, he had offered to replace the rotten boards on the front porch. Today, he came with tools and wood in the back of an old, black pickup. While Albert unloaded the planks, Cleotha took two boxes of food into the house.

Carrie was mopping the living room floor and didn't go out to greet him. Curious about what she was doing, Albert went inside looking for her.

"Hey, Carrie. How you doing?"

Carrie didn't look his way. "If you looking for Mama, she ain't here. She went into town. She'll be back in a couple of hours."

"I was looking for you not Miz Ruth."

"I'm busy, Albert," she said, dipping the mop into the bucket.

Albert tromped across the room, trying to get Carrie's attention. "You can stop a few minutes to talk, can't you?"

"I'm trying to finish before the babies wake up from their nap," Carrie said as she sidestepped him and dragged the mop across the floor.

"You see the stuff I brought?"

"Yeah, I saw it."

"A man can't get a thank you?" he asked puzzled.

"Mama will thank you when she get back."

"That's not who I brought it to."

"Albert, we all thank you." Carrie picked up the bucket and went into the kitchen.

"You got a weird way of showing you grateful," Albert complained as she walked away.

Carrie hoped he would leave when he finished the porch, but Albert stayed for dinner and then got comfortable on the couch, watching TV.

"Miz Ruth, you got anything 'round here to lift the spirits? I could use a little nip right about now."

"No, Albert. I used to keep a bottle but not anymore 'cause my older girl, Tandy, kept stealing it. If you tell me what you like, I'll get some and have it for you next time you come."

"There's a package store close to town. I'll go get us a bottle if you don't mind."

"No, go ahead. I could use a little pick-me-up, too."

"Come on and ride with me, Carrie," he said, tugging at her hand.

She removed his hand with her fingertips and said, "I can't leave the babies."

"Carrie, you can go with Albert. Me and Cleotha will watch 'em."

"That's all right, Mama," Carrie said. "Albert can go by hisself." She crossed her arms and turned her back on him.

"Chile, go ahead," Ruth insisted.

Carrie reluctantly followed him to the truck. It didn't seem to bother Albert that she was being forced to go with him. She sat as close to the door as she could, hoping that he wouldn't try anything on their way to the store.

"Why you quiet?" he asked, glancing at her.

"I ain't got nothing to say."

"You ain't got your mama's ways, that's for sure. You ought to try and be more friendly like her." Albert turned off the main road and headed toward the lake.

Carrie panicked. "Why we going down here?"

"I like to look at the stars from back here."

"Well, I don't. Let's go to the liquor store and head back home," she demanded. "Mama waiting for us."

"Ain't no rush. Just relax."

He drove right up to the lake and turned off the engine. Carrie balled her fists, ready to strike him the minute he touched her.

Albert turned sideways, his knee touching her thigh. "Why you so mean?" he asked.

Being close to him made Carrie's skin crawl, and she scooted next to the door. "I ain't mean. I just don't want to be bothered." She turned her body and looked out the passenger's window at the ink-colored sky. There were no stars. The bright crescent moon reminded Carrie of a slice of honeydew melon.

Albert tried to turn her face toward him, but she pushed his hand away. "See, that's what I'm talking 'bout. That was mean."

"Well, don't touch me!"

"You don't mean that," he said, pulling Carrie's hair.

Carrie brushed away his hand. "Albert, I need to get back to Vicki and Victor."

"Miz Ruth said don't worry about them. We got plenty time." He put his arm around Carrie and bent over to kiss her.

Carrie pushed him away. "Stop, Albert."

He kept trying to press his lips against hers. When he pinned Carrie against the door, she stopped squirming and submitted to his advances. Just as he made contact, she bit him.

"Damn it!" Albert howled in agony. He checked his lip in the mirror. "I ought to go upside your head for biting me. All the shit I do for you, and this the thanks I get. You ain't nothing but a cock tease."

Carrie thought about jumping out of the truck and walking home, but she was afraid of snakes and other critters that came out at night. She sat quietly, waiting for Albert's next move.

After examining his lip in the mirror again, he turned the truck around and headed back to her house. "You think 'cause you high yella that you better than me, don't you? See if you can get anybody else 'round here able to do as much as me. That nigga in Memphis didn't want your ass, and you came running back home. Now you try to be siddity and shit, looking down on everybody. There's plenty women I could have, women begging me to spend the night. I don't have to put up with your shit. See if I come back."

Carrie tried not to look too smug, but listening to Albert talking to himself was kind of funny. He roared up to the house in a cloud of dust and stopped so suddenly that her head snapped. Carrie barely made it out the truck before he backed up.

Ruth met her at the front door. "Why y'all back this quick?" She looked past Carrie and saw the truck's taillights. "Where Albert going?"

Carrie stepped inside the house. "He said he had women begging him to spend the night. He must be going to see one of them."

"Uh, uh, uh," Ruth said, shaking her head. "Letting money walk right out the door. You're going to regret it."

Chapter Eight

~

Nadine had been the lady of the house for nearly two weeks, but today it was coming to an end. Miz Esther was being released from the hospital. Cyrus ordered flowers for the dining room and Miz Esther's room. He told the girls to make a "Welcome Home" banner. Nadine spent a whole day cleaning her bedroom and bathroom.

She got up early and cooked a meatloaf, pole beans, candied yams, and a coconut cake. Nadine was feeling a little down and decided to take a long, hot bath. As she soaked in the tub, she tried to get mentally prepared for her new role – nurse. She felt overwhelmed thinking about taking care of Miz Esther along with everything else she did around the house.

After Nadine dressed, she checked on the girls, who were watching TV in the den. "Now remember, Miz Esther needs peace and quiet. I'm expecting y'all to be on your best behavior," she told them.

"Do we have to stay in our room?" Jocelyn asked.

"No, but you can't have the TV this loud," Nadine said, turning down the volume. "Keep it right here."

"I can't hear it," Salena complained.

"I hear it just fine," Nadine said.

Shortly after two o'clock, Cyrus tooted the horn on Miz Esther's ivory Cadillac. Nadine and the girls went outside to greet them. Cyrus picked up Miz Esther and brought her into the house because she couldn't manage the steps. She giggled like a new bride. The girls thought it was funny, too. The sight of them made Nadine nauseous.

"Welcome home, Grandma," Jocelyn said.

"Look at our sign," said Salena, pointing to the wall.

"How you feeling today, Miz Esther?" Nadine asked.

She didn't look Nadine's way but said in a garbled voice, "I'm tired. I need to lie down."

"I'll take you back to your room, Mama," Cyrus said.

Nadine decided to wait until Miz Esther got settled before asking if she needed anything. From the kitchen, she could hear Cyrus going over the medication schedule and doctor's orders. Cyrus came out of her bedroom and asked, "Have you finished dinner?"

"Yes, everything is ready. I cooked her favorite meal."

"Ask her what time she wants to eat," he told Nadine.

Nadine knocked lightly on Miz Esther's door. "I fixed dinner," she said. "When do you want to eat?"

"I'll ring," Miz Esther said.

"Ring?"

Miz Esther held up a white porcelain bell trimmed in gold. "Cyrus got this," she said smiling.

"Yes ma'am," Nadine said, backing out of the room. When she returned to the kitchen, Cyrus wasn't there. She checked outside, and his car was gone. Nadine heard the bell ringing and ran back to Miz Esther's room.

She was sitting in bed watching TV. "You need something, Miz Esther?"

She didn't answer at first, making Nadine wonder if her hearing had been affected by the stroke.

"Cyrus still here?" she asked.

"No, ma'am, he's gone."

"Good because we need to talk," said Miz Esther, who seemed to have suddenly recovered her voice.

Nadine fumed inside. She suspected that Miz Esther faked her inability to talk and walk to keep Cyrus at her side but didn't dare mention it to him. "Shouldn't you be resting?" Nadine asked in an even tone.

Miz Esther pointed at the chair. "Sit down, Nadine."

"I'll stand if you don't mind," she said, refusing to take orders.

"Suit yourself," Miz Esther said. She took a sip of water and moved the paralyzed hand from her side onto her lap. "I just want to get a few things straight. I am still the woman of this house. Don't think for a minute that this stroke made me feeble and you can take over."

Nadine didn't blink. She remembered what happened the last time she argued with Miz Esther and decided to keep her mouth shut. Miz Esther continued though she appeared to have difficulty sometimes collecting her thoughts and putting them into words. Nadine snickered to herself each time Miz Esther faltered.

"I told Cyrus that I want Vera to look after me for a while because you have your hands full with the girls," she explained. "I don't want to be neglected because you're braiding hair or something."

Nadine was happy to hear Vera, a church member, would be playing nurse to Miz Esther. "Whatever you want," she said.

"And one last thing. Don't ever bring up moving out of this house again. The only way that will happen is over my dead body," she said, "and I plan to be around for a very long time."

Nadine felt like slapping the smile off Miz Esther's droopy face, but she maintained her composure. "Just let me know when you're ready to eat," she said, before turning to leave. Nadine went to the den and turned on the TV just in time to watch *As The World Turns*.

Chapter Nine

~

Cyrus looked at the little calendar on top of the console in the den. His eyes lingered on the date. January fourth, nineteen hundred and sixty-eight. Almost nine months had passed since Miz Esther had a stroke. It was now or never. Cyrus straightened his back, squared his shoulders, and headed to Miz Esther's bedroom. The door was closed, but he could hear music from the radio he bought her for Christmas. He tapped on the door.

"Come in," Miz Esther said.

"How's my favorite girl doing tonight?"

"Worn out from the holidays, but not bad for a sixty-one-year-old, handicapped woman. Pull up a chair." Miz Esther got her cane, walked over to the vanity and sat on the stool to brush her hair.

"Look at you," Cyrus said beaming. "You get around better than some young people."

"This old leg is stiff as a board," she said, resting the brush after a few strokes. She tried raising her right leg, but it only moved a few inches off the floor. "I guess it'll never be the same. Other than that, I'm fine. But I do still seem to get tired up in the day."

"The fatigue could come from the blood pressure pills. I'll ask Dr. Adams about it," he said.

Cyrus wanted to gauge his mother's physical condition before he brought up his marriage. Since she was in pretty good spirits, he broached the subject. "Mama, I want to talk to you about me and Nadine."

"Uh-huh," Miz Esther said, rising to turn off the radio before getting back into bed.

Cyrus wanted to help her but knew she would swat his hands. He let her do it on her own and waited until she had gotten comfortable. Cyrus swallowed hard. His mouth felt dry and his tongue heavy. He wiped his sweaty palms on the front of his pants. "You know, Mama, if Nadine hadn't been pregnant, I wouldn't have married her because she didn't measure up to my standards or yours."

"I don't like where this is going, but go on," Miz Esther said.

Cyrus moved from the chair to the foot of her bed, resting his back on one of the bedposts. He looked pitiful, like a child confessing that he had broken a neighbor's window. "I tried, Mama, but it just hasn't worked. Nadine is more of a caretaker for you and the girls than she is a wife. I need somebody who is more outgoing, who can get us invited to the right social functions." He stopped and ran his hand through his crimped hair. "You know how much being a member of the Commodores means to me, right? When I told Nadine to join the auxiliary, I thought it would lead to us being on the A-list for dinners and parties, but that hasn't happened. She goes to the meetings, but I think she just sits in a corner, not talking to the other wives, which is the whole point of her being there." Cyrus twisted his mouth into a frown. "I've been thinking about hosting a dinner/dance during the Cotton Makers Jubilee at one of the hotels downtown, but I don't see Nadine being able to pull that off, do you?" Cyrus didn't wait for Miz Esther's response. "She's just not a doctor's wife, plain and simple. It's time to call it quits."

Miz Esther's jaw tightened. She narrowed her eyes. "A divorce? Have you lost your mind?" Slowly and with great effort, Miz Esther swung her legs onto the floor. She sat on the edge of the bed. "You, of all people, should know what it's like not having a father around. Why would you want to inflict that pain on your children? Does Nadine want a divorce, too?"

"I haven't talked to her about it yet."

"Well, don't because you're not splitting up my family," Miz Esther said emphatically. "It doesn't make sense for you to tear this family apart and uproot your children from the only home they've ever known. No sir, I'm not having it!"

"Mama, what's the point of us staying married? There's no love between us," he declared. "And don't go dragging the girls into this. They'll be provided for."

"Giving them a couple of dollars a week for child support is not my idea of being a good father," Miz Esther said, pointing her finger at him. "If they aren't living with us, who'll see to it that they grow up right? Nadine didn't come from a family of means. She doesn't know the proper things that girls should be doing. Jocelyn's cotillion is in a couple of years, and we've got to get her ready for all the parties. How is it going to look if the two of you aren't married when she's presented to society? If you and Nadine are having problems, then figure out a way to patch things up. There'll be no divorce in this house. Do you understand me?"

Cyrus didn't expect Miz Esther to get agitated, and he worried that her blood pressure might shoot up. He gently took her hand and enclosed it in his hands. "Mama, people get divorced every day," he said softly. "Look in the paper, you'll probably see somebody's name you recognize. You won't be shamed or anything if we break up. It's not a big deal any more. I wish you'd try to see my side of this."

"What's your side, Cyrus?" she asked, pushing him away. "Have you found some big butt nurse who told you that you're the greatest thing since sliced bread?"

"No, Mama," Cyrus said. He buried his head in the palms of his hands.

"I hope you haven't been messing around. Women who sleep with married men will do anything, and I mean anything, to get some money. Keep your dick in your pants. You don't need to be dragged down to court by some hussy claiming she had your baby."

Cyrus threw up his hands in frustration. "Mama, you've gone off on a tangent now."

"I've made myself pretty clear about this divorce business. You and Nadine will stay together, and my granddaughters will grow up in this house with both parents. They deserve the best, and you'll give it to them. That's all I have to say on the matter." She fluffed her pillows, eased back into bed, and turned off the lamp.

"I guess this conversation is over then," Cyrus said.

"You guessed right. Good night."

Cyrus went back to the living room and slumped on the sofa, upset that the discussion hadn't gone his way. Miz Esther had always given him what he wanted, except her permission for a divorce. He was angrier with himself for not being man enough to get one without asking.

He knew a divorce would shatter Miz Esther's dream of having the picture-perfect family. She lived vicariously through them, enjoying the life she wanted with Cyrus's father but never had because his parents wouldn't let him marry Miz Esther when she got pregnant.

Frustrated, Cyrus grabbed his hat, coat and car keys, and went for a ride. He ended up in the place where he always went to clear his head, the banks of the Mississippi River. The pitch-black water of the mighty Mississippi was churning near the shoreline. The river looked like it was in turmoil, much like Cyrus's personal life.

He stood on the banks of the muddy waterway trying to make sense of things. The cold wind slapped him in the face and stung his eyes. The river usually relaxed him and helped him think, but tonight as he peered into the darkness, it made him anxious. It was almost as if the water sensed his mood and tossed it right back at him.

If Cyrus had listened to his best friend, Skeeter, he wouldn't have gotten tangled up with Nadine. Skeeter warned him, but Cyrus was horny and looking for an easy lay.

"Check out Nadine over there, looking all fine," Cyrus said. His eyes followed her as she left a meeting room at the community center."

"Man, you going backward or what? She ain't even graduated high school yet," Skeeter said as he tied his shoelaces.

"She ain't too much in the looks department, but that shape makes up for it," Cyrus said.

"Her old man will shoot your nuts off if you pop that cherry," Skeeter cautioned. "I wouldn't mess with her if I was you. Let's just play ball and get outta here."

"Sit tight while I get her number," Cyrus said.

He regretted that decision every day of his married life. Miz Esther's concern about his daughters' welfare was understandable but not warranted. Cyrus would never neglect his children the way his father had done him.

He seldom thought about his daddy, and when he did, it was with bitterness. The only time Cyrus saw him was at his high school graduation. His father was a quiet and reserved man who showed no interest in Cyrus. It was an awkward meeting for both of them, especially Cyrus who hoped that they could develop a relationship.

Later, he learned from Aunt Lillian that his father initially declined the invitation but changed his mind after Miz Esther begged him to see his firstborn child and only son.

Cyrus never got over being rejected by his father. For that reason alone, he was steadfast in his pledge to be involved in his children's lives

– all of them. Any woman who wanted to be with him had to accept his offspring.

He didn't anticipate that being a problem with Mamie, his latest love interest who worked in her family's funeral home business in Cincinnati. She was Dr. Adams's cousin, and they met when he attended a medical conference last year in her hometown. Dr. Adams invited Mamie to join them for a night out. Mamie and Cyrus flirted with each other the whole evening.

Although she made it clear that she didn't date married men, Cyrus considered himself the exception. He had no plans to stop pursuing her. Cyrus envisioned her lithe, olive body lying naked in his arms. He wondered if Mamie had fine or bushy pubic hair. The thicker the better. He liked the scratchy feel of it against his fine pubic hair.

The sound of a police siren snapped Cyrus out of his daydream. He had a hard-on and walked peg-legged to his car. He got in, unzipped his pants, and jacked off. He was satisfied but not fulfilled. The time had come for him to live life on his own terms. He left the river determined to make that happen.

Chapter Ten

~

After the twins were put to bed, Carrie went to the living room and sat in a chair next to Ruth, who was warming her feet in front of the heater. Both women sat quietly, each wrapped in her thoughts.

Carrie walked to the window and stared into the blackness. Beyond the house lay the barren cotton fields, which had been harvested in October. On her days off, Carrie had been among the pickers, dressed in her brother's old pants and long-sleeved shirt rolled to her elbows with a rag tied around her head. She spent nine hours hunched over rows of stalks bursting with bulbs of white, fluffy cotton that she stuffed in a nine-foot canvas sack that dragged behind her.

At day's end, she pocketed eleven dollars. Even now, just thinking about the back-breaking work made Carrie's whole body ache. She arched her back and rotated her shoulders. Cold air seeping through the window gave her goose bumps.

Carrie stepped away from the window and tugged at the arms of her sweater. She picked up an old *McCall's Magazine* on her way back to the chair but put it down after a few minutes. Carrie turned on the TV, switching channels back and forth before finally turning it off.

Ruth watched Carrie flitter around the house and finally spoke up. "What's troubling you?"

"Nothing."

"Then why you restless?" Ruth got up, broke off a straw from the broom, and picked her teeth. "You been moping 'round here and complaining all week."

"No, I haven't."

Ruth gave her a stern look. "So, I must be blind and deaf?"

"No."

"Enough of this play acting," Ruth said. "I know what the problem is. It's you."

"Me?"

Ruth stood in front of Carrie and gave her a tongue-lashing. "I'm sick and tired of you acting like Miss Ann. For the last nine months, you been talking 'bout you don't like this and you don't want that. Seems like ain't nothing good enough for you. What are you going to do about it? What's the plan?"

Carrie wasn't in the mood to argue with her mother. She started to get up and leave but knew Ruth would just follow her into the bedroom. "My plan is the same as it has always been. Work and take care of my babies. Things going good right now. I got a few steady customers at the beauty shop. I ain't making a killing, but I'm keeping up."

Ruth bent down so that she was eye level with Carrie. "I can see that, but you ain't happy. And don't lie and tell me you are."

"I'm fine, Mama. I don't know what else you want me to say," Carrie said in exasperation.

"All you do is work, go to church, and tend to your children. You too young and smart to be stuck here. You can make more money in Memphis fixing hair than you can down here. This ain't no place for y'all. The babies need a proper upbringing. They need to live in the city and go to good schools. And you need to find a man to be a daddy to those children."

"I don't need no man," Carrie said indignantly. "I had one and look what happened."

"He wasn't for you. I'm talking 'bout a decent man who gonna look after y'all. Treat you nice. Buy you things. Fix you up a nice place. Albert could've done all that, but you didn't give him the time of day."

"I don't want no man, and I definitely didn't want Albert," Carrie bellowed.

Ruth dropped to her knees and took Carrie's face in her hands. "Listen to me. Every woman need a man. Don't let the babies' daddy turn you against all men. He's moved on to somebody else, and you sitting 'round all by yourself. That don't make no sense. The reason you ain't taken up with nobody here is 'cause you don't think they good enough for you."

"Mama, I'm fine just the way I am." She removed Ruth's hands and returned to the window.

"Well, I ain't happy with you being here," Ruth said, following Carrie. "I sent you to Memphis for a reason. I wanted you to do better than me and be somebody important. I won't let you give up 'cause of some nigga."

Carrie wanted to put her hands over her ears, but she was afraid Ruth would slap her for being disrespectful.

"Ain't nothing down here for y'all. I'll be living in the country 'til the day I die, but there's no reason for you to be here. See, you was supposed to be the way out of Mississippi for Cleotha. I was going to send her up there to go to school like I did you. I promised myself that my last two children would do better than the first two."

Carrie turned quickly and said, "Mama, I've thought about going back to Memphis, but I just don't know. The timing ain't right."

"It's right. Start making plans to go back." Ruth walked over to the heater and rocked on her heels. "The longer you stay here, the harder it'll be to leave. We may all need to move the way things are going."

"Why you say that, Mama?"

She motioned Carrie toward the chairs, and they sat facing each other. Ruth spoke in a hushed voice. "The white folks is all stirred up about the civil rights workers coming through here registering colored folks to vote. The KKK threatening to kill Dr. Martin Luther King if he come back."

"But Dr. King ain't hurting nobody," Carrie said. "He's just trying to make things better for us."

"Chile, they don't want nothing to change," Ruth exclaimed. She became animated, gesturing with her arms. "If colored folks get the right to vote, that means we'll have some power and be equal to white folks. Do you think those peckerwoods in town ready for that?" She grabbed the blanket and threw it across her shoulders. "Look, we done got all off the subject," she said with a dismissive wave. "If you don't want to go back to Memphis, you got a cousin in Chicago who would be glad to let you stay with her. Now, that's just a suggestion. I think you better off in Memphis, but the decision is yours."

"I don't want to leave."

"But you going," Ruth said in a steely tone that told Carrie not to argue with her.

Carrie stalked out of the room and went to her bedroom, where she lay in the dark, mulling over the conversation. It felt good being back home. Now, Ruth was pushing her out.

To go where? That was the question. She had never been to Chicago but heard it was big, windy, and cold. She didn't want to go back to Memphis to live with Nee Mama again, cleaning up her vomit, watching her passed out on the bed, and smelling her body odor when she was too drunk to wash herself.

Flustered, she went back to the living room, where Ruth was waiting. "Mama, I don't see how I can do it. Where would I live? Work? Who would look after the twins?"

"Leave them with me until you get on your feet." The look on Carrie's face told Ruth that she wasn't thrilled with that idea. "It's just for a little while. I believe children should be with their own mama."

She knew Ruth was right. She had gone about as far as she could go at Tess's Beauty Shop. There was no future for her and the twins in Mississippi. It was time to leave. "Okay, Mama."

***

A week later, Carrie took a Greyhound bus to Memphis. She rented a room from Miz Lula, a petite woman with toffee-colored skin who wore a curly wig that was crooked most of the time. She found Miz Lula through Miz Ida Mae, who stayed at the house on weekends.

Miz Lula was a nice lady but a little eccentric. A widow and retired cook, she lived in a neat three-bedroom house on Fenty Avenue in Hyde Park. It was close enough to visit Nee Mama when she felt like it but far enough away to keep her grandmother from dropping by in one of her drunken stupors.

At first, Carrie thought the house with its brown shingle siding was a little spooky. Miz Lula kept the curtains drawn, and there were plants everywhere – on the floor, in the windows, and hanging from the ceiling. Carrie couldn't figure out how they grew without sunlight.

The oddest thing, however, was that Miz Lula saved every greeting card and postcard, and tacked them on the walls. There were Christmas cards, birthday cards, sympathy cards, Easter cards, get well cards, anniversary cards, thank you cards, and postcards from her son who had been in the Army. Some were faded and dry-rotted, which gave the house a dusty smell.

There were good things about her home. When Carrie peered out the kitchen window, she could see a pumping station atop a hill in the middle of a huge field. It felt like she was back home whenever she looked at the field.

Miz Lula charged Carrie ten dollars a week, and she laid down the law. No drinking. No smoking. No cussing. No men. Carrie could use the kitchen, but she had to clean up after herself. Carrie had no problem with the rules, especially since she didn't plan to stay there very long.

For three weeks, she visited the beauty shops that were supposed to be the best in town. Some didn't have openings. Others wanted her to do some more training, which made no sense to Carrie considering she had been doing hair on her own for two months.

The bad weather made looking for a job even more difficult. Freezing temperatures, accompanied by ice storms, made this the coldest January in the city's history. She was ready to give up and go back home when Miz Lula's friend told her that the Tri-County Publishing Company needed help in the cafeteria.

Carrie had never worked in a restaurant, but she had certainly cooked enough meals. On the day of the interview, she arrived at nine o'clock, half an hour early. A muscular man in a blue uniform greeted her when she stepped inside the door. His skin was smooth, a reddish brown, like an Indian. He had a pretty smile and a chest the size of a small refrigerator. His nameplate read Cleary E. Pollard.

"Good morning, ma'am," the guard said, touching the tip of his cap. "How can I help you?"

"I'm, I'm here to see Mr. Thomas Williams about a job," Carrie said through chattering teeth.

"What department he in?"

"He's the cafeteria manager."

"You at the wrong door. This entrance is for deliveries." He stepped from behind his desk, took her elbow, and guided her to the exit.

Carrie thought he was short sitting down, but when he stood they were about the same height.

"Go 'round the back of the building, and you'll see a door that say 'Employees,'" he said.

"Thanks," Carrie said.

"Have a nice day," he said, tipping his hat again.

Chapter Eleven

Nadine checked the pantry and the refrigerator, and jotted down what she needed from the grocery store. She went back to Miz Esther's room to see whether she had enough ginger ale and soda crackers. The bedroom door was closed, but Nadine heard the radio blasting. "Miz Esther, you need anything from the store?" she yelled.

"No."

"I'm going to the beauty shop and the store. Vera is here, okay?"

"Stop shouting," Miz Esther said. "I'm not deaf."

"Sorry, I didn't know if you could hear me over the radio. I'll be back around three."

No response. Miz Esther had been in a bad mood all morning, but Nadine wasn't going to let that ruin her day. She went into the dining room, where Vera was polishing Miz Esther's silver flatware. "She's all yours."

"How's she doing today?" Vera asked as she rubbed gray paste on an elegantly carved knife. A tawny, tall woman with fine features, Vera was in her early fifties. She worked for some of the most prominent white families in Memphis until a terrible automobile accident crushed her right leg. Now, she did light housekeeping and sat with the sick and elderly.

"She's not in a good mood," Nadine replied.

"Me neither. We'll get along just fine today."

Vera treated Miz Esther like she was the First Lady, and Miz Esther played the role to perfection. Nadine was glad they got along, and the girls liked Vera, too.

Soon as Nadine put the key in the ignition, she remembered that Cyrus asked her to take two suits to the cleaners. She ran back upstairs, got the suits, and left them on a chair in the living room. Nadine was about to knock on Miz Esther's door to see if she had any clothes for the cleaners but stopped when she heard her name.

"I told Cyrus to forget about a divorce. They've been married sixteen years, and it doesn't make sense to break up at this point." Nadine put her ear to the crack between the door and frame. "I'm just not letting him do that to my grandbabies."

Nadine started to burst into the room, snatch the phone out of Miz Esther's hand, and tell her to stop lying, but she gathered the suits and left the house. Inside the car, Nadine replayed the conversation in her head. It occurred to her that Miz Esther had actually stuck up for her.

She was furious with herself for not seeing that her marriage was in trouble. She gripped the steering wheel and fought back tears. She needed someone to talk to, and the only person she could think of was Lydia Cooksley, a member of the Commodores auxiliary. Although they talked at meetings, Nadine realized that she didn't know her well enough to share such a personal matter.

The only person she trusted was her best friend, Frannie, who knew all her secrets. Frannie never liked Cyrus or Miz Esther because she thought they acted snobbish. She begged Nadine not to marry him.

Nadine didn't tell Frannie everything that happened in their marriage, but Frannie knew she wasn't happy. She needed her friend's advice and was tempted to call her long distance but decided it would be too expensive. Instead, she wrote Frannie a letter.

February 2, 1968

Dear Frannie,

How are you? I am not doing too well. Things have gotten really bad between me and Cyrus. I heard Miz Esther talking on the phone, and she said that Cyrus wants a divorce. Believe it or not, Miz Esther told him that she is not in favor of him getting a divorce. If he decides to do it anyway, what will happen to me, Jocelyn and Salena? He may put us out on the street. Where would we go and how would we live? This is all my fault. If I had been a better wife, he wouldn't be trying to divorce me. I haven't been performing my wifely duties, if you know what I mean. I'm sure this is the reason he wants to leave me. I am so scared that I can barely eat or sleep. If you have any ideas write me back right away.

Love always,
Nadine

When Frannie's letter arrived, Nadine locked herself in the bathroom before she tore open the envelope.

February 6, 1968

Dear Nadine,

I am doing fine. I'm sorry that you're having problems, but I think you would be better off without Cyrus. You deserve to be happy and free of him and Miz Esther. You are too good for them. I know you are worried about being on your own, but you can make it. There are plenty women who don't have a husband and do just fine. They get a job and pay their own bills. Cyrus will have to give you some money to take care of the girls so don't worry your head off. If he asks you for a divorce, just sign the papers and say good riddance. I'll even come to Memphis and help you move out of that house. I

will be praying for you.
    Yours truly,
    Frannie

She read the letter again. It seemed that Frannie had more confidence in her than she had in herself. Nadine decided to stop worrying and pray that everything would turn out in her favor.

***

Nadine was sitting in the den, towel drying Salena's hair and thinking about Frannie's advice when Jocelyn sidled up to her.

"If I ask you a question, will you say yes?" Jocelyn asked.

"I can't say yes without knowing the question," said Nadine, who parted Salena's hair in four sections, dipped two fingers in a can of Royal Crown, and spread the hair dressing on her scalp.

"Okay, okay," Jocelyn said. "Just don't get mad."

"I will get mad if you don't spit it out before next Christmas," she said.

Jocelyn took a deep breath and blurted out, "Mama, can I go to the Elite Debs dance with Ronnie Tilson?" She closed her eyes tight and then opened one to see Nadine's reaction.

Nadine stopped brushing Salena's hair and busted out laughing. "Can you do what?"

"Come on, Mama. You heard me."

"What is the Elite Debs?"

"It's that club Daddy said I couldn't join last year. They have a Sweethearts Ball every year, and everybody's going." She grabbed Nadine's hand. "Please, can I go?"

Nadine gave Jocelyn a look of disapproval. "No dating until you're seventeen," she said. "By my math, that's another two years."

"Ow!" Salena squealed. "Mama, you're hurting."

"Sorry, baby," she said, loosening the braid. "I'm annoyed by this whole discussion. I didn't mean to take it out on you."

"Mama, this is special," she explained. "All my friends are going."

"With boys?"

Jocelyn began picking at her fingernails. "No, not all of them."

"Why do you have to go with one?"

"Mama, Ronnie is the cutest, most popular boy in school," she said, resting her head on Nadine's shoulder. "And he's the captain of the football team. All of the girls wanted to go with him, but he asked me."

Nadine looked at her curiously. "How did you end up being the lucky one?"

"I don't know. I guess he thinks I'm cute." She giggled. "I mean, I guess he thinks I'm nice or something."

"There you go, Salena," Nadine said, patting down the last braid. "Now go tie up your hair." She turned back to Jocelyn. "Who are this boy's people?"

"His daddy lives in Forrest City, Arkansas, and his mama is a social worker."

"When is the dance?"

"A week from Friday. Can I go, please, Mama?" she said with her hands clasped in front of her. "We won't be by ourselves. There'll be teachers and parents chaperoning."

Nadine thought about it for a few seconds. "Well, I don't see why not as long as there'll be some adults there. Let me talk it over with your daddy."

Jocelyn pouted. "I know what he's going to say. No!"

"How do you know? Are you a mind reader?"

"I know him. He gets mad whenever I mention the b-word."

"You may be surprised this time. Let me talk to him first."

"Okay."

Nadine gave her a playful smack on the bottom. Thinking back to high school, Nadine recalled that she was Jocelyn's age when she went to her first dance with a boy. She didn't see any harm in letting Jocelyn go but still had to run it by Cyrus.

That night, Nadine was sewing a button on one of Cyrus's shirts while he sat across from her reading the afternoon newspaper. "There's an activity at Jocelyn's school in two weeks. I'm thinking about helping out unless there's something you have planned."

"What date is that?" Cyrus asked.

"February ninth."

"I have a meeting in Nashville on the ninth and tenth. You can do whatever you want."

Nadine wanted to jump for joy. Cyrus would never know that Jocelyn went to the dance with a boy. It would be their secret. She began thinking about what kind of dress Jocelyn would wear to her first social. Nadine wanted her to be the prettiest girl at the dance and planned to shop at the exclusive boutiques in midtown to find the perfect dress.

***

When Ronnie Tilson and his mother came to pick up Jocelyn the night of the big dance, he was speechless. She looked like a fashion model in a rainbow-colored, chiffon dress that floated around her body as she glided across the room on light green kitten heels. Miz Tilson promised to have Jocelyn home by ten-thirty. As she left, Nadine whispered into her ear, "You'll be the prettiest girl at the dance. Have a good time, baby."

"I will, Mama. Thanks."

Nadine got teary as Jocelyn hooked her arm through Ronnie's arm, and they walked out the door. Salena was trying to get her attention, but Nadine's mind was on Jocelyn and how grown-up she looked.

"Mama, can I have some ice cream?"

"Yes, you can have two scoops tonight," she said, pinching Salena's cheeks.

"I can? Why?"

"I'm in a good mood, but if you don't want it, I'll eat it."

"No, I want it," Salena said, running to the kitchen.

After they ate ice cream, Nadine and Salena watched TV until it was Salena's bedtime. Nadine couldn't wait to climb into bed with the latest copy of *Jive* magazine. Thirty minutes later, she heard the front door open. She grabbed her bathrobe to go downstairs and thank Miz Tilson. As she descended the stairs, she bumped into Cyrus.

"Where are you going in such a hurry?" he asked.

The shock of seeing him caused her to stumble on the stairs. "What are you doing home?" she asked, looking up at him. She tried to sound normal, but her voice was two octaves higher.

"I haven't been feeling well and decided to come back early. I must be coming down with something."

Nadine nervously clutched the top of her bathrobe.

Cyrus walked past her and said over his shoulder, "Bring me a glass of water so I can take a couple of aspirin."

She went to the kitchen and began walking in circles, trying to figure out how to explain Jocelyn's whereabouts. Cyrus walked into the kitchen and looked around. "Where's Jocelyn? She's not in her room."

Nadine got a glass, filled it with water, and handed it to Cyrus. "She had an activity at school."

"Weren't you supposed to go with her?"

"Yeah, but they had so many chaperones that I decided to stay home." Nadine wet the dishrag and wiped the stove.

Cyrus set the glass on the counter. "You know I don't like her to be out at night. When is she coming home?"

"Miz Tilson said she would bring them back around ten-thirty."

"Who is Miz Tilson?" he asked.

Before Nadine could answer, the front door opened. Cyrus pushed Nadine aside and headed to the living room. He got there just as Ronnie was giving Jocelyn a good night kiss.

"Nigga, get your hands off my daughter!" he yelled.

He lunged at Ronnie, but Jocelyn stepped in front of him. "Daddy, he was just—"

"I saw what he was doing," Cyrus said, pushing Jocelyn aside. "Get out of my house, boy, before I hurt you."

"Sir, I didn't mean no disrespect," he said. "I'm Ronnie—"

Cyrus cut him off. "Get out!"

Ronnie turned to Jocelyn and said, "I'm sorry if I got you in trouble." He hurried out the door.

Cyrus slammed the door behind him. Nadine stood speechless, afraid of what Cyrus might do next. Miz Esther hobbled out of her bedroom to see what the commotion was about.

"Daddy, you didn't have to be mean to Ronnie. He didn't do anything wrong."

"He had his hands all over you. The two of you were making out right in my living room."

Miz Esther gasped. "They were doing what?"

"He didn't have his hands all over me," Jocelyn said.

"Look at you," he said, eyeing her with disgust. "It's no wonder he was treating you like a slut. You got your face all painted, and you're wearing that see-through dress. You look like a whore."

Jocelyn started crying. "I hate you!" she shouted.

"What did you just say?" Cyrus raised his hand, and before Nadine could step between them, he slapped Jocelyn.

"Stop it, Cyrus," Nadine yelled.

Cyrus started toward her. "Shut up, bitch. You shouldn't have let her go out. You think you can do stuff behind my back and get away with it?" He pushed Nadine until she backed into a corner. Then, he slapped her. His class ring raked her left eye, causing her to cry out in pain.

Something took hold of Nadine. She attacked Cyrus, kicking him in the groin and punching him in the chest. Cyrus pushed Nadine off, held her back, and slapped her repeatedly. Stunned by the blows, Nadine fell backward.

"Daddy, stop!" Jocelyn pleaded.

"Stop it, Cyrus, before you kill her," Miz Esther screamed as she tried to pull him away.

Cyrus stood above Nadine with wild eyes. His face was flushed and sweaty. He jerked his head sideways like a boxer.

Jocelyn squeezed between them. "Mama, are you okay?" she asked, stooping to examine Nadine's face.

She lay crumpled on the floor, blood trickling from her nose and mouth. She tried to get up, but her legs gave way, and she slumped back to the floor. Jocelyn stood Nadine up and took her to the couch.

"This is what you get," Cyrus said, shaking his fist at Nadine. "Don't you ever do something like this again."

"That's enough, Cyrus," Miz Esther said. "Go get a pan of cold water and some towels."

Cyrus didn't move.

"Didn't you hear what I said?"

"You clean her up." Cyrus snatched his coat and car keys, and left the house.

For the next few minutes, Miz Esther and Jocelyn tried to calm Nadine, but she cried hysterically.

"Hold your head back, Nadine," Miz Esther said. "You're getting blood all over everything."

"Leave me alone," she said, pushing away Miz Esther's hand. "I don't need your help."

"Mama, you look hurt real bad," Jocelyn said. "Do as Grandma says."

Nadine struggled to her feet and walked a few steps, but her vision was impaired. "Oh, God!" she shouted. "He put my eye out!"

Miz Esther felt sorry for Nadine, but she was losing her patience. "Sit down, Nadine. Your eye is just swollen. You aren't blind," she said.

"Please come and sit down, Mama. I need to clean your face and put some medicine on it," Jocelyn said. She tried to guide her back to the couch, but Nadine broke free and staggered toward the front door. She lost her balance, hit the floor, and bumped her head.

"Mama!" Jocelyn shrieked as she rushed over to Nadine. Jocelyn tapped her on the cheek. No response. She shook her. Nothing. Jocelyn screamed, "Grandma, I think Mama's dead!"

Miz Esther limped over to Nadine and put two fingers on the side of her neck, checking for a pulse. "She's still alive. She probably just knocked herself out. Go get the smelling salts from my medicine cabinet. It's in a brown bottle."

Jocelyn ran to Miz Esther's bathroom and came back with two bottles. "I didn't know which one," she said, both of her hands shaking.

Miz Esther read the labels and took the smallest bottle. She opened the bottle and waved it under Nadine's nose. Her eyes opened, she coughed, and looked at them terrified. She began clawing at Miz Esther.

Jocelyn grabbed her hands. "No, Mama, don't." Nadine's body went limp, and she began whimpering. "Grandma, we need to get her to the hospital."

"That won't be necessary," Miz Esther said. "I'll call Dr. Adams."

He arrived within the hour. He examined Nadine and determined it was safe to move her upstairs. After he cleaned her face, he discovered that Nadine wasn't as bad off as she looked.

"Your face is going to be swollen and sore for a while, but you'll be fine after that. It doesn't look like anything is broken," Dr. Adams said. He removed a bottle of pills from his satchel. "I'm going to give you two pills for the pain, and I want you to get some sleep. You can take two pills every four hours if you need to."

"What about my eye?"

"After the swelling goes down, your vision may be a little blurred, but it should clear up. If it doesn't, come and see me."

After Dr. Adams packed up his bag, he turned to Jocelyn and said, "Take good care of your mother. She's been through a lot. Good night."

"Thank you," Jocelyn replied. She covered Nadine and got into bed with her.

Chapter Twelve

~

Cyrus drove his Thunderbird like he rode his women. Hard. Long. And sometimes fast. He crisscrossed the city, ending up at the riverfront. He stopped for a few minutes to collect himself, but the water rendered no solace. He sped away.

When Cyrus got to Second Street and Vance Avenue, he saw a couple of prostitutes standing on the corner. One of them sashayed over to his car while he waited for the light to turn green. She wore a fake leopard coat, fishnet stockings, and black leather boots. She was short and bowlegged. Cyrus rolled down the window. Her black minidress was cut so low that her breasts tumbled onto his forearm when she leaned into the car.

"Hey, handsome, looking for me? A fine man like you need somebody to keep him warm on a cold night like this. How about me and you go on a date?" she asked, flipping back the red wig that hung to her butt.

Cyrus looked at the hooker, unsure whether he should push her off his car or invite her in. She looked clean and didn't talk nasty like a lot of the streetwalkers. Actually, she was kind of pretty. She had smooth cocoa skin, a round face, and light brown eyes. He guessed that she was in her early thirties.

"Well, are you going to have me standing here all night or what?" she teased, stroking her breasts.

Cyrus leered at the hooker. "How much will the date cost?"

"Ten and two."

"And what do I get besides the pleasure of your company."

"That's cute," she said smiling. "We can discuss that in my room."

"Where would that be?"

"Over there," she said, pointing to the Skyview Hotel across the street.

"Is there a back door?"

"You one of them back door men, huh? That's okay, sugar. Drive 'round back of the hotel and park in the alley. I'll let you in the back door. Don't be long."

Before Cyrus got out of the car, he checked the alley to make sure he wasn't being set up for a robbery. The hooker opened the emergency exit and beckoned him. They walked up a narrow, dimly lit stairway to the second floor.

The hallway reeked of urine and smoke. She unlocked the door to a small room that smelled like bleach. There was nothing fancy about the accommodations. A faded green bedspread. A beige vinyl chair. The only light in the room came from a tiny lamp atop the bedside table. "It ain't the Holiday Inn, is it? Take off your jacket and get comfortable."

"What's your name?" Cyrus asked as he sat on the bed.

"Senorita."

"Please to make your acquaintance, Senorita," he said, offering his hand.

She shook it and curtsied. "Me, too," she said. "You look kind of tired. Been working hard?"

"I just came back from a trip, and I haven't been feeling well."

"Maybe I can help you feel better."

Senorita did a little strip dance as she peeled off her clothes. Cyrus lay on his stomach, and she straddled him, massaging his neck and shoulders. Her hands were quick and soothing. After a few minutes, he became aroused and turned over. Senorita slid her hands up and down his manhood.

Cyrus reached out to touch the breasts that had teased him, but they were out of his reach. He pulled her down on the bed and got on top. Cyrus pumped and pumped his body into hers until it felt like a dam had broken inside him. Panting and tired, he fell flat on Senorita.

"Hey, you're not gonna die on me, are you?" Senorita said, shaking Cyrus.

"I need some rest," he mumbled.

Senorita got out of bed and picked up her clothes. "You have to pay eight dollars if you want to stay all night."

Cyrus staggered out of bed, got his wallet, and paid for her services and the room. Sweating and feverish, he flopped across the bed. Sleep came quickly, but Cyrus was tormented by dreams of demons stabbing him with pitchforks as he hung above a vat of boiling hot sauce.

He tossed and turned all night long. One minute he was screaming for help; the next he was apologizing to Nadine and Carrie. The monsters came and went. Eight hours later, a loud knocking awakened him.

"Party's over, buddy. Time to go," said a gruff voice outside the room.

"Huh? What?" Cyrus said underneath the tangled covers. He was lying crosswise in bed on the damp and foul-smelling mattress.

"Get moving," the man said.

"What time is it?" Cyrus called out.

"It's morning. Time for you to hit the road."

"Okay, okay. Let me get my clothes on."

Cyrus dressed quickly and left the same way he came. Luckily, his car was still parked in the alley. Slowly, scenes from last night came back to him. Nadine bloody on the floor. Jocelyn crying. He couldn't believe that he had hit Nadine. He felt bad about what he had done but still angry with Nadine for deceiving him.

Miz Esther was sitting in the living room when he got home. She took one look at him and frowned. "You look like hell warmed over. Where have you been all night?"

"Mama, I—"

"Nadine is in bad shape, Cyrus. I called Dr. Adams after you went storming out of the house. He said you might have busted her eardrum."

"Why did you call him?"

Miz Esther picked up her cane and threw it at Cyrus. "What else was I supposed to do? Take her to the hospital and have everybody asking me a bunch of damn questions?"

Cyrus picked up the cane and laid it next to her. "Did Dr. Adams ask what happened?"

"Of course he did, but I didn't tell him anything. He could tell from looking at her that she didn't get those injuries falling down the stairs."

Cyrus sat in the chair and rubbed his forehead.

"Was that your way of getting Nadine to divorce you?"

He blinked rapidly and shook his head. "No, this has nothing to do with the divorce. I don't know what happened. Something just snapped. I didn't mean to hurt her. When I came out of the kitchen and saw Jocelyn kissing that boy, I just lost it."

"Nadine was wrong to let Jocelyn go out, but you can't go around beating your wife. Think of what would happen if word of this got out. Dr. Adams will keep his mouth shut, but you never know who is listening and watching."

"I know, Mama. You're right. I'll never do this again. I promise."

"I'm not the only one you need to make up with. Nadine needs to see how remorseful you are. Go upstairs and apologize even if you don't mean it."

Cyrus kissed his mother on the cheek. She got a whiff of him and pretended she was having a coughing spell. She shooed him away.

Inside their bedroom, Cyrus found Nadine lying on her side facing the window. Jocelyn was asleep on her stomach next to Nadine. He shook Jocelyn, and her eyes fluttered open.

"Go to your room," he whispered.

"Huh," she said half-awake. "Daddy, don't…"

"Do as I say."

Jocelyn threw back the covers, pushed down her party dress, and rushed out of the room.

Cyrus walked around the bed to wake Nadine but recoiled at her appearance. One of her eyes was swollen shut, and her face was purple and puffy. He touched her arm lightly.

"Nadine," he said.

Groggy from the painkillers, Nadine lifted her head. "Get away from me!" she yelled.

"Quiet, Nadine. I'm not going to hit you," he said, backing away. "Listen, I didn't mean to hurt you, but you shouldn't have gone behind my back and let Jocelyn go out. You know how I feel about her courting. If you don't want this to happen again, I suggest you don't do it again." Cyrus stopped talking briefly unsure whether Nadine had fallen asleep. "Did you hear me?"

"I heard you," she murmured.

"Let's just put this behind us," he said, heading for the bathroom. "I forgive you."

***

After his last patient, Cyrus got comfortable in his chair and dialed Mamie's office. "I can't wait to see you. When are you getting here?"

"It looks like I won't be able to get away until May."

"That's three whole months. You're killing me," he said, feigning pain.

"I don't know if I want to see you again. In case you forgot, there's still this issue of you being married."

"Why is that a problem?" Cyrus asked. He removed his necktie and unfastened the top button. "We're just two people enjoying each other's company."

"Are you seriously asking me why I don't want to go out with a married man?"

"Lighten up, please. There's nothing wrong with going out with a friend, is it?"

"No, as long as *you* understand the rules," she said. "We can talk and drink all night, but that's as far as it goes."

Cyrus smirked. "I hear you loud and clear."

"Well, I've got to head out for a meeting. I'll talk to you later."

"Yes, you will," he replied. "Take care."

Cyrus liked a challenge, and Mamie playing hard to get turned him on. He had no problems letting her think she was controlling the relationship. He couldn't wait to see her. The more time he spent with her the harder it would be for her to resist him.

Chapter Thirteen

~

The job in the cafeteria was okay, but Carrie had no intention of growing old there. Her shift started at seven o'clock in the morning. She took orders and cleared the tables for the breakfast and lunch crowd. Carrie brought home thirty-eight dollars a week in salary and tips. After expenses and sending money home, she saved about nine dollars a month.

Carrie missed her babies. She longed to hug them, pinch their soft cheeks, and smooth down their curly hair. She imagined them doing something crazy with their hair when they became teenagers, like trying to wear the new Afro hairstyle. She laughed to herself.

"What are you smiling about?" asked Cleary, the security guard. He walked past her and hopped on a stool.

"Nothing."

"Oh, it was something all right. Had you grinning from ear to ear."

Carrie smiled again. So did Cleary. "When do you work? Every time I come up here you sitting down sipping coffee like you the boss lady. Didn't your mama tell you that coffee make you black?" he teased.

"I been drinking it a long time, and ain't nothing happened yet," she said in a sassy voice. "What you having today?"

Cleary said in a low voice, "If I told you, would you give it to me?"

"Don't be coming in here with no mess today," she said, waving a towel at him. "I ain't in the mood."

"I'm just playing with you. Give me a scrambled egg sandwich with mayonnaise and ketchup, and a grape drink. And don't burn my toast this time."

"It wasn't burnt the last time. You said make it dark, didn't you?" She wrote down his order and took it to the window.

"Uh, uh, uh," he said, shaking his head. "I don't know how no man put up with you. You need a good whupping."

Carrie put her hands on her hips and walked toward him. "How no man put up with me? I don't put up with no man, and ain't nobody laying a hand on me."

"Well, I can see that. So, you don't have a man, huh?"

"That ain't your business," Carrie said, setting the silverware on the counter. "Did I ask you if you had a wife?"

"No, but I ain't married," he said.

Carrie filled a glass with water and set it in front of him. She pretended to be busy while the cook was making his sandwich. She didn't want Cleary asking any more questions. Nor did she want to be mean and run him off. He was nice to her, always had something funny to say.

Most of their conversations had been pretty general except for the day when they got on the subject of kids. Cleary told her that he had a nine-year-old son but had not seen him in five years. He was living with the boy's mother when she ran off with another man.

Now, he wanted to know if she had a man in her life. Carrie set his food down and went to get a grape Nehi soda. When she returned, she said, "No, there ain't nobody I'm seeing right now, Mister Nosy Rosy. Anything else you want to know?"

Cleary swallowed quickly, gulped down some soda, and nearly choked trying to get out the words. "That'll do for now. There's a lot more I'd like to know, but we can talk about that somewhere else. Why don't you let me take you out Saturday?"

"Out where?" she asked. "I don't want to be sitting up in one of those juke joints you probably hang out in all night 'cause I got church Sunday morning."

"We don't have to be out all night unless you want to be. I got church, too. I'm in the choir." Cleary started singing "Swing Low, Sweet Chariot." "How does that sound?"

"Bad, real bad," Carrie said laughing. "I bet you ain't darkened a church in I don't know how many years. You going to hell for lying, boy."

"So, we on for this Saturday?"

Carrie extended her index finger to her cheek, turning her head from side to side. "Well, I guess you can take me out, but you better behave."

"Like I said, I'm a church boy," he said, bowing his head in prayer.

"Eat your lunch. I've got to get back to work."

"Girl, you don't be doing no work. Who you fooling?"

Carrie threw the towel over her shoulder and turned up her nose at Cleary on her way to the kitchen. As she put away the clean dishes, she had second thoughts about going out with him. She remembered her vow not to get involved with another man. Then again, she thought it might be nice to have somebody to talk to beside Miz Lula, Miz Ida Mae, and Nee Mama.

When Cleary got ready to pay his check, Carrie wrote down her address and phone number. She told him to honk when he got to her house, and she would come out to the car. She didn't want Miz Lula to think that men were about to start trotting in and out of her house.

***

Carrie stood at the window until she saw Cleary's blue Galaxy coming down the street. She was at the curb so fast that he didn't get a chance to blow the horn. Cleary rolled down the window. "Excuse me, I'm looking for Carrie Boyd. She's probably wearing a blue uniform with a white apron and black hairnet. Have you seen her around here?"

"Stop playing, Cleary, it's cold out here. Unlock the door and let me get in the car before I freeze to death."

Cleary gazed at her in awe as she climbed into the car. "Wow," he said. "Your hair looks nice. I'm not used to seeing it hanging down."

"Thank you. I have to keep it pinned up at work for sanitary reasons," she said.

"Who would've thought that underneath that hairnet and big dress was such a pretty girl? I'm just glad nobody else noticed."

She tried not to blush from all the compliments, turning her head toward the window so that he wouldn't see her red cheeks. "Let's go. We'll be late if you keep sitting here trying to fill my head."

"I'll keep my thoughts to myself," he said, smiling at Carrie.

When they got to Curry's Club Tropicana, the place was packed. There was a long line at the front door, but Cleary ushered her to a side entrance. He tapped on the door four times, and a burly man wearing a shiny gray suit let them in. They were in an area behind the stage. The walls and ceilings were painted black, and the floor was black and white tile. Carrie could hear the crowd clapping.

"Here's the coolest cat around. Cleary, my man, what's going on?" The men shook hands and gave each other a half hug.

"I see y'all got a full house tonight."

"Yeah, man. The Memphis folks love them some Bobby 'Blue' Bland. He could pack this place seven nights a week."

"Swift, this here is Carrie," Cleary said.

Swift nodded in her direction. "How you doing, Carrie?"

"Fine, thank you. It's nice to meet you, er, Swift."

"My real name is Calvin, but the cats at the gym call me Swift 'cause

I'm fast," he explained, punching the air like a boxer.

Cleary put a hand over his mouth and doubled over in laughter. "That ain't the real reason. He got that nickname when he was in seventh grade and got knocked down by a punching bag. A trainer was trying to show him how to use it. When the dude hit the bag, he told Swift to move, but he didn't get out of the way fast enough."

"Man, that bag knocked the daylights out of me. Just talking about it makes me see stars."

Carrie laughed.

"Y'all come on and get your seats," he said, leading the way. "I saved some good ones down front. Bobby will be coming on in about twenty minutes." When they got to their seats, Swift turned to Carrie and said, "It was pleasure meeting you. Enjoy the show."

Cleary and Swift shook hands, and he disappeared behind the curtain. Cleary ordered ice and soft drinks for the fifth of whiskey he brought with him. He drank his straight; she mixed hers with a little Coke.

By the time Bobby 'Blue' Bland came on, Carrie could tell that Cleary was feeling pretty mellow. He had that look in his eye that said everything was copacetic. Carrie had relaxed, too, and really got into the show. Bobby brought the house down singing bluesy tunes about love and betrayal. He ended the ninety-minute show with one of her favorite songs, "That's the Way Love Is."

"Do another one," Carrie shouted as the crowd gave Bland a standing ovation. She let out a loud whistle that made Cleary crack up. "Bobby, Bobby," she chanted with the crowd.

Bland returned to the stage and sang two more songs. After he finished, the DJ began spinning records. Carrie and Cleary hit the dance floor. They did the boogaloo on "I Heard It Through the Grapevine." Hand danced to "Chain of Fools." And slow danced on "I Wish It Would Rain."

Cleary pressed his body hard against Carrie, and she could feel his erection. She was glad when the record ended because Cleary's hand had slipped close to her butt. She didn't want him to get the wrong idea. They danced two more fast songs and left the club around one-thirty. Carrie was nervous when he walked her to the front door. She thought he might try to kiss her.

"Well, Carrie, here you are safe and sound," Cleary said. "I enjoyed being with you tonight." He stood a respectable distance with his hands in his coat pocket.

Carrie wanted to hurry and get inside. "Me, too," she said, searching her purse for the house key. She found the key, slipped it into the lock, and opened the door.

Before she went in, Cleary said, "I'm game for doing it again. What about you?"

"You behaved yourself so I guess we can go out again," she said.

Cleary moved closer, and Carrie knew what that meant. To thwart any romantic overtures, she pecked him on the cheek like she would her brother. "Thanks for taking me out," she said. "I had a good time."

If Cleary was disappointed, he didn't show it. "Better get inside and lock the door. I don't want you saying I made you miss church. You know I got to be there early to sing."

"God is going to strike you down for lying. I'll see you Monday. Good night."

"Good night, Carrie."

Carrie went inside and peeped through the curtain as Cleary walked back to his car. She had to admit that Cleary was a nice, easy-going guy. She liked the fact that he treated her like a lady and didn't expect anything in return for taking her out. She didn't know what Cleary had in mind, but she knew that they would be good friends, nothing more.

Chapter Fourteen

~

Nadine's physical wounds healed in about ten days, but she wasn't quite herself after the beating. She became quiet and withdrawn. Ashamed to admit that she had been beaten, Nadine stopped writing letters to Frannie because she couldn't pretend everything was fine. Frannie would see right through her lies, demand to know what was wrong, and pressure her to leave Cyrus.

Although they were like-minded in many ways, Frannie didn't understand the conviction of a wife and mother. Nadine had to do what was best for her children, and that meant staying with Cyrus.

Her only joy these days came from taking care of her daughters, and she made sure they were happy and healthy. She also started volunteering at church. One day, Reverend Tyson asked her to work in the Fellowship Hall, where they were setting up a food distribution center for striking Negro sanitation workers.

When she walked into the room, it was in such disarray that she almost turned around and went home. "Who's in charge here?" Nadine asked a woman wearing an orange floral apron.

"You are if you want to be," the woman replied. "All I know is that I was told to take in donations."

Boxes and bags of food were sitting on the floor, chairs, and long tables lining the room. Nadine looked in one box, which held cans of green beans, corn, pork and beans, Spam, and potted meat. Brown bags were filled with grits, rice, and cereal.

Nadine turned to the woman. "Where did all this food come from?"

"Good people who support the colored garbage men," she said.

"Even some white people, if you can believe that," said a man, who came up behind Nadine.

"Pardon my bad manners. I'm Nadine Mitchell. Reverend Tyson asked me to help out over here."

"I'm Joe Johnson and this here is my wife, Susie. Just tell us what you want, and we'll do it to the best of our ability."

Nadine hadn't planned on overseeing the whole project, but there was no one else. Besides, she was good at organizing things. "Let's start by sorting the canned goods from the packaged food," she instructed. "The cans go on the tables on the right and everything else on the left."

Two hours later, they had organized half the food in the room. Nadine turned to the couple and said, "I have to go now, but I'm coming back tomorrow. Will you be here?"

"Yes, ma'am. We're both retired and ain't got nothing else to do," Susie said. "I'll ask some more church members to join us. Now that there's a system, we'll be able to put stuff away soon as folks bring it in."

Nadine looked around the room. "We're going to have this room looking like an A&P grocery store pretty soon," she said.

On her way home, Nadine stopped by Greenberg's grocery store. As she looked over the fruit, she saw one of the bag boys staring at her. He followed her when she rolled her shopping cart over to the dairy case. Nadine was ready to give him a piece of her mind if he accused her of stealing.

"Excuse me, ain't you Nadine?"

"Yes, I am," she said, searching his face for some sign of recognition.

"You don't remember me, do you?" He took off his cap, smoothed down his hair, and turned sideways.

Nadine broke into a grin. "Willie Lee? Willie Lee Griffin?"

"Yeah, Pookie, it's me. Ain't you a sight for sore eyes," he said, taking in her body. "Unh, unh, unh, you looking good, girl."

Nadine was surprised that Willie Lee remembered her pet name. "Nobody's called me Pookie in years. In fact, nobody called me that but my daddy."

"I know. Remember, I used to work for your daddy. I pitied the man that married you cause he spoiled you rotten. You were the only girl I knew who got an allowance. The rest of us had to do work around the house 'cause Mama made us. We didn't dare ask to get paid."

"Hush, I remember you were always begging me for jaw breakers. I knew you took a few from the display case when Daddy wasn't looking."

"Shh! Don't say that too loud. The boss man might be listening." Willie Lee put the cap back on. "Your daddy was the best boss I ever had. I heard he died a while back."

"Yeah, Daddy and Aunt Bessie Mae both passed away," she said, resting her purse in the shopping cart. "I come in here all the time, but this is the first time I've seen you. How long you been working here?"

"I been back about six months. I'm usually in the stockroom," he explained, pointing to a door behind him. "One of the boys broke his leg so I'm helping out front for a while."

"Your folks moved up North after tenth grade. Where did you go? Chicago?"

"No, we went to East St. Louis, where my mama's sister lived. I sure didn't want to go. It was hard leaving all my friends."

"What was East St. Louis like?"

"It was okay," he said. "After high school, I worked in the stockyards during the week, but the fun came on the weekend when I worked at my uncle's tavern. We danced all night long. There were more pretty girls than you could shake a stick at."

"I see some things haven't change," she joked. "You were always chasing girls."

Willie Lee looked at her with bedroom eyes. "Who, me?" he asked, raising an eyebrow. "You got me mixed up with somebody else. I've always been a one-woman man."

"Yeah, yeah, I'll believe it when I see it," Nadine said. "What made you come back to Memphis?"

Willie Lee was slow to answer the question. He stared at the floor, and when he raised his head, he had a somber expression. "My wife passed away, then my uncle died. After he died, my auntie closed the tavern."

"I'm sorry to hear that," Nadine said, wondering if she should ask any more personal questions. Since they were old friends, she didn't think he would mind. "How long were you married?" she asked quietly.

"Ten years."

"You have any children?"

Willie Lee's face lit up. "Yeah, I got a boy, nine. He's back in East St. Louis with my cousin. I'm going to bring him down here to start school in the fall. What about you, any crumb snatchers?"

"Yes, two girls. One just turned fifteen; the other is eight," she said proudly.

"Who was the lucky guy you married? Anybody I know?"

"Nah, he was a little older than us. His name is Cyrus Mitchell. He's a doctor."

"All right then, but I hope you ain't on his case like you were on mine."

"No, nothing like that," Nadine said with a nervous laugh. "Well, it's good to see you again, Willie Lee. I hope everything works out for you here."

"You, too, Nadine. Take care."

Willie Lee still had the same boyish good looks – caramel skin, freckles, and dark brown curly hair. Although he was short, Willie Lee had an athletic build that he maintained over the years.

Her daddy had been very fond of him. They talked baseball all the time, and her daddy let him drink half a bottle of beer when they discussed baseball teams and the great sluggers.

Nadine recalled that Frannie had a crush on Willie Lee. In fact, Frannie liked just about every boy she met. She made a mental note to write Frannie and tell her that she ran into one of her old flames.

Chapter Fifteen

~

Cyrus rushed his last patient through her exam so that he would have time to freshen up before a meeting of the Commodores, a prestigious club for professional Negro men. He had been nominated for vice president, and voting would be held tonight.

His sponsor, Judge Lucious Jacobs, had been quietly garnering support for Cyrus, who had been in the club only five years. His opponent was a dentist who had been a member for twelve years. Judge Jacobs told Cyrus that he was a shoo-in with his support.

The Commodores played an important role in colored society. Each year, the group sponsored the Cotton Makers Jubilee. With formal parties, a parade down Main Street, and a carnival on Beale Street, the Jubilee was the social event of the year. Cyrus looked forward to the day when Jocelyn would be crowned carnival queen and ride on a float.

He arrived at the Cotton Bowl Hotel early to do some last-minute campaigning for vice president. Cyrus squared his shoulders, held his head high, and strolled into the meeting room. When he saw the judge, he walked over to him and pumped his hand. "Good evening, Your Honor. How's everything looking?"

The judge squeezed Cyrus's hand firmly and quickly. He placed a hand on Cyrus's shoulder. "I'm glad you got here early. I need to talk to you. Walk with me."

As the two men headed for the hall, Cyrus sensed something was wrong. He tried not to let his imagination run away, but he couldn't help but think the judge had some bad news. When they reached a quiet spot, Jacobs stopped and started to speak but hesitated.

"What's wrong?"

"We may have a problem getting enough votes tonight. There's a rumor going around that you have some problems at home."

Cyrus squinted at Jacobs. "What are you talking about?"

The judge took out a handkerchief and wiped his forehead. "I don't want to get into your personal business, Cyrus, but some of the members think you need to wait a while and get this matter behind you."

"What matter? And how do they know what goes on in my house?"

"It makes no difference, son," he said. "The point is, you don't have enough votes and should withdraw from the election."

Cyrus became incensed. "Withdraw? Why? You haven't given me any reason to withdraw. All I'm hearing you say is somebody started a rumor about me having some problems at home. I don't know what they're talking about."

"Look, I don't want to get into a lot of hearsay but…"

"I want to know what was said," Cyrus demanded.

The judge looked Cyrus in the eye. "There's talk that you beat your wife during an argument."

"It's a damn lie. I don't know who is spreading this shit, but it's not true."

"Regardless…"

"No regardless, Judge. Somebody's lying on me."

"Cyrus, I'm not passing judgment. I'm just telling you that the right thing to do is drop out of the election. Trust me on this."

He knew Jacobs was only trying to spare him from the embarrassment of a crushing defeat, but withdrawing was out of the question. There was no point in trying to persuade the judge that he wasn't a wife beater.

How did the Commodores find out? He knew the answer immediately. Nadine must have blabbed to Lydia, who was married to John Cooksley, a longtime Commodore and president of the largest colored life insurance company in the Mid-South.

Lydia and Nadine worked together on the Commodores' service projects. When Cyrus suggested that Nadine get to know her better, he thought it would boost his standing in the Commodores, not destroy him. He would deal with Nadine when he got home.

"Thanks for your help, Judge Jacobs, but if I bow out now, people will think it's true. Would it be proper for me to make a statement before the vote? Not about the rumor, per se, but about being dedicated and hardworking."

"That would be out of order. There are no speeches prior to the vote. I wish you would rethink this. There will—"

"All due respect, but I am the most qualified candidate. I can't see pulling out because somebody is spreading malicious lies."

"Well, I've done all I can. Good luck," he said, giving Cyrus's shoulder a squeeze.

"Thank you, sir. I appreciate your support."

Cyrus was so furious that he could hardly keep his composure. He went to the men's room to get himself together. Luckily, it was empty. If Nadine had been there, he would've choked her to death. She knew how much being an officer meant to him.

He gathered his thoughts and headed to the meeting room. He had thirty-five minutes to persuade as many members as he could that he was an upstanding man. Cyrus shook hands and asked about wives, mothers, daughters, and sons. He offered to send a letter of recommendation for the son of a member applying to Meharry.

By the time the meeting started, Cyrus's shirt was wringing wet.

Voting was halfway through the agenda. When he heard his name being called as one of the candidates, he stood and put a hand to his brow in a little salute. Cyrus figured he had a fifty-fifty chance.

When the members finished voting, tellers took the ballots to another room. Cyrus didn't hear anything else that happened at the meeting because his mind was on what was happening in the next room. Finally, they returned with the results but didn't reveal them until the end of the meeting.

One by one, the president called the names of the new officers, and they took their place in front of the head table. Cyrus held his breath and waited to hear his name.

"Commodores, greet your new officers," the president said.

Cyrus stood and applauded the ten men standing at the front of the room. He caught a glimpse of the judge, who clapped excitedly, which made Cyrus wonder if he had voted for his opponent.

When the meeting adjourned, Cyrus didn't hang around for the social hour. He was humiliated. It was the first time he had ever lost anything in his life. He sat in his car outside the hotel for the longest time.

Cyrus was hurt. Being vice president meant that he would be in line to become president. Since he lost, chances were that he wouldn't be nominated again anytime soon.

He didn't consider himself a vindictive man, but nobody took anything from him without paying for it.

If any of those men knew the circumstances surrounding him hitting Nadine, they would've understood. However, he couldn't risk explaining what happened because it would be an admission that he had beaten his wife. Something a Commodore would never do.

Cyrus thought about getting out of the club, but that was too drastic and would make him look like a sore loser. Everybody knew that rumors died eventually. He decided to ride this one out. Still, he had to deal with

Nadine, and he wasn't sure what he would do to her when he got home.

On the way, he stopped by Sonny's bar to get a drink. Sonny was one of Miz Esther's oldest friends and like an uncle to him. A bronze, heavy-set man who favored a conk hairstyle, Sonny owned several businesses in colored neighborhoods. His bar used to be packed every night of the week. Cyrus couldn't recall the last time he saw it crowded. Tonight, there was a couple at a corner table and a man sitting at the bar talking to Sonny.

The bar really needed some fixing up. The walls were cracked and peeling. The bar stools and booths needed to be reupholstered, and there was a hole in the water-damaged ceiling.

Sonny had already hit the bottle a few times because he was running off at the mouth about the garbage workers' strike, which was in its second week. Cyrus sat next to the other patron at the bar and ordered a beer.

"Doc, what you think about this? The garbage men out there hauling cans all day, and the white boys don't let the colored ones ride inside the truck, even when it's raining. Ain't that some shit? Crackers think they can treat us any kind of way. They can kiss my black ass."

Cyrus knew the conversation was going to go in circles but decided to weigh in anyway. "It's a shame how they've been treated – bad working conditions, low pay, long hours, and no overtime. Two more workers had to get crushed to death before the city acknowledged the trucks had defects."

"It don't make no goddamn sense. I'm behind them all the way even if I have to take my trash out back and burn it," Sonny said, slurring his words. "I'm sick of this shit. Anytime we want something we got to bow and scrape. Every nigga on this street had to pay some cracker under the table to get a liquor license or a permit. They make us jump through all kinds of hoops and charge us twice as much for everything."

Cyrus had heard most of this before in one of Sonny's tipsy tirades. When Cyrus got tired of the conversation, he said good night. At least Sonny had gotten his mind off the Commodores. All Cyrus wanted to do now was go to sleep. He didn't want to talk to anybody. Nadine wouldn't ask any questions, but Miz Esther would be waiting for him. She wanted to see him win more than he did.

When he got home, Miz Esther was in the den reading a book. "Well, how's the vice president of the Commodores? Have you been out celebrating?" Miz Esther inquired cheerfully.

"I can't tell you how the vice president is doing because I'm not him," Cyrus said as he sat next to Miz Esther.

"Stop playing, Cyrus."

"I'm serious, Mama. I didn't win," he said disheartened.

Miz Esther stopped smiling. "What happened? I thought this was a done deal."

"It probably was until they got wind of that little incident with Nadine."

Miz Esther gasped and put her hand to her throat. "How did they find out about that?"

"My guess is that Nadine told her buddy, Lydia, and she ran straight to her husband. That's the only way it could have gotten out."

"I don't think Nadine would be that stupid. Besides, I don't think she knows Lydia that well," Miz Esther said. "It could've been somebody who saw her face when she went to the grocery store or beauty shop. I certainly hope Jocelyn didn't tell anyone."

"It was Nadine. She told Lydia just to get even with me."

"What did the judge say?"

"He told me to drop out, but I've never backed down from anything and wasn't about to tonight. He thinks I can run again, but I don't know. People don't forget that kind of stuff."

"Just try to put it behind you, son," Miz Esther said, patting his hand. "Are you going to say something to Nadine?"

"Not tonight. I just want to get some sleep."

"You'll be president of the Commodores one day, Cyrus. This just wasn't your time," she reassured him.

"Thanks, Mama. Good night."

"Good night, son."

Cyrus changed into his pajamas, but his mind wouldn't rest until he confronted Nadine. He shook her shoulder hard. "Nadine, Nadine."

"What?" She turned slowly toward Cyrus, foggy with sleep.

"What did you tell Lydia about us?"

"I don't know what you're talking about," she said, lying back on the pillow.

Cyrus threw the bedcover off. "Wake up, Nadine, before I—"

"Don't hit me!" she cried, covering her face and head with her arms.

"Put your hands down. I'm not going to do anything to you. Just answer my question."

"What question?" Nadine asked.

"I want to know what you told Lydia about me," he demanded.

"Nothing. I didn't tell her anything."

"You're lying," Cyrus said between clenched teeth. "If I find out that you told her I hit you, you'll wish you never laid eyes on her."

"I didn't tell anyone about that night. Why are you coming in here accusing me of stuff?"

"You're the reason I lost the election. I would've won if you had been more supportive." He poked Nadine hard in the chest with his hand. Her back hit the headboard. "You were so busy following up behind Lydia that you couldn't do what all the other wives do for their husbands."

Nadine spoke softly and chose her words carefully, hoping that Cyrus would cool down. "How was I supposed to know what you wanted me to do? All you said was that it would be good for me to join the women's auxiliary."

"You were supposed to make friends with the wives so they could talk me up to their husbands, who would vote for me when I ran for office. My God," he said, grabbing his head. "I thought you had sense enough to know what to do. You've been listening to me and Mama talk about the Commodores for years. Don't sit there and play dumb."

"Cyrus, I didn't have anything to do with you losing the election. Now, if you don't mind, I'm going back to sleep." She scooted down in the bed and got under the cover.

"Lydia had better keep her distance," he warned.

From the moment he laid eyes on Lydia, Cyrus suspected she was a troublemaker. He didn't understand what her old man saw in her. She was thin as a rail and had bulging eyes. Every time he saw Lydia, she had a cigarette in her hand.

He hated women who smoked. They stank and got smoke all over his clothes and in his hair. "The only thing you better say to Lydia from now on is hello and goodbye," Cyrus ordered. "And I better not hear about you telling anybody what goes on in this house. If I do, you'll have hell to pay."

Cyrus went downstairs and poured himself a drink. He had wasted time and money on this election. The envelope that Nadine dropped off at the judge's house several months ago contained one thousand dollars. Although Cyrus's note said the money was for one of his charities, both men knew it was payment for helping him win the election. Jacobs wouldn't return the money, which fine with Cyrus because that meant the judge owed him a favor.

Chapter Sixteen

~

Carrie woke up feeling depressed. She washed up, put on her blue uniform, and headed to work, hoping it would take her mind off her money problems. When the cafeteria grew quiet after the breakfast rush, Carrie started feeling down again.

It had been only a month since she left Mississippi, but it seemed like she had been gone much longer. Without her children, she felt like a piece of her was missing.

She dipped a rag in the sink, squeezed out the water, and wiped the coffeemaker. Carrie heard someone laughing, looked up and saw the white reporter, Bob, walking toward her with one of the photographers. He worked at the morning newspaper, *The Sentinel*.

At least twice a week Bob sat at the counter and bent her ear about some big story he was working on. All that white folks' business didn't concern Carrie, but she listened politely.

Bob was an odd duck. He was just under six feet tall with a medium build and the tightest, brown curly hair she had ever seen on a white person. He looked like a schoolboy in his tweed jackets and black leather loafers.

"You're going to scrub off the color at the rate you're going," he said, taking a stool in front of her.

She continued cleaning the coffeemaker and didn't make eye contact.

"What can I get you today?"

"A pastrami sandwich on rye with mustard and a Coke." He unfolded a newspaper and spread it on the counter. Carrie brought the drink back, set it down hard, and turned to go. "Hold on a minute. What's wrong? Did I say something to upset you?"

"No, I got a lot on my mind."

"Like what?" he asked, shoving the newspaper aside. "Maybe I can help. I'm good at solving problems."

"Thanks, but I'll be okay. Let me go check on your order."

She brought his sandwich and went to ring up another customer's bill. Carrie was on her way back to the kitchen when Bob motioned for her to come over.

"Have you been going to any of the rallies for the garbage workers at Clayborn Temple?"

"Nope."

Bob took a bite of his sandwich, chewed quickly, and wiped the mustard from the corners of his mouth with the back of his hand. "I hear the garbage men are planning to do something big, but I haven't been able to find out what."

"Why don't you just go down there?"

"They aren't letting white folks in the church."

Carrie couldn't suppress her laughter.

"What's so funny?" he asked.

"Nothing."

"Must be, you're laughing."

She didn't have the nerve to tell him that there was finally some place that colored folks could go and white folks couldn't.

"Well, if you hear anything, let me know, okay?"

"Yeah," Carrie said. She doubted she would hear anything. If she did, Bob would be the last person she would tell. Whatever was going on at the church was colored folks' business.

Carrie thought she was through with that discussion, but a couple of days later Bob was back at the counter begging for a favor. "All I need you to do is go to the meeting tomorrow night, listen to what they're saying and tell me."

"I don't know, Bob. I have to get up early, and that meeting will keep me out too late."

"There's nobody else I can ask. If the meeting goes long, you can leave," he promised.

"Let me think about it."

"Okay, I'll come by tomorrow. We can talk about it some more then."

Bob was getting on her nerves. She sympathized with the thirteen hundred garbage workers and didn't want to spy on them. She saw a copy of *The Sentinel* in one of the booths and walked over to get it. She flipped through the pages until she found Bob's article about the city's refusal to bargain with the strikers.

Carrie knew that Bob would keep bugging her until she agreed to go so she decided to help him one time. She didn't plan to tell him anything that would hurt the garbage workers.

A letter from Ruth was waiting for Carrie when she got home. Her mother had enclosed a photo of the twins sitting on the couch in matching outfits. Carrie got teary when she read the letter.

February 28, 1968

Dear Carrie,

I hope this letter find you feeling good. We're doing good. The babies are getting big and walking, Victor gets into everything. Vicki watches him like a hawk and smiles all the time. We had a little party for their first birthday. I will send you the pictures when I use up all the film. Cleotha act like she their mama and take good care of them. Tandy back home, and she watch them when I'm at work. Have you been able to find a beauty shop job? I hope you haven't given up looking. There must be a lot of women up there who need their hair fixed. I got to run.

Love,

Mama Ruth

Carrie got homesick after reading the letter. She went straight to her room and took a nap. She would have slept right through dinner if Miz Lula hadn't knocked on her door. "Carrie, you feeling okay?"

"Yes, ma'am," she said, sitting up in bed. "Come in."

Miz Lula entered the room with a worried look. "Why you sleeping this late up in the day?"

"I was tired. They been running me ragged at work."

"Poor thing. You need a good meal. I cooked a big pot of greens, neck bones, and a pan of cornbread. Come on and get it while it's hot."

"Yes, ma'am. That sounds good. Let me throw some water on my face. I'll be right out."

Carrie felt better after she had put some food in her stomach, but the loneliness and pain of being separated from the twins left an ache that couldn't be satisfied by anything except their reunion.

"Baby, what's troubling you? You don't seem like yourself tonight," Miz Lula asked after they finished eating.

"I miss my babies, and it will take me forever to save enough money and bring them up here."

"You ain't got nobody to help you? What about their daddy?" Miz Lula said. She took their dirty plates to the sink.

Carrie shook her head. "We don't talk, and I don't want to beg him for nothing."

"Chile, put your pride behind you, and do what you have to for your children's sake."

"It's not that easy, Miz Lula."

"I know it ain't, but he owe it to you 'cause you didn't make those babies by yourself. He might come sniffing around for some, but you ain't obligated to give him the time of day."

Carrie was so tickled that she almost dropped a plate she was drying. "Why Miz Lula, you give better advice than Ann Landers." She had never heard Miz Lula, a devout Baptist, carry on about men. "You make a good point. I'll think about it."

"If he a decent man, he'll give you the money."

Carrie decided to follow Miz Lula's advice. She rehearsed what she would say to Cyrus before she went to bed. She planned to make it clear that they wouldn't be romantically involved, but she needed his help.

After her shift ended the next day, she called his office from a pay phone near the employee lockers. She told the receptionist that she was a patient. While Carrie waited for Cyrus to pick up, she chewed her fingernails and practiced what she would say.

"This is Dr. Mitchell, how can I help you?"

When Carrie heard Cyrus's voice, she forgot her whole speech.

"Hello, anybody there?" he asked. "Hello."

Carrie hung up. She grabbed her belongings from the locker and went to the elevator, angry with herself for considering such an idea.

"Hey, Carrie, wait up." She glanced over her shoulder and saw Bob. "I've been looking all over for you. What did you decide about the meeting?"

"I can't go tonight. I have some personal business to take care of. Maybe some other time."

"Please, I really need your help. Can't you put off whatever it is? I'll do anything in return."

"There ain't nothing you can do for me!" she said. "Leave me alone!"

Carrie opened an exit door and ran down the stairs.

She couldn't wait to get home though she knew Miz Lula would be waiting with a million questions. To her relief, Miz Lula had left a note on the refrigerator saying her sister had come down with the flu, and she would be staying at her house for a couple of days.

Carrie made a cup of hot chocolate, kicked off her work shoes, and propped up her feet on the coffee table. She calculated how many more months it would take to save enough money for the bus ride home, an apartment, and furniture. Too long was the answer.

Feeling desperate, Carrie changed clothes and caught a bus downtown. She knew Cyrus frequented Sonny's and thought she might be able to catch him before he went home. When Carrie got downtown, it was six-thirty. Main Street was crowded with shoppers and people getting off work.

After walking up and down Main Street tossing things around in her head, Carrie decided not to ask Cyrus for money. She was convinced that nothing good would come out of letting him back in her life.

Carrie found a pay phone, called Bob at the office, and told him she could go to the meeting after all. She changed her mind more out of interest in the strike than a desire to help him get a story.

It took her about twenty minutes to reach Clayborn Temple, which was walking distance from Main Street. She stepped into the crowded sanctuary just as one of the garbage workers approached the podium. She looked all over the room but couldn't find space on a pew so she stood against the back wall. Hundreds of men, women, and children sat shoulder-to-shoulder, eyes on the speaker.

Carrie turned her attention to the man talking down front. He was about six feet tall and weighed more than two hundred pounds. His voice was deep and melodious. "I'm forty-one years old and been hauling trash since I was twenty. After all these years, I ain't making but a dollar and seventy cents an hour. I done seen white boys come in younger than my boy and get more money than me. Some of them get to be the boss and ain't never picked up a can in they life. That's 'cause they white."

Someone in the crowd yelled, "Speak the truth, brother."

The man continued. "No matter how old we be, they call us boy. They wouldn't call no white man my age boy. Why they say it to me? I am a man!" he yelled.

The crowd applauded.

"Amen," said one man.

"Here, here," said a woman.

The strikers became more excited as the night wore on, rising to their feet and waving clenched fists when one strike leader called for a mass turnout at the next City Council meeting. "Let's march into City Hall and show them we will stand tall no matter how long it take," the man yelled. "We won't go back to work until we get decent pay and bargaining rights."

The crowd began chanting, "I am a man! I am a man! I am a man!"

Carrie looked at the wall clock. It was nearly ten, and she had been standing more than two hours. Her feet were tired, and her back hurt. She decided to leave and call Bob. There was a phone booth in front of the church, but she used one a block away to make sure no one heard her conversation. She dialed the number, and Bob picked up on the first ring.

"Bob Levine."

"Hey, Bob. This is Carrie."

"What happened at the meeting?" Bob blurted out.

Carrie was taken aback by his rudeness. He was usually very pleasant. When she phoned to tell him she could go to the meeting, he was beside himself. Now, he was curt. "Well, a lot of people got up and talked – a preacher, a white man from the union, and some garbage men who told everybody about stuff that happened to them at work."

"Like what?"

"You want to know everything they said?"

"Was there one guy who had a lot to say that you found interesting?"

"Probably the first man."

"Tell me everything he said. Do you remember his name?"

"It was Nathaniel something. I don't remember. Why do you need that?"

"It's good to have a name with the information that I'm writing."

"You not going to put my name in there and say that I was at the meeting are you?"

"No, reporters don't put themselves in the story. Now, let's go back to Nathaniel. What did he say?"

Carrie recounted in detail everything that she could remember about Nathaniel and the other speakers at the rally. "Oh, I almost forgot. They plan to protest at the next City Council meeting," Carrie said.

"Really? Thanks, Carrie. This is going to be the lead story in tomorrow's paper."

"Okay, Bob. I'm tired. I got to get home."

"Thanks again, Carrie."

"Just remember this when you leave your tip tomorrow."

"Not to worry. Good night, Carrie."

"Bye."

Carrie hung up the phone and rested her back against the glass wall of the phone booth. She was exhausted and cold. The wind whipped through her coat. She tightened her scarf and stuffed her hands in the pockets on her way to the bus stop.

About an hour before quitting time the next day, Bob came rushing in waving the newspaper. "Hey Carrie, did you see the front page? My story about the march on City Hall next week was the lead story. I scooped everybody."

"No, I ain't seen it."

"Here, let me read it to you." Bob sat on a stool and unfolded the newspaper.

"Bob, I ain't no baby. I can read," she snapped.

"I'm sorry," he said. "I'm just excited. I couldn't have done this without you, Carrie."

"Yeah, well, I went for my benefit, too."

"The strike leaders have decided to let white reporters attend the meetings because they need the publicity, but my editor thinks it's a good idea if you keep going to report from the Negro perspective. That way I can concentrate on what's happening at City Hall."

Carrie threw her notepad on the counter. "I can't go to a meeting every night. I'm half dead now 'cause I didn't get enough sleep," she said angrily. "You don't have to be at work at seven o'clock in the morning like I do."

Bob's face turned red. "I really appreciate what you did," he said, looking down at his hands. "I'm sorry if I came off unsympathetic. That was not my intent."

"Forget about it," she said, hastily grabbing the notepad. "What you ordering?"

Bob looked at the menu again. "A turkey sandwich with lettuce, tomato, and mayo. And I'll take a lemonade." When she came back with his drink, he brought up the subject again. "If you can't go every night, would you consider every other night?"

"You just don't give up, do you?" Carrie said on her way to the kitchen.

"My editor will pay you seven dollars for every meeting."

Carrie did an about-face. "What?" she asked, walking over to him. "He'll pay me?" She put her hands on her hips. "I ain't in no mood for play, Bob. Is this for real?"

"I'm serious as a heart attack," he said.

"All I have to do is go to the meetings and do what I did last night? It's okay if go a couple of times a week and not every night?"

"Yeah," he nodded.

"He ain't expecting me to write a story, is he?"

"No, no. All you have to do is take notes about what was said and who said it, and report back to me. I'll write the story based on your notes and what I pull from my other sources. How does that sound?"

Carrie wiped her forehead with a paper napkin. "I don't know. I'm so sleepy that I can't think straight. Let me sleep on it."

"Okay, just let me know. Here's my home number." He jotted down the number on a sheet ripped from his reporter's notebook.

Cleary came into the cafeteria while they were talking but didn't interrupt. When Bob left, he walked over to the counter.

"Hey," she said, sitting a glass of water in front of him.

"Hi, Carrie. How you feeling today?"

"Sleepy."

"Why? You been hanging out in a juke joint?"

"No, I had a meeting last night and got home late."

"And who is the cat you met with?"

"Who said anything about a man?" she shot back.

"I was wondering if it was that cracker who just left. Every time I look around, he's grinning up in your face. You and him got something going on?"

"You crazy? Ain't nothing going on between me and that white boy," she said in a low voice. "He just asked me to do him a favor."

"What kind of favor?"

"None of your business."

"I'm making it my business."

"Listen, Cleary, don't you and nobody else own me. I can do whatever I want with anybody I want, anytime I want. If you got a problem with that, you can keep on stepping." She turned and went into the kitchen.

Cleary looked around to see if anybody had heard their argument. There were two white women sitting at a nearby table, but they were engrossed in their own conversation. When Carrie came back, Cleary apologized. "I'm not looking for a fight. I—"

"Then, don't start one."

"I'm just trying to figure out where we stand," he said. "I like you a lot, but I can't tell if the feeling is mutual. You hard to read."

Carrie drummed her fingers on the counter. "How about we just be friends. I got a lot going on right now and can't make no commitment."

"If that's what you want." Cleary lowered his eyes and slowly got up from the stool. "I'll see you around."

Chapter Seventeen

~

With Cyrus's permission, Nadine met Lydia for lunch at the South Memphis Women's Club to work on plans for the auxiliary's annual spring fashion show and luncheon. There was the usual small talk, each woman spending a few minutes chatting about what was happening in her life. Lydia was excited about a trip to Detroit at the end of the month. Her husband was attending a convention, and she was tagging along.

"I've got a feeling John is going to buy me a mink coat while we're there." She giggled. "He's been hinting at it all week. I sure wish you and Cyrus could come with us. It would be a lot of fun. We could go shopping and not worry about crossing the picket line. I'll be glad when the garbage workers' strike is over so I can go downtown."

A look of chagrin crossed Nadine's face as she sliced the roasted turkey. "I wish I could go with you, but me and Cyrus don't travel together. He likes to go places by himself."

"Girl, that's the worst thing you could do," said Lydia, who was talking so fast that bits of food flew out of her mouth. "You don't let that handsome husband of yours go anywhere by himself. The women are waiting to pounce at every opportunity. It's a shame the way they throw themselves at our husbands."

"If Cyrus is going to do anything, he'll find a way if I'm there or not,"

Nadine said with resignation.

Lydia stopped chewing and stared at Nadine. "I don't like the sound of that," she said, resting her fork. "What's wrong, Nadine? I could tell something was bothering you as soon as you sat down."

Nadine remembered Cyrus's stern warning about telling family business. However, she felt the need to confide in someone older and more experienced with men. "Things are bad between me and Cyrus. I don't know what to do," Nadine said. She brought a hand to her forehead.

"Honey, you've been married long enough to know that it isn't always easy. This is probably just a little rough patch."

Nadine didn't want to hear any of Lydia's platitudes today. She needed honest, straightforward advice. "It's more than that, and it's been going on a long time," she said.

"If you don't mind me asking, what exactly is the problem?" she asked, leaning closer to Nadine.

"Everything," she said, throwing up her hands. "Living in a house with a woman who hates my guts, bosses me around, and criticizes every thing I do. And having to keep a gun under the mattress because I'm afraid Cyrus will beat me to a pulp again." Everything came out so fast that Nadine didn't realize that she had said too much. By the time she finished, her eyes were glistening.

"What?" said Lydia, her eyes bucked. "Back up. Did you say Cyrus beat you?"

Nadine wiped her eyes with the napkin. "Yeah, it was pretty bad. And he thinks I told you about it, you told your husband, and that's why he lost the election."

"But that's not true," Lydia said. "Why in the world did he hit you?"

Nadine told Lydia the whole story. After she finished, Lydia reached for Nadine's hand. "I'm sorry you had to go through that. It must have been awful."

"I'm okay now, but I get a ringing in my ear sometimes. My lip healed okay. The cut over my eye left a tiny scar. Look," she said, moving closer to Lydia.

"My God, Nadine. He hit you in the face? Cyrus just doesn't seem to be that type of man." Tears came to Lydia's eyes. She got a tissue to blow her nose. "What are you going to do?"

"I don't think he'll hit me again because he knows people are watching him, but he may put me out."

"Why do you think that?"

"I heard Miz Esther tell her sister that Cyrus wants a divorce, but she told him that he couldn't get one."

"I thought you said Miz Esther didn't like you."

"She doesn't, but she has this thing about breaking up a family. I heard her and Miz Lillian talking one day, and it sounded like Miz Esther had a lot of problems with Cyrus's daddy. I think that has something to do with her not letting Cyrus get a divorce. And you know how siddity she is." Nadine pursed her lips and held her head high, mimicking Miz Esther.

Lydia laughed. "If you got Miz Esther on your side, you don't have anything to worry about. But if I were you, I'd still be worried about Cyrus's temper and getting beat up again."

"I am. That's why I got the gun. What if Cyrus doesn't listen to Miz Esther? I don't know what I'll do if he puts me out on the street."

Lydia placed her knife and fork across her plate and pushed it to the side. "Nadine, please get rid of the gun before somebody gets hurt or the girls find it. As for being kicked out, let me tell you something." Lydia crossed her legs and lit a cigarette. "As long as Cyrus is a doctor, you don't have a thing to worry about. I can ask a lawyer friend how much you could get in alimony and child support."

"No." Nadine said. "You can't do that. Cyrus may find out."

"I don't have to tell him who I'm asking for. I can do it in a round-about way."

"Please, Lydia, don't do that."

"Okay, I won't, honey," Lydia said with a weak smile. "I'm just trying to help."

"I appreciate the offer, but I don't want to get on Cyrus's bad side. You have no idea how mean he is."

Nadine didn't want to talk about Cyrus anymore and steered the conversation toward their fundraising project. Lydia respected her wishes and didn't ask any more questions.

After lunch, Nadine stopped by the Fellowship Hall. The food distribution center was busy with volunteers filling boxes. It took Nadine three days to organize all the donations and set up a schedule for volunteers and system for giving away the food.

Nadine saw Reverend Tyson and went over to greet him. "Good afternoon, Reverend Tyson. How do you like our little operation?" she said with a sweep of her hand.

"Sister Mitchell, good afternoon. You've done a fine job here as I knew you would. Now, I have another challenge for you."

"What's that, Reverend?"

"The food center at New Hope Baptist Church in North Memphis could use your help," he explained. "People started dropping off food before the church could set up. I was over there yesterday, and the basement is one big mountain of bags and boxes. Would you go over there and lend a hand?"

Nadine was flattered. "Of course, Reverend. I'll do what I can."

He took out a piece of paper and gave it to Nadine. "Here is the pastor's name, phone number, and church address. He's expecting your call. We appreciate all your work, Sister Mitchell."

"I enjoy doing it," she said. "I just hope the strike ends soon so things will get back to normal."

"We just have to be patient and prayerful," he said.

The next day, Nadine drove over to New Hope on the other side of town. The food center there was not quite as big as the one at her church. There were five volunteers helping the strikers.

"Good morning," Nadine said to one of the women. "I'm Nadine Mitchell from Gethsemane Baptist Church. I organized the food bank over there, and I'm here to help set up this one."

"I'm Clara Barnes," said one woman.

Then, each woman called out her name with a little wave.

"The first thing we need to do is set up some tables. That way we can separate the items as we take them out of the bag. We want to make this room look like a grocery store."

Volunteers came and went, and Nadine repeated her instructions to each new person. As she surveyed the room that afternoon, a woman tapped her on the shoulder. "Hi, I'm Mother Copeland. I'm here to lend my support to the strikers any way I can."

"Hello, Mother Copeland. It's nice to meet you. I'm Nadine Mitchell," she said, shaking her hand.

"I don't think I've seen you at our Sunday service. Are you a new member?"

"No ma'am. I'm from Gethsemane. I'm just here to help organize the food bank."

"Well, welcome to New Hope," Mother Copeland said. "What do you need me to do?"

"Right now, we're unpacking everything in these bags and boxes."

"My, my, there's a lot of food." Mother Copeland walked around the room in astonishment. "Praise the Lord for this bounty."

Nadine showed her the tables. "We're putting each item in one of these five sections," she said, pointing to cardboard signs.

"That shouldn't be too hard for an old lady like me."

"I'll be here for another hour if you have any questions." When Nadine turned, she bumped into a tall, attractive young woman. "Oh, I'm sorry," Nadine said.

"This is my friend, Carrie Boyd," Mother Copeland said. "Do you want her to work over here, too?"

"Yes, that's fine," Nadine said. "Welcome, Carrie. I'm Nadine Mitchell." She extended her hand. "Thanks for coming."

Carrie was tongue-tied as she stood face-to-face with Cyrus's wife. Nadine was the last person she expected to see at the church. Carrie's face turned crimson as she shook hands.

Before Nadine could give her instructions, Carrie grabbed two bags and hurried over to a table. She stole looks at Nadine, wondering what Cyrus saw in this dark, homely woman with bouffant hair. She expected her to be tall and beautiful with long, flowing hair. She looked more like a maid than a doctor's wife.

Nadine came over to say goodbye to Carrie and Mother Copeland, but Carrie didn't look in her direction. "Will you be back?" Nadine inquired.

"Yes, darling," said Mother Copeland. "I'll keep working 'til the strike is over."

"I'll see you next time," Nadine said cheerfully.

Chapter Eighteen

"Excuse me, Dr. Mitchell," said the nurse. "Clara Young is dressed and waiting in your office."

"I'll be there in five minutes," said Cyrus, who was checking the fetal heartbeat in an obese patient. He removed the stethoscope from his neck and slid his hands over the woman's belly to check the baby's position.

"Dr. Mitchell, is the baby okay?"

"Everything's fine, Odessa. I'm almost through. He's a busy one, but I don't have to tell you that, do I?"

"Is that bad?"

"No, they're supposed to be active during the third trimester."

"I'll be glad when he comes. I'm tired of being laid up."

"The bed rest is just a precaution because of the spotting. You're going to long for this bed rest once the baby comes."

"That's what everybody keeps telling me. I been waiting for this child so long that I promised myself I wouldn't complain about nothing he did."

"We'll see," he said, covering her with the sheet.

"Dr. Mitchell, your aunt is on line two," the receptionist said over the intercom.

"My aunt?" he asked surprised.

"Yes, do you want me to take a message?"

"No, I'm done in here. I'll get it in my office. Odessa, I'll see you next week. Stay off your feet." Cyrus rushed to the phone, expecting an emergency. "Aunt Lillian, is everything okay?"

"Yes, Cyrus, I'm fine. I know you're busy, but I had to talk to you about something. I didn't want to bother you at home."

Cyrus sat on the edge of the desk. "What, Auntie?"

"I saw Carrie downtown yesterday. Did you know she was back in town?"

Cyrus stood upright, knocking over the phone. The earpiece fell out of his hand into the trash can. He scrambled to pick it up. "Are you still there, Auntie?"

"Yes."

"You saw Carrie? Are you sure? Where?"

"Yes, I'm sure. She was standing at the bus stop, and my bus passed right by her. I couldn't believe my eyes. You haven't heard from her?"

"No, I haven't," he said, twisting the phone cord around his finger. "Was she by herself?"

"Yes. From what I could see from the tail of her dress, she was wearing a blue uniform. Maybe she works at one of the hotels downtown. I didn't know if you knew, but I was hoping that maybe you had heard from her. I'd like to find out how she and her children are doing."

"You mean *our* children, don't you?"

"You know what I mean, Cyrus. Anyway, I won't hold you. I just wanted to share that information. Carrie looks good. She's slimmed down. I'm sure taking care of two babies from sunup until sundown would make anybody lose weight. If you hear from her, let me know, okay?"

"I will, Auntie. Bye."

Cyrus was thrilled to hear Carrie was back. As each month passed, he worried that she might never return. He had given up hope of seeing his son and daughter again. He had envisioned them as young adults knocking on his door one day.

What was unfolding now was even better. He had to find Carrie. As soon as he got off work, he drove to Klondike to see if Carrie had moved back into her old house. It was a long shot but worth a try.

The neighborhood still looked the same. Someone had replaced the rusted porch furniture with a raggedy couch. He knocked on the door. A woman peered from behind a curtain and said, "May I help you?"

Cyrus saw only a sliver of the woman's face. She didn't look like Carrie's grandmother. "Does Carrie Boyd live here?"

"Nope," the woman said.

"Look, I'm a friend of hers and—"

"Ain't nobody by that name live here. Now get off my porch."

"Thanks."

He sat in his car for a while trying to figure out how he could find her. There were too many hotels for him to call on his own. The only person who might be able to help was Skeeter. His childhood friend had connections everywhere and would be able to find out quickly where Carrie worked.

Cyrus headed to Beale Street, hoping to find Skeeter at one of his hangouts. He would have to explain who Carrie was, but that wasn't a big deal. Skeeter could keep a secret.

***

After a week of lurking near the back entrances of hotels, Skeeter came up empty-handed. Nobody had heard of Carrie Boyd. Cyrus called Aunt Lillian and asked what time of the day and where exactly Carrie was standing. She probably caught the same bus at the same time and location every day.

Cyrus got the information and gave Skeeter a picture of Carrie. It took him three days to find a woman who resembled Carrie standing at the bus stop on the corner of Main Street and Jefferson Avenue. She had a slimmer face than the woman in the photo and her hair was piled high in a bun, but she looked like the girl in the picture.

About the only new information he reported to Cyrus was that the woman might work at the Tri-County Publishing Company because she was holding a shopping bag with that name on the front.

To verify Carrie was an employee, Cyrus called the main number for the publishing company. He told the operator that he wanted to speak to Carrie Boyd, but he wasn't sure what department she worked in. She connected him to the cafeteria.

"Good morning, sir," Cyrus said. "How early do you open?"

"Seven o'clock," he said.

"Thank you."

Cyrus decided to stake out the newspaper building. He parked across the street around three o'clock, the time he thought Carrie might get off work. He saw several colored women leave a side entrance. Cyrus sat up straight and strained to make out their faces. Carrie wasn't among them.

He kept his eyes glued on the door, hoping she would be in the next group. He averted his eyes for a few seconds, and when he looked up again, he saw a tall, slender woman talking to a man loading rolls of newsprint onto a pallet. When she turned in his direction, he saw that it was Carrie.

Cyrus jumped out of his car and walked quickly toward her. She stood stock-still when she saw him. Her whole face contorted with rage.

"Carrie, it's good to see you. When did you get back?"

"What do you want?" she snarled.

Cyrus wanted to hug her, but the tone of her voice told him that was out of the question. He moved closer; she extended her hands to stop him. "I'm happy you're back. Why didn't you call me?"

"For what? You didn't help before. Why should I waste my time? You made it clear that you didn't want nothing to do with us. I don't see where we got much to discuss."

"We got a lot to talk about, Carrie," he said, turning up the charm. "I know I could have done more before, but there was a lot going on back then. I'll do better this time. Let me drive you home. We can talk, and I can see my boy and girl."

Cyrus thought that he had won Carrie over until she laughed in his face. "My children don't know you exist. Don't come 'round here thinking you can sweet talk me 'cause I ain't no dumb country girl no more. Go back to your family and leave me alone."

"Please don't shut me out," he said. "We can work things out. I'll do whatever you want."

She shook her head and walked toward the bus stop. He followed her but gave up after a few steps. It was obvious that she wanted nothing to do with him. He drove off, unsure about his next move.

Chapter Nineteen

~

Carrie had wanted to come off cool and in control when she saw Cyrus again, not angry. She had just gotten over the shock of meeting Nadine, and now she had to worry about Cyrus making demands.

She decided that she wasn't going to let Nadine keep her from volunteering at the food bank. She would simply steer clear of her. She admitted that she was quite fascinated by Nadine. How did such a plain woman keep a man like Cyrus and make him abandon her and the twins?

As for Cyrus, Carrie was confident that she blessed him out so good that he wouldn't bother her again. She stopped thinking about him and concentrated on getting ready for the strike meeting. Carrie liked attending the rallies at Clayborn Temple. Since she was getting paid, she felt obligated to check out the morning and afternoon newspapers every day for the latest news.

Carrie read the stories aloud sometimes, like she did in the sixth grade for Mr. McKinley, the white man who owned their house and half the town. Cataracts had impaired his eyesight, and he gave Carrie a dime each time she read to him when his nephew brought him around to collect the rent.

Although the meetings wore her out, Carrie felt that she was helping the strikers by telling their stories. She had never seen such brave and determined colored men in her life. They had started a movement that would change colored lives in a good way or bad way.

That night, she arrived at Clayborn Temple early to get a seat near the exit. When the time came, she could leave without drawing attention to herself. She was still paranoid about the garbage men finding out she was working for the newspaper though there were several white reporters, TV crews, and photographers in the sanctuary.

Tonight, preachers from other churches addressed the sanitation workers and prayed for them. A petite, fawn-colored woman wearing thick glasses told the workers that the community was behind them.

"Ain't nobody in here gonna starve or be put out on the street because you can't pay rent. We got two food banks, one in North Memphis and the other in South Memphis, and we been collecting money all over town," she said. "The Negro community in Memphis is behind you one hundred percent. Plus, we getting support from people in Mississippi, Alabama, and Georgia."

After she finished, a short, bald preacher came to the podium. He spoke in a singsong voice. "God will make a way out of no way. You've come this far by faith. Keep leaning on the Lord."

The crowd stood and shouted back.

"Amen!"

"Hallelujah!"

"Preach!"

At nine o'clock, Carrie decided to call Bob and give him an update. She walked to the phone booth and dialed the newspaper office. "I ain't got much to tell," she reported. "It was like church, a lot of singing and praying."

"Start from the top and tell me what everybody said."

Carrie shifted the phone to her other ear and got her notebook. "Okay, if that's what you want."

She spent about fifteen minutes describing speaker after speaker. Bob asked her questions, too. He wanted to know how many people were there and the names of preachers.

"I'm going to weave this information into another story I'm working on," he said. "That should do it. Thanks a lot. I'll see you tomorrow."

After Carrie hung up, she walked toward the bus stop. A green pickup with three white boys pulled up beside her. The driver stuck his head out the window and yelled, "Hey, nigger bitch, need a ride?"

Carrie ignored him and kept walking with her head down.

"Maybe she don't like your looks," said a man sitting next to the driver.

"You deaf or something? I asked you a question," the driver said.

"See, I told you niggers in Memphis done got too big for their britches 'cause of them garbage workers. Our niggers in West Memphis know their place," said another voice inside the truck.

"We need to show her what we do to our coloreds when they get out of place," said the driver.

"Uh-huh," said one man.

He laughed in a creepy way that made Carrie shudder. Her heart raced, and she quickened her step. She looked over her shoulder to see if the bus was coming. The street was quiet; just her and the white boys. She made a U-turn at the corner and walked back toward the church. The pickup kept going.

"Lord, Jesus, don't let them crazy crackers come back," she said under her breath.

She slowed her pace. Suddenly, the pickup zoomed down the street, stopping next to her. Two men jumped from the bed of the truck, grabbed Carrie, and threw her in the back. She screamed and swung at their faces.

One of the men punched her in the face. "Shut up, cunt," he said, putting his hand over her mouth. She bit him hard and struggled to get up. "Fucking bitch," he said, hitting her again.

The punch made her dizzy. Her eyes watered. The man straddled her and pinned her against the floor of the truck.

Carrie's face felt numb from the blows, and blood filled her mouth. "Let me go!" she screamed.

"When we through," the man said. "Drive, Kenny."

The truck took off, and Carrie's fear intensified. With all the strength she could muster, she kicked, trying to break free.

"Look a here, this one's a fighter," said the man holding her down.

The other man laughed. "That ought to be fun," he said. "What should we do with her?"

"The same we do to our nigger women."

Carrie flailed her body ferociously, trying to throw the man off. When the truck made a sharp turn, the man holding her was thrown into the other man.

"What the fuck, Kenny?" he screamed at the driver, who stepped on the brake.

Carrie scrambled to her feet, jumped over the side of the truck, and fell to the ground. She got up and ran down the dark alley. She had only gotten a few yards when she was tackled from behind. "Help! Help!" she shouted.

"You really gonna get it now," said one of the men. Each man grabbed an arm and dragged her to the truck. The rocks and broken glass on the ground scraped the back of her legs.

"Help me, please! Somebody help me!" she yelled.

When they got back to the pickup, the two men held her down while a third man pulled down her girdle and panties.

"No, no!" Carrie cried. "Please don't, please!"

"I'll be damned," said the man straddling her. "This bitch is bleeding. She's on the rag." He held up Carrie's sanitary napkin.

"I ain't putting my dick in that," said the man holding her arm.

"Don't make no difference to me," said the man who undressed Carrie. "A pussy is a pussy."

"Yeah, but their blood got all kind of diseases. You want some nigger shit to kill you?" asked the other man holding Carrie's arm.

"Hell, I'll fuck her with a bottle," said the man hovering over Carrie. He searched the area around them.

Carrie screamed and thrashed on the ground. When he returned with the bottle, he stuffed the sanitary napkin in her mouth and spread her legs. "Should I do it the regular way or up the ass?" he asked his friends.

"Ain't nobody here no fucking fag. Do it the regular way," said one of them.

Just as he inserted the neck of the bottle inside Carrie, a band of flashing lights lit up the alley. The man tossed the bottle next to a building.

As two white officers approached them with guns drawn, the three men stood with their hands above their heads. Carrie removed the pad from her mouth and pulled down her dress.

"Officer, they was raping me!" Carrie screamed. "That man in the green coat stuck a bottle up me."

"Step away from the woman," the taller officer said. "Lady, you all right?"

She tried to stand, but her legs were wobbly. She fell on her hands and knees. It felt like the lower part of her body was on fire. One of the officers helped Carrie to her feet.

"No, I'm not all right. That one kept hitting me in the face," she said, pointing to her attacker.

"What's going on here, boys?" said the shorter policeman.

The driver of the truck grinned, showing a row of tobacco-stained teeth. "Ain't nobody raped her. We was on a date."

"A date?" The shorter cop looked at his partner, who shook his head. They holstered their weapons.

"Yeah, our buddies came over here last week and picked up a couple of whores, and they had a good time. We came on over tonight looking for the same," said the driver's friend.

The taller policeman looked at Carrie suspiciously. "What are you doing in the alley this time of night?'

Carrie looked at him in disbelief. "You believe them?" she asked. "I didn't come back here on my own. They brought me back here."

"She's lying. She flagged us down on Beale Street and told us to come back here where it was quiet," said the driver.

"Lady, did you solicit these men?" the officer asked.

"I ain't no prostitute!" she yelled. "I was coming from the strike meeting at the church, and they grabbed me off the street."

"You're one of those strike sympathizers, huh?" the taller officer asked Carrie. "I hope each one of them niggers get fired. They ain't got no business going on strike."

Carrie didn't respond. She knew that the officers didn't care what the men had done to her. She didn't want to say anything that would make them angry. She just wanted to go home.

"From everything I've heard, it looks like we have a case of he-said-she-said," said the shorter officer.

His partner turned to him. "Well, I ain't about to spend two hours typing up this shit. Look lady, I can't tell what really happened here. It's best that you go on home. If we catch you here again, we will arrest you for prostitution."

"I told you what they did to me. Why do you believe them instead of me?" Carrie asked tearfully.

"Just go on home, lady," the cop said. He scolded the men in the pickup. "Your date is over. Get back across the river, and don't come back."

"Wait, my pocketbook is in the truck."

She wanted to cuss out every one of them but feared the cops would haul her to jail. Instead, she ran from the alley and called Bob. "Come and get me," she said in a quivering voice.

"Carrie, what's the matter?"

"I got beat up."

"Where are you now?"

"In a phone booth by Pollack Machine Parts, a block from the church."

"Hang tight, I'll be there right away."

Carrie felt exposed in the phone booth and hid on the side of the building. As she waited for Bob, warm menstrual blood trickled down her leg. She wiped it with a piece of notebook paper. She felt a sharp pain in her vaginal area and wondered if she was cut inside.

She could feel the right side of her face swelling from the blows. The inside of her mouth felt shredded, and bits of skin stuck to her tongue. She got angrier the more she thought about how the cops treated her.

Suddenly, the doors of Clayborn Temple opened, and people streamed out to their cars and the bus stop. She walked back to the bus stop and stood in the crowd, careful not to make eye contact. She didn't want anyone to see her battered face.

She spotted Bob's car and stepped off the curb to flag him down. "What happened? Who did this?" he asked. Bob was visibly shaken and outraged by her appearance.

"Just drive, Bob. Get me away from here." As they drove through downtown, Carrie explained most of what happened.

"You need to get checked out at the hospital," he said. "I'm taking you right now."

"No," Carrie said. "I'll be okay."

"And I think you should go the police department and file a report about the assault and a complaint against the cops," he said.

"That won't do no good," she said. "I told you they thought I was a prostitute."

"When I tell them that you were working for the newspaper that will make a difference. They don't want any bad press."

Carrie shook her head. "They'll just make up some lies about me and give me a bad name. Then, I'll lose my job. Just forget about it."

"No, Carrie," he said, hitting the steering wheel. "If you don't stand up and do something, the same thing will keep happening."

"I said no!" Carrie shouted. "This is my business. They didn't beat you and stick, uh, uh, just leave it alone."

When Bob stopped at a red light, he said, "I've got something to ask you, and please tell me the truth, Carrie."

"What?"

"Did they rape you?"

Carrie started to tell him about the bottle but changed her mind. "They were 'bout to, but the cops came."

"Thank goodness," Bob said, collapsing over the steering wheel. "I would never be able to live with myself if that happened. I feel bad enough because you wouldn't have been down there if it hadn't been for me. I'm sorry, Carrie." He reached over to touch her hair, but she jerked her head.

Carrie wasn't upset with him. She was feeling what the garbage workers had been talking about - being invisible and powerless. The only difference was that they were doing something about their problems.

When they reached her house, Bob ran around to open the door for Carrie, but she beat him to it.

"You're probably going to be sore and black-and-blue tomorrow. You may want to think about staying home."

"I can't miss no days. If I don't work, I don't get paid."

"You must have sick days, don't you?"

"Yeah, but I'll need them when I'm really sick."

"Carrie, you're not going to be in any shape to work tomorrow. I can tell from looking at your face."

"I'll be fine."

Bob walked her to the front door and waited for her to go inside. When she turned to say good night, his face was red, like he was about to cry. "I'm so sorry this happened, Carrie."

"Bob, it's not your fault. Stop apologizing."

"If you need anything, call me. Okay?"

"Yeah, okay. Bye."

Inside the house, all the lights were turned off except the one in the hall, which meant Miz Lula was asleep. Carrie was glad she didn't have to explain how she got the bruises until morning. She checked her face in the bathroom mirror. It wasn't as bad as she thought. Her right eye was red and swollen, and would turn into a black eye in a few hours. Both cheeks were puffy and turning purple. Bob was right. There was no way she could go to work looking like she had been in a bar fight.

Normally, she wouldn't take a bath on her period, but she wanted to get the smell of the men off her body. She scrubbed until her skin burned. She set her alarm for the usual time but only to call in sick. Carrie planned to tell the boss that she had gotten mugged and needed to take a couple of days off to recover from her injuries.

Chapter Twenty

After Nadine found out Willie Lee worked at Greenberg's, she looked forward to grocery shopping twice a week. They had lengthy conversations about everything, ranging from the garbage workers' strike to religion to raising children.

Nadine was evasive when Willie Lee asked about her marriage. She didn't want him to feel sorry for her or think she was a fool for staying in an abusive marriage. Willie Lee had always put her on a pedestal, and that is where she wanted to remain.

"Do you think you'll ever get married again?" she asked as they chatted in his office.

Willie Lee swiveled in the burgundy leather chair, contemplating the question. "Maybe," he said.

"I'm surprised you haven't been snatched up by one of the women who shop here. I'm sure they come in here flirting with you. I can just see them." Nadine looked over her shoulder seductively and batted her eyelashes, giggling at herself afterward.

"You are so silly," he said, chuckling. "I don't see anybody because I'm usually in the back. Besides, most of the women around here got men. I ain't got time for no foolishness."

"You don't want to wait too long and get set in your ways," Nadine warned.

Willie Lee picked up two boxes in the corner and set them on the desk. "I'm not in a hurry. I'm waiting for the right woman to come along," he said with a hopeful look. "You know, I had the biggest crush on you in high school."

"Really?"

"I didn't have the nerve to tell you," he said. "You didn't even see me back then. All you did was boss me around the store."

"And look who's telling me what to do now," Nadine said.

Willie Lee made Nadine feel like a schoolgirl again. She enjoyed listening to him talk about the food industry. "One day, I'm going to open my own store - Griffin's Grocery," he said, framing an invisible sign in the air.

"That has a nice ring to it. Well, I need to get going. Thanks for the donation."

Willie Lee picked up the two boxes of produce, put them in a cart, and followed Nadine to her car. "Let this be our little secret," he said. "If you need anything else, let me know."

"I appreciate your help, and the garbage workers thank you, too. I'll see you next week." Nadine touched him on the shoulder before getting into the car.

"I'm counting on it," he said, closing the door.

As she drove over to New Hope, Nadine sang along with the radio, tapping the steering wheel. She was always in a good mood after seeing Willie Lee. She also looked forward to working with the women at New Hope. She felt free to be herself around them.

There was one young woman in particular who piqued her curiosity because she seemed sad and withdrawn. Nadine planned to seek her out today and make her feel welcome.

The parking lot of New Hope was packed, forcing Nadine to find a spot two blocks away. Inside, there were a few new volunteers among the familiar faces. She spotted Mother Copeland and Carrie working in a corner.

"Good afternoon," Nadine said. She deposited the box of produce from Willie Lee on a table. "I got some fresh vegetables and fruit that we can give out today. Carrie, would you help me unfold another table?"

Carrie expected Nadine to show up but didn't think she would remember her name. Until that moment, Carrie didn't know how she would react when she saw Nadine again. She quietly set up the table and went back to her station.

Nadine soon drifted over to where Carrie was packing food. "We got almost twice as many strikers this week than last," she said, passing Carrie canned vegetables. "And the food just keeps coming."

"Uh-huh," Carrie uttered.

"I saw Mother Copeland earlier this week. She told me that you'd probably come today since you were off."

Carrie didn't respond.

Nadine took the box they had just filled to another table and came back. "How long have you been a member of New Hope?"

"I started coming a few weeks ago when I came back."

"From where?"

Carrie didn't expect this kind of attention from Nadine. It was unnerving. Although she wanted to cut her off, Carrie couldn't be rude because Miz Lula was nearby. "I was in Mississippi," she said grudgingly.

"You lived here before?"

"Yeah, uh, excuse me, I have to use the ladies' room."

"I have to go, too," Nadine said. "Too much coffee this morning."

On the way to the restroom, Nadine peppered Carrie with more questions. When she asked Carrie whether she had children, Carrie told her about the twins, who had turned one.

"I have two girls. My oldest, Jocelyn, is fifteen and working my last nerve. My baby, Salena, is eight."

"Uh-huh," Carrie replied. She tried to drown out Nadine's incessant chatter.

"I can't imagine having two babies at the same time," Nadine said from the next stall. "I used to want three children, but my husband said two were enough. I kind of wish I had a boy."

When Carrie exited the stall, Nadine was standing there smiling. She moved out of the way so Carrie could wash her hands.

"Why did you leave and come back to Memphis?"

"It's a long story," Carrie said. She hoped Nadine took the hint that she didn't want to talk, but she kept asking questions as they walked back to the food bank.

"Do you work?"

"Uh-huh."

"Who keeps the children?"

"They're in Mississippi with my mama."

Nadine gave her a sympathetic look. "That must be really hard. I don't know what I'd do without my girls."

"You survive and do the best you can," Carrie said in a deadpan tone.

"If you don't mind me asking, where is their daddy?"

Carrie wanted to slap Nadine and tell her that she was the reason Cyrus walked out on them, but she maintained control. "He said he had a lot on his plate and couldn't be the man I needed him to be."

Sick of Nadine prying into her business, Carrie walked faster. Nadine's short legs had to do double time to keep up. "That's too bad. You couldn't work things out for the children's sake?"

Carrie stopped unexpectedly and faced Nadine. "What was I supposed to do?" she asked with a raised brow. "He didn't want to be with me. I got enough sense to know that if a man don't want you, it's time to leave."

"I guess younger women have a different way of looking at things than women my age," Nadine said.

"Age ain't got nothing to do with this," Carrie pointed out. She had reached her breaking point with Nadine.

Nadine saw that Carrie was getting upset. When she reach the food bank, Nadine left Carrie alone in the back of the room while she assisted families up front.

Carrie was angry and ready to go home, but she had told Miz Lula she would stay at the church until after her Mother's Board meeting. She felt stupid for coming back to the food bank and swore she wouldn't return.

As far as she could tell, there was nothing special about Nadine. She was a dowdy woman whose life revolved around her daughters. She probably had no idea that Cyrus was cheating on her.

Before Nadine left, she went over to Carrie. "Me and some of the other ladies are talking about going to a strike meeting next week. Would you like to come with us?"

"No, thank you," Carrie said, refusing to look at Nadine. "I'll be working."

"Maybe some other time. It was good talking to you."

Nadine didn't know if Carrie was brave or stupid for trying to raise two children alone. She decided that the best thing she could do was listen to Carrie if she felt like talking about her problems.

When Nadine got home, Jocelyn was watching TV, and Salena was playing with her dolls. She went to check on Miz Esther but stopped when she got to the door because she heard Miz Esther shouting.

"You know better than this. I'm not going to tolerate this nonsense," she shrieked.

She knocked on the door and entered at the same time. "Miz Esther, are...?" Nadine paused when she saw that Miz Esther was fully dressed in one of the knit suits she wore to school. "I've summoned the principal to handle this situation," Miz Esther said, pointing at Nadine.

"Miz Esther, why are you dressed like that? You don't teach school anymore. And there is nobody in here."

"Get out of my classroom, heifer," Miz Esther yelled. "You lie just like the rest of them."

"Maybe you need to lie down. Let me help you get in the bed."

As Nadine led Miz Esther to bed, she pushed Nadine into the wall. "Get your hands off me before I call the police."

"Okay, I'm leaving," Nadine said, backing away.

She listened on the other side of the door to make sure Miz Esther had come back to her senses. After a while Miz Esther turned on the TV and got quiet. Nadine went back to the kitchen puzzled about her bizarre behavior. She really didn't care what Miz Esther was doing as long as her mother-in-law didn't bother her.

As she sliced a cabbage, Nadine made a mental note to find out what time the meetings were held at Clayborn Temple. She thought it was time the girls learned about the civil rights movement as it was unfolding in Memphis. However, that wasn't the only thing on her mind. She thought about Willie Lee and how much she liked being around him.

Chapter Twenty-One

~

"Son, I'm glad you came home early tonight. I haven't played gin rummy in a long time," Miz Esther said as they sat in the den. "And for the record, I didn't let you win tonight."

"I was wondering if you were holding back. This was fun. I don't get much time to relax these days. It's good that I'm busy, but this practice is wearing me out."

"You should think about taking on a partner. I'm sure one of the doctors at Meharry could recommend someone."

Cyrus sat back in the chair and rubbed his chin. "That's not a bad idea. Maybe I'll look into it." He inserted the deck of cards in the box and looked at his mother. Something about her seemed a bit off. "You been feeling okay, Mama?"

"So, so. I'm not sleeping through the night." She massaged the fingers of her paralyzed hand. "I nod off, and an hour later I'm wide awake."

"I can give you a sleeping pill," he offered. "Anything else bothering you?"

Miz Esther thought about it for a moment and shook her head. "No, I can't think of anything." She hesitated and then said, "Well, there is something I'm not happy about."

"What?"

"I don't like the way Nadine is cooking my food. It tastes like cardboard. No flavor, no nothing. I'd rather starve than eat the food she's putting on my plate."

He gave Miz Esther a disapproving look. "You know what the doctor said about your diet. You're not supposed to eat a lot of salt and greasy food because of your blood pressure."

"That doesn't mean no seasoning at all. There are plenty of things Nadine can put on the meat to make it taste better. I got a mind to start cooking my own food."

"Oh, no you won't," Cyrus said. "I don't want you fiddling around in the kitchen."

"I'm not making any promises."

"I'll talk to Nadine and tell her to make your meals a little more appetizing. Anything else? You seem preoccupied by something. Spit it out."

Tears brimmed in her eyes. "It's nothing. I'm just feeling sorry for myself," she said.

"Come on, tell me what's wrong."

"I miss not being able to get up and go when I want," she said. "Lillian was over here earlier today and told me about all the things happening around town. I'm getting cabin fever stuck in this house."

Cyrus looked confused. "I thought you didn't want to go anywhere, but if you've changed your mind, I'll see to it that you get to wherever you want to go."

Miz Esther patted him on the cheek. "You're such a good son."

"That's not what you told me when I was a teenager."

"That's because you were the devil incarnate back then," she said.

Cyrus hugged Miz Esther. "I know it's been rough since you had the stroke, Mama. I'm proud of how you've handled all the changes. I'm going to do all I can to make your life as comfortable as possible even if we don't see eye-to-eye on certain things."

"Please don't bring that subject up tonight," she said frowning.

"What if I told you that I've found the perfect woman to be my next wife – one who will catapult us in social circles and help me become president of the Commodores?"

"I'd say you've lost your mind. What is wrong with you?" She stared at him with contempt. "A family is not like a car that you trade when the new models come out." She shook her head. "If I didn't know better, I'd swear you were raised by a pack of wolves."

Miz Esther picked up *The Memphis Clarion*, the afternoon newspaper. After she read each page, she tossed it on the floor in front of her. Bewildered by her behavior, Cyrus waited for an explanation.

"How much money do I have in the bank?" she asked.

"I don't know offhand," Cyrus responded. "Do you need something?"

"I need you to stop asking me all these damn questions. It's my money. I can do whatever I want."

"Mama, I was just asking. You don't have to get upset," Cyrus said. "Tell me how much you want, and I'll get it tomorrow."

"Why can't you go now?"

"Because it's almost ten o'clock. The bank is closed."

Miz Esther grew quiet and stared at a page. Slowly, a smile crept across her face. "Aha!" she said, pointing to a travel advertisement. "We're going to Mexico. I think Jocelyn and Salena would like that, don't you?"

Cyrus couldn't tell if Miz Esther was serious or joking. "I'm sure they would one day," he said. Cyrus watched Miz Esther as she carefully but clumsily creased the page, tore out the ad, and handed it to him. "What do you want me to do with this?" Cyrus asked.

"Go to your room," she said, pointing to the hallway. "I don't want to hear another peep out of you tonight." She grabbed her cane and went to her bedroom.

Cyrus balled up the ad. He surmised that either Miz Esther was losing her mind or trying to run him crazy.

***

While Cyrus was shaving, he heard Nadine walking back and forth in front of the bathroom because she needed to use the toilet. However, he didn't care if she peed on herself or lost her bowels. It had gotten to the point where he couldn't stand the sight and smell of Nadine. The more she tried to make herself invisible around him, the more she stood out.

Nadine served as a constant reminder of the biggest blunder in his life. Cyrus didn't know how much longer he could take being miserable in his own home. He turned up the radio to drown out Nadine's footsteps.

She knocked on the door. "Are you almost done?"

"Not yet."

"I need to use it."

Cyrus clipped his mustache and splashed on after-shave lotion. He rubbed Duke pomade in his hair, combed and patted it until waves formed in even rows. When he unlocked the bathroom door, Nadine was crouched in the corner holding her stomach.

"It's all yours," he said.

She rushed passed him, slamming the door. When Nadine came out of the bathroom, Cyrus asked her to come into the bedroom, where he was getting dressed for work.

Nadine stood behind him as he knotted his tie, and he studied her in the mirror. She looked like a field hand wearing a head rag, housecoat, and black orthopedic shoes.

Cyrus turned to her. "Do you ever think about fixing yourself up when I'm home? You look like somebody picking cotton every time I see you."

Nadine looked down at her clothes. "I don't see no point in dressing up today because I'm not going out. I'll just be cleaning and waiting on

Miz Esther all day."

"You just don't get it, do you?" he said. "What man would want to come home to a woman looking like you every day?"

Nadine turned to leave, but Cyrus stopped her. "I'm not through," he said. "I called you in here because Mama said she doesn't like how you're fixing her food. You need to make it taste better."

"But you told me not to put any salt and bacon in her food."

"I know what I told you, but can't you add something else to make it taste better? You've got all those cookbooks downstairs. Go read them. You can read?"

Nadine's jaws tightened. "Anything else?"

Cyrus looked her up and down and said, "No, there's nothing you can do for me. Absolutely nothing."

On the way to his office, Cyrus's spirits were lifted when he saw a billboard advertising the grand opening of a new hospital in the medical complex. He had planned to tour the hospital before it opened but had been too busy. Cyrus heard some of the white doctors marveling over the state-of-the-art equipment. He couldn't wait to see it.

Since the University of Tennessee College of Medicine operated the hospital, he was confident that he would get privileges without delay. The college enrolled Negro medical students and trained Negro doctors who worked at John Gaston Hospital and Collins Chapel Hospital.

Chapter Twenty-Two

~

When Carrie told Cleary that she had been assaulted, he was furious and blamed Bob for putting her life in danger.

"I can't believe you let that white boy talk you into going to those meetings. It's dangerous for a woman to be out late at night with everybody all riled up over the strike. You need to quit before you get killed."

Carrie was worried about her safety, too, but felt she didn't have a choice. "I can't quit. I need some extra money. Anyway, it's not like I'll be doing it forever. The strike will probably end soon," Carrie said.

"You don't have to do this," he argued. "I can help if you're in a jam. I got a little money saved up."

"I appreciate the offer, but I can't let you be responsible for my burdens. I'll figure something out."

"What? I want to hear your plan before you get off this phone," he said.

"I…I…I don't know right now," Carrie stammered. "Maybe I'll leave the meeting early or something."

"If I could, I'd go with you. But you know I have to turn in early because I have to be at my post before daylight."

"I don't expect you to be my bodyguard. I know you need your sleep, which is why I'm hanging up right now. Good night."

"Carrie, be careful. I don't want anything to happen to you. Good night."

***

When Carrie returned to work, she had to explain how she got the bruises on her face to everyone she served. She left out the part about going to the strike meeting at Clayborn Temple.

Bob came into the cafeteria with a serious look as she was clearing her last table. Carrie got a feeling that she was about to get fired. "Hey, got a minute?" he asked.

Her heart started racing. "Yeah, what's wrong?"

"I've been thinking. What if I met you at the church, got the information for my story, and then drove you home?"

"That's a good idea," she said, relieved that she wouldn't have to fuss with Cleary about being out on the street late at night. "But when would you write your story?"

"I would have most of it written before I left the office and just add whatever you got from the meeting. Then, I would dictate the story over the phone."

"Okay."

"See you tomorrow night," he said.

Unfortunately, things didn't quite work out as planned. Bob picked up Carrie from the meeting the next night, but the editors were too busy to take his dictation. They ended up going back to the office.

The good thing was that it was a Friday night, and Carrie was off the next day. She went to the restroom to see whether her face looked any better. It was still discolored. Luckily, the bottle hadn't caused any internal damage. It felt normal down there.

When Carrie went back to the newsroom, she found Bob and a copy editor bent over a typewriter. They talked for about ten minutes before Bob came back to his desk. "I'm clear. Let's get something to eat."

"How about taking me home?" she told him.

"Not yet, I'm hungry. You know any barbecue places on Beale Street?"

Carrie looked askance at him. "What do you know about Beale Street?"

"One of the reporters told me they had good barbecue down there," he said with a nonchalant shrug.

"Yeah, there's one place still open. But ain't too many white folks on Beale Street with the strike going on."

"I'm not scared if you're not."

Ten minutes later, they pulled up to The Cue, a small white stucco building trimmed in red. Two colored men stood at the take-out window. One guy elbowed the other one when they saw them. For a moment, Carrie was afraid that they might jump on Bob for being in their neighborhood.

"Maybe we should go someplace else," she said, her eyes on the men.

"Why?" he asked. "I thought you said the barbecue was good."

"I don't think it's safe for you to be down here."

He spotted the men, who were staring them down. "Don't worry, Carrie. I know how to take care of myself. What do you want?"

She had lost her appetite. "Nothing."

"Come on, you haven't had dinner. Aren't you starving?"

Carrie wanted to hurry and leave before the men started trouble. "Get me a mild pork shoulder sandwich with extra slaw, a bag of potato chips, and a Champale."

"I'll be right back." He got out of the car and strolled up to the take-out window like it was no big deal. Carrie rolled down the window to hear what was going on. "How y'all doing?" he asked the men.

"Cool," replied one guy, who was dancing to music blaring from loudspeakers.

The other one, dressed in a peacoat and skullcap, didn't open his mouth. He sized up Bob like he was an opponent in the ring. Carrie got nervous.

"Hurry up, hurry up," Carrie said.

Bob, who was oblivious to the man, waited patiently at the window until the waitress filled their order. On the way back to the car, he told the men, "Y'all take it easy."

"You, too," replied the friendlier man.

When Bob handed Carrie her food, he said, "See, nothing happened. You worry too much."

He insisted that they eat their sandwiches in the parking lot. Carrie sipped the Champale and watched the men, who were talking and laughing with the girl at the window. Slowly, the malt liquor calmed her nerves. "Bob, do you mind if I ask you a question?"

"No, shoot," he said.

"Why you like being 'round colored people?"

"What?" The question made him blush. "I don't get what you mean."

"Most white people scared of us or pretend they don't see us, but you don't act like that."

Bob took a swig of beer. "Really, there's nothing to be scared of. You're people just like anybody else. I learned that from the lady who took care of me. She was a Negro and worked for my family on Long Island for twenty-five years before she died. She was like my second mother."

"You from an island?" Carrie asked in astonishment.

"Sort of. Long Island is close to New York City. You never heard of it?"

"No, but I've seen pictures of New York and all those tall buildings."

"That's Manhattan, which is nothing like Long Island. We have more houses than skyscrapers where I live."

"Oh, I see," said Carrie, who felt like a dummy. "Did you go to her funeral?"

"Whose funeral?"

"The colored lady."

"Yeah, as a matter of fact, we did," he replied. "Why did you ask?"

"I was just wondering."

What she really wanted to say was that no matter how much white folks claim you're part of their family, they never act like your real kin people. After Carrie ate half her sandwich, she turned the tables and played reporter with Bob. "Do you think Dr. King coming here will help the garbage men?"

"It can't hurt them," he said. "They need to do something big at this point to make the city agree to their demands. Dr. King has been pulling large crowds wherever he goes."

"Yeah, he's brave for standing up to white people."

"I admire him for that," Bob said, guzzling the beer.

Carrie looked out the window and said quietly, "I get scared for him sometimes."

"He has his own security guards. And the police are always somewhere watching him, trying to figure out his next move. They don't know what to make of Dr. King. They've never come up against a well-spoken, educated Negro who isn't afraid of the white man."

"Dr. King make colored people feel powerful, like we can do anything we set our minds to."

"And that's why whites are scared of him," said Bob, reaching for a napkin to wipe the barbecue sauce that dripped onto his shirt. "He has too much influence over Negroes."

Carrie drank her Champale and mulled over Bob's words. She had a newfound respect for him after his comments about Dr. King. She didn't think white folks thought highly of any colored person.

During the drive to her house, Carrie found herself doing most of the talking. She even told him about Vicki and Victor, and their no-good daddy. However, she regretted it right away because she didn't want Bob's sympathy.

"Don't worry about me. Covering these meetings will give me enough money to bring my babies to Memphis," she said, sitting in front of her house.

"I'm sorry you have to do all this by yourself. I admire you for that." Bob reached over and tucked a stray hair into place. He stroked her cheek. His hand was soft, like a baby's. Carrie liked the way it felt.

She rested her face in Bob's hand and closed her eyes. His touch reminded her of Vicki and Victor. When she opened her eyes, Bob's mouth was inches from her lips. He kissed Carrie. Softly. Timidly. His tongue touched hers. The shock of them kissing made her draw back.

"I shouldn't have done that. I'm sorry," he said, slapping his forehead.

"I'll see you tomorrow," she said, flinging open the car door. She was horrified by what had just happened. She dropped her keys in the grass and had to feel around for them in the dark.

Carrie went straight to the bathroom, brushed her teeth twice, and gargled with Listerine. She didn't know what kissing Bob would do to their working relationship. If he tried it again, she would stop him. She didn't want to get in trouble at work for messing around with a white man.

Chapter Twenty-Three

~

After everyone was out of the house, Nadine poured herself a cup of coffee and drank it slowly. She was in no rush to start cleaning. She sat at the kitchen table daydreaming before she realized forty-five minutes had passed. She went to check on Miz Esther before starting her chores.

Miz Esther's bedroom door was slightly ajar. She was standing in front of the radio with nothing on but her bra and panties trying to dance. Her paralyzed leg dragged behind her, causing her to stumble.

Nadine rushed into the room and helped her to a chair. "Miz Esther, where are your clothes? You need to get dressed and sit down before you hurt yourself."

"I'll do as I damn well please. Don't disturb me and my gentleman friend again," Miz Esther said.

"Yes ma'am," Nadine said, deciding to let her do whatever she wanted. She didn't have time for crazy today.

Nadine went to get a can of Johnson Wax from underneath the kitchen sink. She mopped and waxed the living room floor. Vera rang the bell just as Nadine knelt to do the dining room.

"Hey, Vera," said Nadine, reeking of sweat and wax. "How you doing?"

"I'm fine, and yourself?" said Vera, who stepped carefully on the freshly waxed floor. "How's Miz Esther today?" she asked, removing her coat.

"She refused to come out of her room for breakfast."

"Is she feeling okay?"

"As far as I know," Nadine said.

"She's a stubborn old mule."

"You ain't said nothing but the truth," Nadine agreed, raising her hand to the sky.

She ran upstairs, washed up and changed into a navy dress with a white Peter Pan collar. On her way out the door, she said, "When the girls come home from school, there's some fried chicken and potato salad in the icebox for their snack. See if Miz Esther wants some for lunch."

"I will. Take your time."

Nadine drove to Greenberg's, where there was a lot of commotion in the parking lot. Two attendants were loading a white man into the back of an ambulance. Nadine walked inside the store and found Willie Lee on the phone in the main office.

After he hung up, he motioned for her to come inside. "You won't believe what happened," he said, rubbing his forehead. "Looks like Mr. Greenberg had another heart attack."

"Another one?"

"Yeah, his wife said he had one three years ago." Willie Lee took off his apron and flung it on the desk. "Shit, Mr. Greenberg knew he wasn't supposed to be fooling around like that."

"Fooling around how?" Nadine asked.

"You can't tell anybody what I'm about to say," he whispered. "Mr. Greenberg was at the duplex he owns around the corner humping Bertha, the lady who rents it."

Nadine gasped. "You got to be kidding. Mr. Greenberg?"

"It ain't no secret, except from Miz Greenberg. When he starting having some chest pains, Bertha came running in here screaming like somebody was after her with a butcher knife. You should have seen him. He was naked, all red, and sweaty. We got him dressed and put him in the truck. I was afraid that he was gonna die on the way back to the store. I called the ambulance soon as I got here."

"Well, you did the right thing," Nadine said, touching his arm. "Miz Greenberg better off not knowing all that."

"I hope he pulls through. If he don't, ain't no telling what will happen to this store."

"Willie Lee, don't start worrying about that now," she admonished him. "Wait and see if the man makes it."

"You're right, Nadine. I'm glad you stopped by." He sat on the edge of the desk and took her in with his eyes. "You look nice today. Where you headed?"

"Actually, I was on my way here. When I saw the ambulance, I got scared and thought something had happened to you."

"Worried about me, huh?" He pinched her on the cheek.

"Go on, Willie Lee." She giggled. "You better get back to running this store since you're the boss man for real now."

"Ain't that the truth."

When Nadine got home, she found Vera sitting at the kitchen table knitting some booties. "Is everything okay?"

"Something's not right with Miz Esther," Vera said. "She was half-dressed when I went to check on her, and she gets me mixed up with other folks. Have you noticed that?"

"Yeah, she's been a little confused lately. It's probably her blood pressure medicine. Dr. Adams has changed it a couple of times."

Vera put the knitting needles and yarn in a cloth sack. "I know how that is," she said "The doctor gave Mother some heart pills that made her crazier than the law allows. It was funny at first, but I finally told him to change that medicine 'cause she was acting too big a fool. Well, let me get going. Call me if you need me."

"I will. Thank you, Vera," she said, pressing a five-dollar bill in her hand.

The next morning, Nadine waited for everyone to leave before she called the store.

"Hey, this is Nadine. Just checking to see how Mr. Greenberg is doing," she said when Willie Lee picked up the phone.

"He didn't make it."

"Oh, no. I'm sorry to hear that."

"His son said he had a massive heart attack. They worked on him a long time but couldn't save him."

"What are they going do about the store?"

"His son told me to close it tomorrow for the funeral, but open back up the day after. He said they're going to put it on the market."

"Why can't the son run it?"

"Mr. Greenberg's children ain't never been interested in running the store. They got other jobs. I don't think they like dealing with colored people. I wish I had enough money to buy it."

"How much you think it's worth?"

"I ain't sure, but it's more than I got right now. I know the bank won't give me a loan. They laugh colored people right out the door."

"I'm sure things will work out."

"You know something I don't know? Anyway, I've got to run and take care of something. Thanks for calling."

Nadine began to think the worse as soon as she hung up. If Mr. Greenberg's family sold the store, Willie Lee would be out of a job unless the new owner kept him. He could end up taking a job across town, which meant Nadine wouldn't see him. Her friendship with Willie Lee made living with Cyrus bearable. She couldn't stand the thought of him being far away.

***

From the kitchen, Nadine could hear Miz Esther singing loudly and off-key. When Nadine went into her room, Miz Esther was wearing a blue cocktail dress, mink cape, several necklaces, and bracelets up to her elbows. A white straw hat was perched on her head. She looked like a child playing dress up.

Nadine quietly closed the door and walked down the hall, where Jocelyn was sitting on the floor talking on the phone. She hung up quickly. "Mama, can I run over to Sandra's house to borrow a book?"

"You get it, and come right back," Nadine told her. "I don't want you out too late."

"I won't be gone long," Jocelyn said, racing out the door.

An hour passed and Jocelyn hadn't come home. Nadine went to Jocelyn's room and found her address book. She called Sandra. "This is Mrs. Mitchell. Is Jocelyn over there?"

"No, ma'am," she said.

"Have you seen her this afternoon?"

"Uh, uh…"

"Was she there or not?"

"No, ma'am," Sandra said.

Nadine slammed down the phone, grabbed her car keys, and pocketbook. "Salena, I'll be right back."

"Where you going, Mama?"

"To get Jocelyn," she said. "I won't be gone long."

It was almost dark, and Nadine was getting angrier by the minute. If something bad happened to Jocelyn, Cyrus and Miz Esther would never forgive her. Nadine's life would be over.

She drove past Sandra's house to the end of the street. No Jocelyn. She turned the corner and spotted a couple walking arm-in-arm. Nadine pulled along side of them and rolled down the window. "Jocelyn, get your butt in this car!" she shouted.

"Mama?" Jocelyn stood on the sidewalk terror-stricken.

"In the car, right now!" Nadine said.

Jocelyn climbed into the front seat and pouted.

"Where have you been? And who was that boy?"

"I went over to Sandra's, but she didn't have the book. Then, I—"

"Stop lying. I called Sandra's house. You better tell me the truth before I stop this car and whip your tail."

Jocelyn began talking fast, her sentences running together. "Mama, I knew if I told you that I was going over to Danny's house to get the book that you would say no. I didn't do nothing. His mama was at home. We just talked in the living room, and he was walking me home."

"Yeah, I see how he was walking you home. Y'all all hugged up. What else did you do?"

Jocelyn shook her head. "Nothing, Mama. We didn't do anything."

"I told you before that you're too young to date, but I see you decided to sneak and do it anyway. You better be glad your daddy didn't come looking for you."

"I wasn't sneaking," Jocelyn protested.

"Well, what do you call it when you lie about where you're going?"

"You saw me walking down the street. If I was sneaking, I wouldn't have been out in public." She crossed her arms and turned her body toward the passenger's door.

Nadine slammed on the brake, grabbed Jocelyn by the ponytail, and twisted her head around until they were face-to-face. Jocelyn's eyes were wide with fear. "Girl, I will slap the taste out of your mouth. Don't you ever talk back to me. And if you lie to me again, you'll regret the day you were born. Do I make myself clear, Jocelyn Rene Mitchell?"

"Yes, ma'am," Jocelyn said.

Nadine took a deep breath and drove off. She couldn't get over Jocelyn mouthing off. From now on, she would have to keep a foot on her neck or risk her becoming a rebellious teenager.

***

A couple of days after Mr. Greenberg's funeral, Nadine went to the store. She found Willie Lee smoking a cigarette in the stockroom.

"Hi," she said from the doorway.

Willie Lee looked up but didn't bother getting up from a crate. "What do you need?" he asked with an icy stare.

Nadine wasn't used to seeing Willie Lee in a bad mood. He hadn't shaved and wore a soiled smock. "What's wrong?" she asked.

"Everything, but don't any of it concern you," he said.

"Come on, we're friends," she said, walking toward him. "You can tell me anything."

"Don't worry about it. Go home."

"Willie Lee, why are you talking like this? Did Miz Greenberg make a decision about the store?"

"She wants to sell it for thirteen thousand dollars," he explained. "If she can't find a buyer in a couple of months, she's going to shut it down."

"You think she'll be able to sell it that fast?"

"I don't know," he said, dropping the cigarette on the concrete floor and stubbing it out with his shoe. "She wants to get her money out. Can't say I blame her. It doesn't make sense to have a business and never come around to check on it. See, she don't mind going to the other store because it's in the white part of town, but she never really liked this one because of where it is."

"You can find a job somewhere else," she assured him. "This isn't the only store in town."

"It's probably the only place that will let a colored man run the store. I do everything around here. Mr. Greenberg just came in to sign the checks and went around to his woman's house. What other white man gonna let a nigga do all that? All they want us to be is bag boys. I'm too old to be pushing grocery carts for quarter tips." Willie Lee lit another cigarette. "All my plans shot to hell. That Jew should've kept his dick in his pants."

It hurt Nadine to see him in such a bad state of mind. "Don't give up, Willie Lee. We just got to pray that this will work itself out."

"Yeah, we'll see."

Nadine walked over to Willie Lee and caressed his shoulder tenderly, wishing she could make all his worries disappear.

"I'll be all right," he said, removing her hand.

As Nadine lay awake that night, she realized the answer to Willie Lee's problem was a few steps away.

She sneaked out of the bedroom, went to the same closet where she had stored the gun, and retrieved a white cotton washcloth from the top shelf. Nadine uncovered a beige satin pouch that contained a passbook. She took it to the bathroom, where there was light. She checked the column of numbers, resting on the last figure - three thousand five hundred and eighteen dollars.

Her daddy had left her most the money. Over the years, she had skimmed a few dollars from the family's food and clothing allowance. It was enough to put down on Greenberg's store, but she had reservations about handing her life's savings over to Willie Lee, a man who wasn't her husband or even a relative.

The more Nadine thought about it, she concluded that the store would be a good investment and the key to her independence. Her daddy trusted Willie Lee, and she had no reason to think that he would run off with her money. She put the passbook back in the closet, confident that she had made the right decision.

After Vera's ride dropped her off the next morning, Nadine hurried over to Greenberg's. At first, she didn't see Willie Lee when she searched the aisles. She walked over to the office and saw him on the phone, slicing the air with his hands. Nadine entered quietly and sat on the couch. He was fussing at a supplier about a late shipment. She was impressed with how he handled the problem.

He hung up and shook his head. "Maybe I don't want to be bothered with this business after all. It ain't nothing but one headache after another," he said. "I'm glad you came back. I'm sorry about yesterday. I was feeling sorry for myself and took it out on you."

"That's all right, Willie Lee. I understand," she said. "I came by to give you a present." She handed him her passbook.

"What's this?"

"Open it."

Willie Lee read each page. When he got to the last page that showed the balance, he looked at Nadine and said, "I don't understand."

"It's your down payment on the store," Nadine said smiling.

His jaw dropped. "There's more than three thousand dollars in here."

"I know," Nadine said proudly. "If you give Miz Greenberg cash, maybe she'll let you buy the store on time."

"I can't take your money, Nadine." He shoved the passbook in her hand. "Something could come up, and you might need it. Besides, Cyrus will notice all this money is missing."

Nadine pressed the passbook against his chest and held it there with both her hands. "He doesn't know I have it. Daddy left me this money. I can do whatever I want. It ain't doing no good sitting in the bank. I trust you to turn it into something Daddy and me will be proud of."

Willie Lee took the passbook and covered it with his hands. "Nadine,

I don't know what to say. I can't believe you would do this for me."

Nadine switched from side-to-side and clasped her hands in front of her like a little girl. "I have a selfish reason for giving you this money."

"What?"

"I want to be your partner, be in business like my daddy. I want something of my own," she explained. "But we can't tell anybody. This has to be our secret."

"That's a deal." He turned his head to keep Nadine from seeing how moved he was by her faith in him.

"All I'm asking is that you turn this into the most successful grocery store in town," Nadine said.

Chapter Twenty-Four

~

Cyrus decided on the spur of the moment to check out the strike meeting. He read the newspaper every day but didn't trust everything written by the white press. The weekly Negro newspaper, *The Memphis Gazette*, did a better job of reporting what was really going on. But Cyrus wanted to find out for himself how close they were to settling the strike because garbage was piling up behind his office.

He arrived at Clayborn Temple around eight o'clock and stood along the wall. Cyrus soon became bored with the speeches. He looked for a familiar face in the audience of men, women, and teenagers.

As he scanned the sanctuary, he spotted Carrie sitting at the end of a row. His first reaction was to rush over, but he waited to see if she was with the man sitting next to her. After a few minutes, he casually strolled over and knelt beside her. "Carrie, can we go outside and talk?"

She cringed at the sight of him. "Have you been following me? I don't have anything to say to you. Leave me alone!" She looked straight head, ignoring him.

"Please, just a few minutes."

Carrie jumped up and knocked Cyrus off balance. She ran into the vestibule and hid in the ladies' room. Cyrus followed her but lost sight in the crowded lobby.

Unbeknown to both of them, Nadine witnessed the whole scene. She and four volunteers from the food bank had come to the meeting. She brought Jocelyn and Salena with her. They were sitting one section over from Carrie.

"Mama, I have to use the bathroom," Salena said.

"Can you wait a few minutes? We're leaving after the man finishes talking."

There was a disturbance to the right of Nadine. Two policemen stood at the end of a row pointing to a young man.

"You, in the black cap and glasses, come with me," one cop ordered.

The man didn't move.

"Get up!" the officer commanded.

He drew his gun, and his partner moved in to arrest the man. When the policeman reached for the man, someone sitting in the pew tripped the cop.

"Get out of here, pigs!" someone yelled.

A woman stood and shouted, "Stop harassing us!"

The crowd began throwing wads of paper and other objects at the officers.

POP!

It sounded like someone had set off a firecracker. Pandemonium broke out. Women screamed. People ran toward the exits.

"Get down!" Nadine yelled. She leaned over to shield Salena and Jocelyn from being trampled.

When she thought it was safe, Nadine raised her head and looked over the pew. "Let's get out of here," she said. She noticed that the bodice of Salena's dress was ripped and bloody.

"Oh, my God! Salena, you're bleeding! Somebody call an ambulance!" Nadine screamed. "Call the ambulance! My daughter's hurt!" She touched Salena's chest looking for a wound but didn't feel anything. "Baby, where does it hurt?"

"Right here," Salena said, pointing to her shoulder.

"Help me, somebody! Please!" She looked at Jocelyn. "You okay?"

"Uh-huh," she said, staring at Salena's bloody chest.

Salena started crying. "It burns."

"It's gonna be all right." Nadine looked around the room. "Is the ambulance coming?"

A man came over and took out his handkerchief. "Ma'am, the ambulance is on the way." He placed the folded square on Salena's chest. "Little lady, how you doing?"

Salena closed her eyes.

"No, no! Salena!" Nadine shouted. "Oh, God, no!"

Through the fear and confusion, Nadine heard a familiar voice. "I'm a doctor, let me through, please."

"Cyrus, Cyrus!" Nadine screamed. "Salena…"

When Cyrus saw her cradling Salena, his face turned ashen. "Out of the way," he said, pushing Nadine. "What are you doing here?" He snatched off the handkerchief and examined Salena. "I need to get her to a hospital."

"Cyrus, is she…?"

"Meet me in the emergency room at John Gaston."

"I'm going with you."

"Do like I told you!"

Two policemen broke through the crowd that had gathered around Nadine and the girls. "We got a report that someone was shot," one officer said, looking over Cyrus's shoulder. "Is this the victim?"

"Yes, my daughter has been hurt. I'm a doctor. I'm taking her to John Gaston. My wife will tell you what happened."

"You should wait for an ambulance," said the second officer.

"There's no time for that," Cyrus said. He sprinted past the cops, lay Salena on the backseat of his car, and sped to the hospital.

When Carrie heard all the commotion, she opened the bathroom door to a sea of frightened faces. "What happened?" she asked a man pushing his way through the double doors.

"Somebody is shooting in there."

"In the church?" Carrie joined the fleeing crowd and called Bob from the nearest phone booth.

"The police reporter is on his way," Bob said. "We got it from here. I'll come and get you."

"No, it's early. There are a lot of people out here. I can take the bus," she said.

By the time Nadine arrived at the emergency room, she was beside herself with worry. "Where's Salena Mitchell?"

The clerk was on the phone and motioned for Nadine to wait. Instead, she ran down the hall and looked behind each curtain until she found them. Nadine stood with her hands cupped over her mouth as the doctor worked on Salena.

"Cyrus?" she said in a faint voice.

His face was blank.

Nadine plodded toward the bed. A heaviness settled around her chest. She forced herself to look into her daughter's face.

"Mama!" Salena tried to sit up.

"Hold still, young lady," the doctor said. "I'll be through cleaning you up in a few minutes."

Salena beckoned Nadine with her free hand. Nadine grabbed it and held on tightly. "My poor baby. How are you feeling?"

Salena looked at her arm. "It stings," she said. "Daddy said I fainted."

"Yes, you did. It scared me to death," Nadine said softly.

"She was lucky. The bullet grazed her, but she could've been killed," Cyrus said brusquely. He gripped Nadine's arm, pushing her toward the hall.

"Daddy," Jocelyn called out.

"Stay with your sister."

Cyrus dragged Nadine into a stairwell. He raised his hand to strike her but caught himself. He grasped her face, digging his fingernails into her skin. "You don't have a damn bit of common sense, taking the girls out this time of night. They had no business at that meeting."

Nadine sobbed. "I'm sorry. I didn't think it was going to be dangerous. I just wanted them to hear some of the speeches."

"Now you see what can happen. Don't take them to any more of these strike meetings."

"I won't," Nadine said. She leaned against the wall and cried, knowing that she had come close to losing Salena. "I'm so sorry."

Cyrus sat on the steps with his hands dangling between his legs. He wanted to kill the policeman responsible for injuring his daughter. In his heart, he knew Nadine wouldn't intentionally put the girls in harm's way.

"Do your volunteer work at the church and leave it at that. Don't come to any more meetings. It's not safe," Cyrus said.

"I won't."

He got up and opened the door for Nadine. "I hope you didn't leave Mama alone."

"Vera's there."

"You and Jocelyn go on home. I'll bring Salena."

Nadine paused outside the exam room. She turned to Cyrus and said, "Thank God you were there. Of all nights, what made you stop by the church tonight?"

"Curiosity," he said nonchalantly.

Nadine wanted to ask him about Carrie, but it wasn't the right time. She would find out another day.

***

Cyrus bought the morning newspaper to see what was written about the shooting. Buried inside the main strike story was a paragraph about a policeman accidentally discharging his weapon during the meeting while trying to arrest a burglary suspect. The story reported that the bullet, which lodged in a pillar, grazed a bystander.

"Stupid reporter," Cyrus said. "They didn't mention that it was child who got hurt."

Still worked up about last night, Cyrus called Mamie. "Good morning. I had a rough night and wanted to hear your voice before I started seeing patients."

"What happened?"

Cyrus told her about Salena.

"That's terrible. What's going to happen to the cop?"

Cyrus threw a ballpoint pen across his desk. "There will probably be an internal affairs investigation that will ultimately find he wasn't at fault. They never are when we get injured or killed."

"Why don't you call the newspaper and TV stations, and tell them what happened to your daughter? That will force the police to apologize or do something."

"I don't want to put Salena through that. I just want her to go back to doing the stuff little girls do." He moved a stack of folders from one side of the desk to the other. "I tell you what, somebody is going to be dead before this strike is over."

"Don't say that. I read that the union is turning up the heat, bringing in the big boys from Georgia. It can't go on much longer."

"I hope not. Enough about me. How've you been?"

"Fine. I've been busy working on my sorority's spring gala the third Saturday in April. I'm chairman this year."

"And who will be escorting you to the dance?"

"A gentleman, of course."

Cyrus got jealous. "I could take you."

"And how would I introduce you to my family and friends?" she said. 'This is Dr. Cyrus Mitchell, my married gentleman friend from Memphis.'"

"That's just a technicality for now. Next year, I'm going to take you to that gala. I promise."

"Uh-huh," she said.

"I will. Now, I've got to go. My patients are losing patience."

After Cyrus hung up, he sat at his desk trying to figure out how he could keep Mamie from dating other men until they could be together. He knew that wouldn't be easy considering she was headstrong.

Cyrus didn't know who was more stubborn, Mamie or Carrie. For the latter, he decided to stop being nice and get tough with her. He was determined that no other man would raise his children. The guilt he once felt for not being there when Carrie needed him had turned into obsession. He called her at work.

"Hello, Carrie, this is Cyrus."

"Why are you calling me on my job?"

"I wanted to give you an opportunity to reconsider my offer."

"I told you that I don't need your help. Don't call me again."

"Well, you leave me no choice but to petition the court for custody of my son and daughter."

"You're going to do what?"

"You heard me."

Carrie was incensed. "You don't hold no claim to them."

"I'll drop the petition if you let me see them."

"Go to hell, Cyrus!" She hung up the phone.

Cyrus hadn't expected that reaction from Carrie. He realized that he was dealing with an older, wiser woman, not a simple country girl. Apparently, adversity had made her stronger. He liked that. It even turned him on.

Chapter Twenty-Five

~

Although Carrie thought that Cyrus was bluffing, she knew he was vengeful enough to drag her into court. The headache that had been bothering her all morning grew worse just thinking about a custody battle. She could barely make it through the lunch rush. To make matters worse, Bob came in looking sheepish.

Carrie walked over to him and said, "You eating kind of late today."

"Yeah, I had to interview the mayor."

Carrie took out her notepad. "Know what you want?"

"No," he said, reaching for a sheet with the chef's specials. "You ready for the meeting tonight?"

"The meeting?"

"Yeah, this is the one I told you we needed to cover because the garbage men have some out-of-town civil rights workers coming. I can't go because I'm working on a special section."

"Yeah, yeah, I remember," she said. "I'll be back." Carrie went to the other side of the counter and took an order from another customer. When she came back, Bob was still reading the menu. "How long is it going to take you to decide? I ain't got all day."

Bob looked up at Carrie and asked in a child's voice, "Are you angry with me?"

"No," she replied.

"Then, why are you being short with me today?"

"It's nothing," she said, shifting her weight to the other leg.

"It must be something. Are you upset about me kissing you?" He reached for her hand, but she snatched it from him.

Carrie scowled at him. "Shush," she ordered. "Why are you talking 'bout that here? You want me to lose my job?" she asked, glancing at the man three stools down from him.

"No," he said, looking flustered. "I'm sorry. I wasn't trying to embarrass you. I…"

"Just go 'head and order so people will stop looking at us."

"I'll have a bowl of chicken soup, a grilled cheese sandwich, and some water," he said.

Carrie brought his food and left the check in front of his plate. She didn't say anything else to him during his lunch break. It was her way of showing Bob that he needed to respect her boundaries. She didn't want to lose her job.

Before she left the building, Carrie poked her head out the main entrance, looking up and down the street in case Cyrus might be waiting to ambush her again. There was no sign of him or his car. She crossed the street and boarded the bus.

Cyrus weighed heavily on her mind. She had to stop him from getting custody of the twins. That wouldn't be easy considering she didn't have money for a lawyer. But she did know someone who could help. Carrie got off the bus and crossed the street to catch another bus bound for Castalia Heights.

It had been more than a year and a half since Carrie visited the neighborhood. The red brick house looked smaller than she remembered. Two evergreen trees in the front yard had grown so big that they covered half the house. She knocked lightly on the door.

Miz Lillian peered out. "Lord, as I live and breathe. Carrie?"

"Yes, ma'am. It's me," she said smiling.

"Come in, sweetheart," she said, hugging her. "Mack, guess who's here. It's Carrie."

Mr. Mack looked up from *The Memphis Gazette*. "Carrie?" he said, rubbing his chin.

"Yes, you remember Carrie," she said, trying to jolt Mr. Mack's memory. "She was one of my office aides and helped me around the house."

"Oh, yes," he said, getting up from his chair and extending a hand. "It's good to see you again. How've you been?"

"I'm fine," she said, squeezing his hand. "And the two of you?"

"No right to complain," Miz Lillian said. "I can't believe you're here. It's been such a long time. Let's go to the kitchen. I'm peeling some turnips. Can I get you something to drink?"

Carrie followed Miz Lillian through a small hallway. "Some tea is fine." She looked around the kitchen. Nothing had changed. Two big stockpots for boiling vegetables stood ready on the stove. Cake pans and serving dishes sat on the buffet. Spices were lined up alphabetically on a shelf Mr. Mack built above the stove.

Miz Lillian set two cups of steaming hot tea on the table. "How about a slice of pound cake?"

"No, ma'am. It sure looks good though. I'll take a piece home if you don't mind."

"Not at all. By the time you get ready to go, my apple pie will be done, and you can have a slice of that, too." Miz Lillian put two teaspoons of sugar in her cup and passed the bowl to Carrie. "I'm glad you're back, Carrie. I missed you. I felt so bad when you left. We had no way to get in touch with you. How are things going?"

Carrie blinked back tears. "Not too good. I mean, me and the twins are fine, but I'm having trouble with Cyrus."

"With Cyrus?" she asked surprised. "What kind of trouble?"

"Cyrus is threatening to take me to court if I don't let him see Vicki and Victor."

Miz Lillian set her cup down hard on the table, spilling a few drops of tea on her apron. "Dear Lord, he actually said that?" she asked, dabbing the wet spots with a napkin.

"Yes, ma'am," Carrie said. She sat on the edge of the chair and jiggled her foot as she told Miz Lillian about her last conversation with Cyrus. "He ain't been interested in them all this time, and all of a sudden he want custody. They ain't even up here. They're in Mississippi with my mama."

"Carrie, I don't know what game Cyrus is playing, but I can assure you that he is in no position to make that kind of threat."

"I was hoping that maybe you could talk to him. I don't want to put you in the middle of this, but I don't have nobody else to turn to."

"Don't worry. I'll call my nephew and tell him to back off. But at some point, the two of you will have to reach an understanding. After all, he is the father."

"I know, Miz Lillian. Right now, I'm just trying to work and save money to bring them up here."

"Tell me all about the twins," Miz Lillian said. "They must be so big by now."

Carrie showed her the pictures, and Miz Lillian acted like a proud grandmother. She held the pictures lovingly, staring at each child as if she were trying to commit their image to memory. "They look just like Cyrus," Miz Lillian said. "They got his eyes, his chin, and his mouth. There's no denying who the daddy is."

Carrie smiled. "No, they're the spitting image of him."

When it was time to go, Carrie gave Miz Lillian her address and phone number. She really missed Miz Lillian, who had been more of a grandmother to her than Nee Mama. She had no doubt that Miz Lillian would talk some sense into Cyrus.

On the bus ride home, Carrie leaned against the window and closed her eyes. It had been a long day. Then, she remembered the garbage workers' meeting. There was no way she could make it to the church and get something in time for Bob's deadline. The meeting had completely slipped her mind.

Carrie called him when she got home. As soon as he answered, she could tell he was angry.

"What happened to you tonight? I was expecting you to call me half-way through the meeting," he said.

"Something came up that I had to take care of."

"You should have called. This was a big story. We were counting on you."

"I'm sorry, but I had something important to do."

"Look, if you want to keep this job, you have to be more responsible," he said irritated.

"I don't want this job," Carrie shot back. "And I don't need you bossing me around. You can go to the meetings yourself!" She hung up.

"That cracker ain't got no right yelling at me," she fumed aloud. "Who does he think he is? He can go to hell. I'm through playing reporter."

Carrie had planned to ignore Bob when he came into the cafeteria the next day, but he didn't show up. At four-thirty that afternoon, the doorbell rang.

"How can I help you?" said Miz Lula, standing on her toes to see who was at the door.

"Good evening, ma'am. Is Carrie home?"

"Is she expecting you?" asked Miz Lula, who was wary of white people in her neighborhood.

"No, ma'am. We work together, and I need to talk to her."

"Just a minute, I'll get her." Miz Lula rushed to Carrie's room. "There's a white man on the front porch from your job."

"I don't believe this," she said, tossing aside the letter she was writing to Ruth. "He got a lot of nerve coming to my house."

"Want me to get rid of him?"

"No, I'll handle it," she said, racing to the front door.

When the door opened, Bob started talking fast. "Hi, Carrie. I apologize for showing up like this, but I felt we needed to have another conversation after the last one, which didn't go too well. I totally take responsibility for that."

"Ain't nothing to talk about," Carrie said dispassionately.

"Look, I'm really sorry for yelling at you last night. This strike is driving me crazy. I've got editors breathing down my neck all day, the mayor and City Council members are meeting behind closed doors, and nobody will tell me anything. It's so damn frustrating," he said, running his hand through his curly hair. "But that's no reason to take it out on you. Please accept my apology."

"Bob, I ain't wasting my time being mad at you. I got other things to do."

"You tell him," said Miz Lula, who was standing guard.

"Can we go to my car so we can talk in private," he said, looking past Carrie at Miz Lula.

Her first instinct was to refuse, but she decided to hear him out. "Let me get my coat." Carrie turned and bumped into Miz Lula.

"I'll keep an eye out. If he does anything funny, I'll call the police," Miz Lula whispered.

"I don't think he'll try anything," Carrie said. "But thanks for looking out."

When they got in the car, Bob turned on the engine and cranked up the heat. He rubbed his hands together to warm them. "Carrie, you're one of the few people in the whole building I can talk to. I don't want to ruin our friendship."

"Let's just forget the whole thing. I'm through going to meetings. I ain't no good at this."

"But you are good, Carrie. You just don't realize it. I'll work with you a little more on how to take notes. You have good instincts. All you have to do now is hone your skills."

"See, right there. I have no idea what you talking 'bout," Carrie said, throwing up her hands.

"I'm so used to newspaper jargon that I forget how to speak in layman's language sometimes. What I'm saying is that you can hear a person giving a speech and pick out the most interesting part of it. You know what's important to the reader. That's a skill."

"Really?"

Bob took her hand. "I have another proposition for you."

"What now?" Carrie said as she removed her hand.

"I talked to my editor about hiring you to be a copy clerk. Distributing copies to other departments, ripping the wires, getting coffee, stuff like that."

"You mean quit my job in the cafeteria?"

"Yeah, and work in the newsroom."

"Would I be working for you?"

"You would be reporting directly to the city editor. When you're not busy, I can teach you how to write a story."

Carrie thought about it for a minute and asked, "Any other colored people work up there?"

"No, does it matter?"

"I was just wondering."

"Come on, Carrie, give it a try. If you don't like it, you can go back to your old job."

Carrie frowned at him. "You know they won't keep my job open while I go work somewhere else."

"They probably won't, but that's not going to be an issue because you'll do great."

"How much does the job pay?"

"Forty-five dollars a week."

"That's more than I'm making now," she exclaimed.

"Plus, you'll get a raise in three months."

"Really? For doing that little simple stuff?"

"Yup. See, I'm looking out for you, Carrie. Now, are we friends again?" he asked, offering his hand.

"You crazy, Bob." She shook his hand. He gave her the same look that he did the night they kissed. Carrie's heart skipped a beat.

Bob glanced at his watch. "I've got to run. My editor wants to talk to you. Can you come up to the newsroom when you get off tomorrow?"

"But I haven't decided anything."

"Take the job, Carrie. It'll be good for you."

"I'll think about it," she said.

"Call me tonight if you have any questions."

Carrie weighed the pros and cons and decided to take the job. All she had to do now was impress Bob's editor. She went to her closet and pulled out her lucky outfit – a green and brown plaid dress that she wore for her cafeteria job interview.

***

March 15, 1968

Dear Mama,

How are you and my babies? I am fine. I started a new job at the publishing company. I'm a copy girl in the newsroom. I help out the people that write newspaper articles. One of the white reporters said he's going to teach me how to write stories. He's the one I help out sometimes by going to meetings. I'm making more money now, and I'll be able to come and get Victor and Vicki this summer. Give them a big kiss and hug for me.

 Love,
 Carrie

Carrie put the letter in an envelope along with twenty dollars and addressed the front. She was in a good mood and excited about riding with Cleary to West Memphis, where he was buying fish for his church's fish fry tomorrow night. She was curious about West Memphis, but the real reason she wanted to go was to spend some time with somebody colored.

She was around white people all day, listening to them whine about stuff that she didn't give two cents about. Carrie cleaned off her desk and went to the restroom to freshen up. She applied a fresh coat of lipstick, combed her hair, and hurried to meet Cleary, who was parked at the employee entrance.

Cleary's eyes brightened up when she opened the door. "Hey, Miz Lady, you ready to hit the road?"

"Yeah," she said. "Can you stop by the post office?"

"You expect me to let you mail a love letter to some other man?" said Cleary, pretending to be offended.

"This ain't no love letter. It's to my mama."

"Uh-huh, tell me anything. The only reason I'm doing this is 'cause it's on the way to the fish house." He backed out of the parking space and headed to the downtown post office.

"I appreciate it, kind sir," she said.

"So, how you been?"

"Fine. Just working hard, trying to stay out of white folks way."

"You like this job better than the other one?"

"It's more interesting 'cause you get to know what's going on before anybody else, but it's harder 'cause I got to work with some prejudiced white people. They'll say nigger in a minute, and I could be standing right in front of them." She shook her head. "They something else."

"They can't all be like that."

"No, not everybody, mainly the old men on the copy desk. It don't bother me much as it did the first few days. I just do like they tell me."

"What about that white boy I see you talking to, can't he say something to them?"

"Who, Bob? He don't have nothing to do with them. He's a Jew. They don't like them too much neither."

"I didn't know that. I ain't had the pleasure of talking to Mr. Jew Bob," he said sarcastically.

Cleary's remark confirmed what Carrie had suspected all along. He didn't like Bob. "How much farther we got to go?"

"Another fifteen minutes. Why, you need to get back home or something?"

"No, I was just asking. I've never been to West Memphis," said Carrie, looking past Cleary.

Her mind flashed back to the white boys in the truck and how she was afraid they would drive her over here and dump her lifeless body in the swamp. So far, she hadn't seen anything that looked like a swamp.

"Ain't much happening here 'cept the dog track. It's just another hick town. But they got the best fish around."

"I'm still waiting to taste this fish you claim you can cook," Carrie said, cocking her head.

"I didn't think you was still interested. You surprised me twice yesterday. First, you came by my office to say hi. And second, when you said you wouldn't mind riding over here with me."

"Why you surprised?"

"You so busy nowadays that I thought maybe you and Mr. Jew Bob might have plans."

Carrie's mouth flew open. "I ain't going with Bob. He's white or didn't you notice?"

"That don't make no difference to some folks."

"Well, it does to me. I got my babies to think about." Carrie covered her mouth and squeezed her eyes shut.

Cleary swerved to the side of the road, put the car in park, and turned to her. "Say what? Babies? You got children?"

Carrie stared at the floor mat.

"Do you mean to tell me that all this time we been talking you're just now telling me that?"

"I was going to tell you..."

"When?" he asked, raising his voice.

"I don't know," she replied defensively. "I just hadn't found the right time."

"How many you got?"

"Just two. Twins. Victor and Vicki. They're thirteen months old."

"I'll be damned," Cleary said, shaking his head. He steered the car into traffic. "Where are they?"

"Mama keeping them until I can bring them up here," she explained. "That's why I been working like a slave."

Cleary made a sharp left turn into the gravel parking lot of the fish house. "Where's their daddy?"

"He ain't in the picture."

"You full of surprises lately," he said. "Anything else?"

"No, that's it."

"Let's get this fish and get back across the river." Cleary got out of the car and walked ahead of Carrie.

After they bought the fish, they drove straight back to Memphis.

Cleary still hadn't said much, and Carrie was angry with him for getting an attitude. Before she got out of the car, he said, "Carrie, you don't have to hold nothing back from me. Just be truthful from now on."

"I will," she said.

Cleary turned her face toward him. "One day you'll realize I ain't like those other niggas you been fooling with. I'm the real deal."

Chapter Twenty-Six

~

Nadine cleaned Salena's wound and applied antibiotic cream as the doctor instructed, keeping an eye out for signs of an infection. Although Salena was eager to go to school and show off her bandage, Nadine made her stay home for three days.

While she did her household chores, Nadine couldn't get Cyrus and Carrie out of her mind. She concluded that the only reason they might know each other is if Cyrus delivered her twins. However, that still didn't explain why she ran away from him.

She went back to New Hope looking for answers. "Good morning, Mother Copeland," Nadine said.

"How you doing, baby?" Mother Copeland said.

"It's been a busy week, but I'm fine. Is Carrie coming today?" Nadine asked in a tight voice.

"No, she had something else to do."

"We'll have to carry on without her," Nadine said, trying to hide her disappointment. "It looks like we have plenty of volunteers today."

"And we know how to get people in and out, thanks to you."

Nadine decided against asking any more questions because Mother Copeland might get suspicious. "Let me get to work. I'll talk to you later."

Throughout the morning, Nadine racked her brain trying to

remember whether Carrie disclosed where she lived or worked. It occurred to her that she had done all the talking, and Carrie hadn't divulged any information about herself. It would be another week before she could ask her about Cyrus if she showed up for volunteer duty.

***

Nadine piddled around the kitchen waiting for Cyrus to come downstairs. It was taking so long that she finally went upstairs to see what was keeping him. She stood in the doorway watching him hold neckties against a white shirt under a gray patterned jacket. "Are you eating with us tonight?"

"No, I've got a meeting," he responded without looking at Nadine. "Why?"

"I need you to take a look at Jocelyn."

Cyrus stopped knotting a tie and turned to Nadine. "What's wrong with her?"

"She has a little rash on her cheeks, and she claims her legs and arms hurt. I don't see any sores or bruises."

"Nadine, take the child to the doctor if she's sick. Don't sit around waiting for me to come home and examine her. I have enough to do," he chastised her.

"I just thought maybe you wanted to check her first to see if it was serious," she said.

"She seemed fine to me earlier, but I'll look at her before I leave."

"It's probably nothing but growing pains as Aunt Bessie Mae used to say," Nadine added.

"Go to Jocelyn's room," Cyrus said dismissively. "I'll be there in a few minutes."

Before Nadine could tell Jocelyn that her daddy was coming to examine her, Cyrus strolled into the room. "I hear you're not feeling well. What's the matter?"

She closed her science book. "It's nothing," she said, clicking a ballpoint pen.

"That's not what you told me," Nadine interjected. "Go ahead and tell him what's hurting you."

"Your mother said you have pain in your arms and legs."

"Sometimes."

"Did you fall or hurt yourself in gym class?" Cyrus asked.

"No."

"Show me where it hurts."

Jocelyn pointed to the back of her knees and the inside of her elbows. Cyrus bent her knee and gently pushed it toward her chest. "Does this hurt?"

"Uh-huh." He repeated the motion with her other leg. Same response. Then he raised each arm and bent it toward her shoulder. Jocelyn told him that each movement was painful. "How are you feeling otherwise? Do you have a sore throat or headache?"

"No," she said. "What do you think it is, Daddy?"

"I don't know," he said, cupping her chin. "How long have you been feeling like this?"

She shrugged. "Two weeks, maybe."

"Well, your mother is going to take you to see Dr. Adams. He'll take good care of you." He kissed her on the cheek.

Nadine followed him back to their bedroom. "What do you think it is?" she asked anxiously.

"I don't think it's serious, but Dr. Adams will run some tests and tell us more." Cyrus began undressing. "I'll be home late," he said.

"Yeah, I figured that."

"You figured right for a change," he said with a smirk.

***

Out the corner of her eye, Nadine saw the tail of a light blue dress float across the hallway. She closed the refrigerator and went to investigate. She found Miz Esther running her finger along the baseboard in the dining room.

"Miz Esther, is everything all right?"

"No," she said, holding up a finger. "Look at all this dirt. Why haven't you cleaned the baseboard? You know I don't keep my house like this."

"Yes, ma'am. I'll get right on it," Nadine said. "Can I get you anything?"

"Just clean my house. You never know who's coming by." Miz Esther stepped on Nadine's foot deliberately and shuffled back to her room.

Nadine shook her head. One minute Miz Esther was crazy as a loon; the next she was back to her old hateful self.

While Nadine was crawling along the floor wiping the baseboard, the phone rang. "Dr. Adams called with the lab results," Cyrus said as soon as she answered.

"Already," she said, bracing herself for bad news. "What did he say?"

"Jocelyn has a disease called systemic lupus erythematosus."

"System lupus, what?" Nadine asked, her voice rising with each word. "I've never heard of that. Is it serious? Is she going to be okay?"

"Calm down," Cyrus said. "Lupus is a disease that causes the body's immune system to attack healthy tissue, like the joints, which is why Jocelyn is experiencing some pain. It can also affect the kidneys, brain, heart, and other organs."

"Is there any medicine for this lupus?"

"Dr. Adams can prescribe oral prednisone to treat her symptoms. Unfortunately, there is no cure…" Cyrus said, his voice trailing off.

"Oh, my God," Nadine cried. "Are you saying that Jocelyn is going to die?"

When Cyrus opened his mouth to speak, he got choked up. "Right now, Jocelyn has a mild case of lupus, but it could get worse. And it can be fatal. Dr. Adams doesn't know how the disease will progress in Jocelyn because it affects each person differently."

"Poor Jocelyn," Nadine cried. "She's so young."

"She's going to be okay, Nadine."

"How did she get this? Can we catch it?"

"Nobody knows what causes lupus. It's not contagious," Cyrus explained. "Look, I hate to leave you like this, but I've got patients waiting. Pull yourself together before the girls get home. You can tell Jocelyn this afternoon or we can do it together tonight. It's your choice, but you have to be strong for Jocelyn."

"Okay," Nadine said, sniffling.

She hung up the phone thinking that she couldn't break this news to Jocelyn by herself. She would wait for Cyrus because he would know exactly what to say and answer all of her questions.

Nadine went back to cleaning the baseboard, but her mind was on Jocelyn and lupus. Her first thought was to call Willie Lee, but she decided not to bother him at work. She couldn't call Lydia because she was out of town.

With no one to console her, Nadine went upstairs and lay across the bed. She closed her eyes and prayed. *Lord, I need you now. Give me the strength to get through this. Take away my child's pain and suffering and make her whole again, most merciful Father.*

Nadine curled up in the fetal position and hummed a song, "I Need Thee Every Hour," until she drifted off. The sound of the front door slamming woke her up. Nadine got up, washed her face, and pretended that everything was fine.

She cooked smothered chicken, rice and broccoli for dinner but didn't have much of an appetite. Nadine stared at Jocelyn throughout the meal, wondering what her life would be like with lupus. Will she finish college? Find a husband? Have children?

When Nadine felt like she was going to break down, she went upstairs and cried in the bathroom. Shortly after seven, Cyrus walked in the house, looking worried and exhausted.

"How's Jocelyn doing?" he asked.

"About the same as far as I can tell," Nadine said, nervously twisting her wedding band.

"Did you tell her?"

"No, I decided to wait until you got home."

"Give me about forty-five minutes. I want to wash up, change clothes, and get something to eat first."

"I'll go heat up your dinner."

After Cyrus finished eating, Nadine sent Salena upstairs to play and Jocelyn to the den. She and Jocelyn seated themselves on the couch. Cyrus sat in a chair across from them.

"Am I in trouble?" Jocelyn asked, looking from Nadine to Cyrus.

"No," Cyrus said. "I want to talk to you about the pain in your joints."

"It's not bad today," Jocelyn said.

"That's good," Cyrus said, looking at Nadine. He leaned forward in his chair. "Dr. Adams got your test results back. They show that you have a disease called lupus."

"Huh?" Jocelyn said, wrinkling her nose. "What's that?"

"The easiest way to explain is like this: Your immune system is composed of cells, organs, and tissues that work together to fight off sickness. When you have lupus, your immune system mistakes some part of the body as an invader and attacks its own cells. Do you understand?"

"I guess," said Jocelyn, her eyes wide with fear. "Am I going to die?"

"No, baby, we can manage the lupus with medicine, but you have to follow the doctor's advice and take all your medication for it to work."

"What if somebody touches me, will they get it?"

"No, lupus is inside your body. It's going to make you feel tired, sore, and achy sometimes, but nobody will know you have it unless you tell them."

"How did I get it, Daddy?"

Cyrus walked over to Jocelyn, sat on the end of the sofa, and put his arm around her. "Doctors don't know the answer to that question," he said. "We have to stay on top of this. I need you to tell your mother when you're not feeling well. Promise me you'll do that."

"I will," Jocelyn said. "Can I go now?"

"Sure, I know you must have some homework. If you have any more questions, I'll be here."

"Okay."

After Jocelyn left the room, Nadine turned to Cyrus. "Could it have been something I ate or did while I was pregnant that caused the lupus?"

Cyrus lost his patience. "You haven't been listening. I'll say it again. Doctors don't know how people get lupus."

"I'm sorry," she said fretfully. "It's just that I'm having a hard time understanding all of this."

"The only thing you have to remember is to make sure Jocelyn takes her medicine. We're dealing with a lifelong, chronic illness. We need to keep it under control as much as possible."

Nadine rocked with her head down and arms crossed on her chest. "I couldn't bear losing her, Cyrus. I just can't."

Cyrus put his hand on Nadine's shoulder. "Try not to think about that. We have to take this one day at a time."

"I have to be strong for Jocelyn," she repeated three times.

"We'll get though this," Cyrus said.

With no one else to console them, they clung to each other. Nadine drew away first, concerned that she might be sending the wrong signal. She didn't want him to think for a moment that she had any feelings for him.

Chapter Twenty-Seven

Cyrus felt Miz Esther should be told about Jocelyn's illness, but he worried that the news might be too upsetting. Jocelyn was her favorite. She had mapped out her social life through high school, from her escort for the cotillion to her senior prom date. He went to his mother's bedroom and found her looking at a family photo album. "How are you feeling tonight, Mama?" he asked cheerfully.

She passed the album to Cyrus, who put it back on her bookshelf.

"You know, if I died today, I'd be a happy woman. I got you and my grandbabies. Everybody is happy and healthy. I'm glad you dropped that divorce nonsense."

"Well, my feelings haven't changed," Cyrus said adamantly. "I've accepted the fact that I made a big mistake marrying Nadine. I'll be paying for it the rest of my life. "I've found—"

"Shut your damn mouth!" she shrieked. "If you hadn't been such a cock hound, you never would've got yourself in that predicament. You're just like your daddy. Humph. Faulting me for getting pregnant, never once stopping to think that he was as much to blame as I was."

"Mama, take it easy. I didn't…"

Miz Esther narrowed her eyes and fixed them on Cyrus. "After you got what you wanted, you went back to that other woman, the one your mammy was crazy about. You didn't give a damn about what happened to me or my baby!" she screamed.

Nadine came running into the room when she heard the loud voices. "What's wrong?"

"I don't know," Cyrus said as he moved closer to comfort Miz Esther. "Mama, I think you need to lie down. You're talking out of your head." When Cyrus tried to help Miz Esther up, she pushed him, causing him to fall backward over the ottoman.

"Ain't nothing wrong with me," she said, waving her cane. "I'm just telling the truth, and you can't stand to hear it. If you were any kind of man, you would have stood up to your folks and told them you wanted to be with me. You son of a bitch."

Miz Esther came at him with her cane. Her eyes were enlarged. Spit oozed from the corner of her mouth. Cyrus watched in shock as Miz Esther charged at him. He scrambled out of the way. Abruptly, she stopped babbling, fell to the floor, and bawled like a baby.

"Cyrus, do you want me to call an ambulance?"

"No, just help me get her to bed. I'll give her a sedative."

She looked up at Cyrus. "You weren't a mistake, son. I loved him."

"I know, Mama. It's all right. We're going to put you in the bed."

"That's a good idea. I'm tired. Kiss the babies for me. I'm going to get up in the morning and make them some biscuits."

Nadine helped Miz Esther put on a fresh gown. Cyrus brought a sleeping pill and glass of water. She took it without protest.

"Get some rest, Mama," he said, kissing her on the forehead.

"Good night, baby."

Cyrus and Nadine went into the den.

"What caused her to go off like that?" Nadine asked.

Cyrus shrugged his shoulders. "We were having a normal conversation. Has she acted like this before?"

"No, she's in her room watching TV most of the time."

Nadine didn't feel the least bit guilty about lying. In her mind, Miz Esther's crazy spells were payback for mistreating her. She didn't want Cyrus to cure her because the house was peaceful when Miz Esther's mind was bad.

"I'll have Dr. Adams check her out."

"I just hope it's nothing serious," Nadine said, faking concern. "She's been through so much."

When Dr. Adams came by a few days later, Miz Esther was back to normal, chatting about things she had read in the newspaper or seen on TV. Dr. Adams didn't find anything that would explain her odd behavior.

"Miz Esther's mental faculties may have been impaired by the stroke, and she's probably becoming a little senile," he told Cyrus in the living room.

"She's only sixty-one," Cyrus said. "That's kind of young, isn't it?"

"It's more common in older people, but like I said, the stroke could have triggered it."

"Great. Something else I have to deal with," Cyrus mumbled. "Thanks, for coming by."

On the way to work, Cyrus felt a tightness in his chest. He stopped the car, loosened his tie, and took a couple of deep breaths. Between his family's medical crises and his practice, he was under a lot of pressure. It was beginning to take a toll on him. The only way he knew how to relax was between the thighs of a woman. He had to find one soon.

***

Cyrus had noticed the statuesque woman with the warm, amber complexion on previous shopping trips to Goldsmith's department store. Cozette worked as a sales assistant in the Men's Department. She was friendly and knowledgeable about the merchandise. However, her biggest asset was a voluptuous chest, which she encased in tight-fitting sweaters.

Today, the white salesmen were busy waiting on white customers so Cozette offered to help him. She followed him from rack to rack, holding his selection of suits. When she was out of earshot of the other salesmen, she whispered, "It's about time you let me help you. I thought you were one of them uppity Negroes who don't like their own kind."

"Not at all," he said, forcing a smile. "I just want white folks to treat me with respect. I spend a lot of money in this store."

"I understand what you're saying," Cozette replied, "and I respect you for it."

Cyrus knew from the way her hand lingered on his shoulder while helping him into a jacket that she was available after store hours. "Dr. Mitchell, you look like a million bucks in that suit," she purred. "I'd let you operate on me any time."

He shot her a glance. "Is that right? And what else would you let me do?"

She leaned against the wall, flipped her shoulder-length brown hair and stuck out her chest. "What else do you want to do?"

His eyes lingered on her body. "You'll just have to come to my office and find out."

"You know, I been meaning to go see a doctor. I been having some pain down there, but I can't afford to take off in the middle of the day."

"Why don't you come by my office tomorrow after you get off work."

"I'll do that," she nodded. "I can be there around six thirty."

Cyrus looked at himself in the mirror and turned sideways. "I need a forty-six. This isn't fitting the way I like."

"Umm," she cooed. "I like a man who knows what he wants."

"And I like a woman who knows how to please a man."

"Then we're going to be real good together," she said in a throaty voice.

***

Cyrus decided to wear his lab coat to impress Cozette. He was looking forward to servicing her in his office, which he hadn't done in a long time.

At six thirty-five, there was a light tap on the door. Cyrus unlocked it, and Cozette strutted in, wearing a red and black striped blouse, black skirt, and black high heels.

"Evening, Dr. Mitchell," she said seductively.

"Hello," he said, checking out her butt. "You're a sight for sore eyes."

She wandered around the waiting room, stopping to study pictures on the wall and thumb through *Ebony* and *Jet* magazines on a coffee table. "This is a nice office for a colored doctor. I like this turquoise color on the wall. It's soothing and reminds me of the ocean. You've got good taste," Cozette said, winking at him.

"Thank you for noticing," Cyrus said.

"Do you always keep late hours like this?" she asked.

"Only for you."

"I feel real special then." Cozette sat on the receptionist's desk and crossed her legs. Her tight skirt inched mid-way up her thigh, showing off a black garter belt.

Cyrus wanted to take her right there but decided to give her a pelvic exam first to see if she had any serious gynecological problems. "Why don't you step into the exam room on the right. I want to find out why you've been experiencing some pain."

"Whatever you say, Dr. Mitchell." She got undressed, slipped on a pink-checked gown, and reclined on the table. "You sure are acting formal," she said.

"Don't you want a doctor who is professional?" he asked. "Where exactly is your pain? And describe it."

"It's down there," Cozette said, pointing to the space between her legs. "It hurts sometimes is all I can say."

"Before your cycle or after?"

"Whenever it wants to," she explained. "Ain't no special time of the month."

"Do you have heavy bleeding with your cycle?"

"Lord, yes," she said, waving her hand. "I have to change pads every hour it seems."

"Okay, let's see what's going on. Scoot down and place your feet in the stirrups." Cyrus applied some lubricant on his fingers and said, "I'm going to insert my fingers inside to feel your uterus and ovaries, just relax."

"I am very relaxed," she said.

Cyrus put one hand on top of her stomach and felt inside Cozette with the other hand. He moved from the right side to the left side. "Aha!" he said.

"What is it, doc?"

Cyrus removed his hand and wiped off the lubricant. "You have a fibroid tumor."

She jumped up from the table. "A tumor? Is it cancer?"

Cyrus took her by the shoulders and eased her down on the table. "Fibroids are fairly common in Negro women. I don't recommend doing anything about the fibroid unless it becomes too painful or your periods become too heavy. Then, you'll need a hysterectomy."

"Female surgery?" Cozette said. "Lord, have mercy. I don't want to lose my woman parts. That'll kill my desire."

Cyrus sat next to her on the table and continued explaining her diagnosis. "That's just an old wives' tale. You won't dry up and become frigid. Trust me, you can live without your uterus unless you plan on having children."

Cozette shook her head. "I got one boy, and he's more than enough. I don't want no more."

"We'll just keep an eye on the tumor and see what happens."

"You sure that's all it is?"

"I'm positive," he said, caressing her thigh. "Now, let's have a drink. You look like you need one." Cyrus went to his office and got a bottle of whiskey and two glasses. When he went back to the exam room, Cozette was sitting right where he left her. "Here we go," he said, filling their glasses.

Before long, Cozette was tipsy and had forgotten all about the tumor. She put on Cyrus's white coat and told him to get undressed and lie on the table. "Now, it's my turn to play doctor," Cozette said, slurring her words.

"I've got an emergency," Cyrus said, pointing to his erection.

"I got just the right cure." She spread his legs and walked her fingers up his thighs until she reached his penis. She leaned over and took him in her mouth.

"Ooh, baby," Cyrus moaned. "This is what I needed."

An ardent lover, Cozette made Cyrus come quickly. "Whoa." His face turned red with embarrassment. "That wasn't supposed to happen. Did it get in your mouth?"

"If it did, it's now in yours," she said, kissing him.

Cyrus got a towel and wiped himself off. He was always in control when he was with a woman. He didn't know what to make of his rapid climax. "You've got a magical touch," he said.

"So I've been told," she said confidently. "I can do a lot of things besides hang up suits. Don't let the tight sweaters fool you. I was number two in my class at Stranahan's Business College. Those white teachers didn't know what to make of me. I should be working in a big law office downtown, but they don't want to hire a colored girl. I'm just working at Goldsmith's until something better comes along."

"I'm impressed," he said, sitting on the edge of the table. "You can tell me all about your business skills later. Right now, I've got some business to take care of." Cyrus couldn't let Cozette leave his office thinking that he was a quick shooter. Tonight, he had to turn in an award-winning performance. "Lie down," he said. "This is one office visit that you won't forget."

Chapter Twenty-Eight

~

The garbage workers' strike was dragging on much longer than Carrie had expected. It had taken a turn for the worse when Dr. King's march through downtown Memphis erupted in violence and looting, forcing him to flee the scene. He vowed to return and lead a peaceful march.

A week later, Carrie was oiling her scalp and swaying to music on WDIA radio when the DJ interrupted the music with a bulletin: Dr. King had been shot to death on the balcony of the Lorraine Motel.

"No, no, no!" Carrie said, dropping the brush on the floor. She ran to kitchen, where Miz Lula was scrubbing a pot. "I heard on the radio somebody killed Dr. King."

"What? Turn on the TV," Miz Lula said.

They stood close to the console waiting for the picture to pop up on the screen. When the anchorman confirmed that Dr. King had been shot to death, Carrie slumped on the couch and cried.

Miz Lula bolted out the front door and stood on the porch waving her hands and screaming. "Lord help us! They done killed Dr. King! They killed him!" Her piercing cries rang out over the grassy hills of the pumping station.

The whole scene was surreal. Carrie could see the TV anchor's mouth moving but couldn't hear the words over Miz Lula wailing. The phone rang. Slowly, Carrie got up to answer it.

"Hello, hello," Bob said.

"Uh-huh."

"Carrie is that you?"

"Yes."

"Are you okay?"

"Yeah, we just heard about Dr. King."

"That's why I'm calling. We need you to get reaction to the slaying."

"What?"

"We want you to interview some people. Start with your neighbors. Ask them how they feel about what has happened to their leader and how this will affect race relations in Memphis."

"How they feel? That's the stupidest question I ever heard. I'm not getting up in nobody's face asking them that."

"Carrie, listen to me. I know you're upset, but you've got to put your feelings aside. This is the biggest story of the year. I need you to help me tell the story of this great Negro leader who was cut down trying to help the sanitation workers."

"I don't know, Bob. You don't understand how we feel right now."

"That's why I want you to interview your neighbors. Let the world feel your pain. Let white people in this town know that you won't stop fighting for your rights just because Dr. King is dead."

After hearing Bob explain the angle, Carrie knew she had to help him. "How many people do you want me to talk to?"

"Interview about ten. Remember what you're supposed to do. Get their name, age, address, and occupation. Make sure you write down every word they say. Tell them to slow down if they're talking too fast. Call me in an hour to let me know how things are going."

"Okay."

"Take your company ID because the National Guard is out there clearing the streets. The city is under a curfew until five in the morning."

"Got it."

Carrie hung up and pulled herself together. She put on a pair of dungarees, a blue shirt, and jacket. When she stepped outside, an eerie feeling came over her. It was dead silent on her street. She walked four blocks to Chelsea Avenue, where she saw three young men standing in front of the sundry smoking cigarettes, ignoring the curfew.

At first, she walked past them, looking for someone standing alone. She changed her mind and doubled back. "Excuse me, did y'all hear Dr. King was killed?"

"Yeah," said the taller of the two boys. "It's a goddamn shame."

"I work for *The Sentinel*. You mind me asking you some questions?"

"When did they get a colored reporter?" said the short, chunky boy.

"I'm really a copy clerk, but I help out sometimes."

"Well, sweet thing, what you need to know?" asked the taller boy. He moved closer to Carrie, smiling and rubbing his hands together. "By the way, what's your name?"

"My name is Carrie Boyd." She took out her pen and flipped open her notebook. "What's your name? How old are you? Where do you live?"

"Why you got to know all that? I don't want no pigs coming after me," he said.

"Everybody's got to give their name," she said.

"Well, first let me see what you're going to write. Then, I'll decide if I want my name on it."

"Don't be wasting my time," Carrie told him. "If you're not going to give it to me, I'll go talk to somebody else."

"My name is Eddie Lewis," said the shorter boy. "I ain't scared of no police. Ask me whatever you want."

"Okay, when you first heard Dr. King had been killed, what did you think?"

"I think he made a lot of white folks mad. He was shaking things up, and they wanted to keep colored people down. They figured the only way to stop him was with a bullet."

The third young man who wore thick eyeglasses spoke up. "They just pissed us off. We gonna see to it that Dr. King's death mean something. We'll march, picket, and burn this muthafucka down if we have to."

"Right on," said the taller boy.

Carrie got more than enough quotes from the men. In the end, they gave their names. She went up and down the street, knocking on doors for reaction. To her surprise, people were anxious to speak their minds. She rushed home and called Bob, bubbling over with quotes and her observations about the mood of the community.

"Whoa, slow down. Let me get some paper in my typewriter."

"Bob, you were right. I didn't think people would want to talk to me, but most of them were nice."

"I knew they would be once they saw that you were serious about getting their thoughts on the record. Okay, give me your best quotes."

"They're all good. I don't know which ones to pick," she said, scanning her notes.

"Start with the one that grabbed you the most."

"There was one elderly lady who got choked up and started crying."

"That's what I want. Give it to me."

Bob sent a photographer to pick up Carrie. They drove to other parts of Memphis to get reaction to Dr. King's assassination. After each stop, she called Bob and fed him her quotes.

When Carrie got back to the newsroom at five o'clock the next morning, she was exhausted. Bob, on the other hand, was still going strong, talking to the copy editor about changes in his story for the final edition.

Carrie asked the city editor if she could leave or if she had to stay and work her regular shift. He motioned for her to go home. "Good job,

Carrie. We couldn't have done it without you. I mean that," the editor said.

She went to say goodbye to Bob, but it looked like he and the copy editor were so engrossed in his story that she decided to sneak out without interrupting them. She left a note on his typewriter, saying she would catch up with him later.

On her way out, she bumped into Cleary, who was making his rounds. "You going the wrong way, ain't you?"

"No, I been working all night on the King story. They let me skip my regular shift. Things quiet in your neighborhood?"

"Pretty much," Cleary said. "Some knuckleheads shot off their guns, but I didn't see any damage when I drove in."

"That's good. I hope things stay quiet. I can't wait to get under the covers."

"Yeah, you look pretty beat," Cleary said. "Get some rest."

"Good night, uh, I mean, goodbye," she said laughing. "See how confused I am."

"You'll be straight by tomorrow," Cleary said, patting her on the back.

Carrie walked to the bus stop proud of what she had done. Until now, she had never thought too much about newspapers and their role in the community. This assignment taught her that newspapers were the voice of the people, colored and white.

The biggest surprise came later that afternoon when Carrie read a special edition of the paper and saw her byline under Bob's name. She read every word of the story, smiling each time she came to a sentence that she contributed. Bob had made it all flow together like a story with a tragic ending.

She showed Miz Lula the story. While she was reading it, Carrie called Bob at work. "Why didn't you tell me my name would be on the story?"

"Because you would've said leave it off. I was too tired to argue with you and just did it."

"It read real nice, Bob. What time did you go home?"

"I haven't. I've been here all night and day. There's a lot happening. Police are looking for a white man who was seen running from the rooming house across the street from the motel. I'm working with the cop reporter on that angle."

"You ain't tired?"

"I don't know what I am at this point. I'm running on pure adrenaline."

"I hope you don't keel over."

"I'll be okay."

"Call if you need me."

"Listen to you, volunteering to do some reporting."

"Why not? This is a big story."

"And it's going to get bigger when they catch the gunman," Bob said. "I'll keep you posted."

"Thanks, Bob. Take care."

Carrie was so happy when she hung up that she walked up to the sundry and bought ten copies of the newspaper. She could have gotten them free at work but didn't want to wait until tomorrow.

As night fell over the city, Carrie sat in the living room watching a TV special on Dr. King. She thought about his children, growing up without a father. For all intents and purposes, her children were in the same situation.

Chapter Twenty-Nine

The day after Dr. King's assassination, Nadine and the girls stayed indoors, watching TV for the latest updates on the search for his killer. She would have stayed home again today, but she needed food for tomorrow's dinner.

Because there had been sporadic outbreaks of looting, Nadine wasn't sure what she would find at Greenberg's. Surprisingly, it looked like a typical Saturday morning with shoppers rushing in and out.

Nadine got a cart and went looking for Willie Lee. He was in the rear of the store near the meat department. When Willie Lee saw her coming, he met her halfway. "Am I glad to see you," he said. "Any problems where you live?"

"Everything is quiet. It doesn't look like you had any trouble here."

Willie Lee shook his head. "Not a cracked window."

"Thank God for that."

Willie Lee started grinning. "I've got some good news."

"It must really be good the way you're beaming. Tell me."

"I don't know if I want to share with you," he said, rocking on his heels.

Nadine pinched his arm. "You'd better tell me or else."

"Or else what?"

"I don't know, Willie Lee," Nadine said impatiently. "Go ahead and tell me."

"Miz Greenberg accepted my offer."

"She did?" Nadine squealed. "Tell me what she said."

"Come in my office and sit down. You want something to drink?"

"No, I'm fine. When did she tell you?"

Willie Lee's words gushed like water from a fire hose. "She called me yesterday. At first, she was talking about how she didn't want to be bothered with trying to run me down every month looking for a payment. I told her it wouldn't be like that because I pay my bills before they're due. I told her she could call my landlady and ask her if I paid my rent on time."

"Did she?"

"I don't know," he said, waving his hand. "She probably did. You know how white folks is. Anyway, she kept saying how she was looking to sell the store outright. I thought she was fixing to tell me that somebody else bought it, but then she said I was a hardworking man, and Mr. Greenberg liked me. She said she was willing to sell it to me, but if I fall behind in the payments, she would take it back."

"What about the papers?"

"Her lawyer is drawing up some papers for me to sign. Her son is bringing them by next week."

"Hmm," Nadine uttered as she pondered whether that was the best way to handle the deal.

"What?"

"I think you need to have a colored lawyer read them, too. You don't want to be gypped out of your money or nothing. You know how Jews can be."

"You mean, your money don't you? I haven't forgot this is your money that's buying the store. I'll pay you back. I promise."

"I'm glad to see that things are working out. You deserve it."

Willie Lee was about to say something else about the store until he noticed that Nadine's mood had abruptly changed. She looked grief-stricken. He leaped out of his chair to comfort her. "Nadine, what's wrong?"

"It's Jocelyn. We just found out that she has a disease called lupus," she said.

He lifted Nadine's chin, wiping her tears with the bottom of his apron. "Is she going to be all right?"

"She has to take medicine every day, but it could get worse. She could even die."

"No," Willie Lee said, holding her tightly. "That can't be. She's just a child. Can't they operate or something?"

Nadine told him everything Cyrus had told her. When she finished, she eased out of Willie Lee's arms and stood. "I'm sorry for dumping all this on you. I've been trying to stay positive, but it's hard."

"You're a strong woman. I saw that when Salena got hurt. You'll get through this, too. I'll be there to help you." He kissed Nadine lightly on her cheek and held her in his arms. She folded her body onto his chest, where she felt safe. They stayed that way until the phone rang.

"I probably need to get that," Willie Lee said.

"And I need to buy some food," she said. "Thanks for listening."

"I'm here whenever you need me," he said before picking up the phone.

Nadine smiled to herself as she shopped up and down the aisles. Willie Lee's kiss, sweet and innocent, had unleashed a longing in her. For him. She had developed feelings for Willie Lee over the last two months. She tucked away those illicit thoughts and finished shopping.

On the way home, Nadine swung by Gethsemane, but the church parking lot was empty. No food was being passed out today. It was probably the same at New Hope.

Nadine decided that she would wait until she heard from the pastor of New Hope before going back. She couldn't wait to question Mother Copeland about Carrie. She was her only link to the mysterious young woman.

***

When Nadine went to Greenberg's a week later, she felt like a schoolgirl, waiting to be noticed by the boy she liked. She did her grocery shopping first, instead of looking for Willie Lee right away as she usually did. He tapped her on the back as she was picking out some mustard greens.

Nadine swung around. "Hey, Willie Lee," she said. "I didn't hear you come up behind me. I thought somebody was fixing to tell me I was in the way. How are you?"

"I'm good. What about you? Feeling better?"

"I am," she said. "I was really worried about Jocelyn. You know how it is when your child gets sick. Your whole world stops."

"I understand. Just remember that she's getting the best care from you and the doctor. She's going to be okay. Hey, I got some stuff that came in early this morning. Come and pick out what you like," he said, leading her through a door near the dairy case.

When they got to the stockroom, Willie Lee took her by the hand and led her to some boxes piled high with fruit and vegetables. She noticed that his hands were rough and calloused, a workingman's hands.

Nadine wondered if he took his time with a woman in bed or if he plowed in like Cyrus. Lately, she had been thinking more and more about sex. She was daydreaming about Willie Lee's naked body when she heard him call her name.

"These collards look better than the mustard greens you got. How many bunches do you want?" Willie Lee asked as he cut a string that held several bunches.

Nadine snapped out of her fantasy when she heard her name. "Huh?"

"How many?"

"About six, I guess."

He stuffed the greens into a brown paper bag. "You were a million miles away just now. What were you thinking about?"

"You," slipped out before she could catch herself.

"Me?"

"Yeah, you've been so nice to me. I appreciate you taking time out to listen to all my problems."

"That's the least I can do considering what you've done for me," he said. "I'm just glad we reconnected after all these years. As my grandmama used to say, 'That wasn't nothing but God's doing.' "

Nadine looked at him stuffing greens into a bag and had an overwhelming urge to kiss him. "Willie Lee?" she said softly.

"This ain't enough?" he asked with his back to her.

"No, that's enough, but," Nadine hesitated, "I want something else."

"Tell me. We got everything, fresh off the farm. Corn, squash, field peas, you name it." Willie Lee turned to face her, waiting for an answer.

Nadine stepped around the crates, wrapped her arms around his neck and kissed him. He dropped the bag of greens, grabbed her by the waist, and they kissed until their lips were numb.

"Let's go to my place," said Willie Lee, smothering her face with kisses. "I'm taking my lunch break in about thirty minutes."

Nadine pulled away. "I'm sorry, Willie Lee. I don't know what came over me, throwing myself at you like that."

"Your real feelings came out. That's what happened." He tried to hold her, but she rebuffed him. "Since that day I saw you in here, I haven't been able to stop thinking about you."

"I've never done anything like that before. I'm a married woman. It was wrong. Forget it ever happened." She picked up the greens and turned to leave.

Willie Lee grabbed her by the arm. "Nadine, I can't forget about it. You obviously have feelings for me. I know you're not happy in your marriage. I saw it on your face the first time I asked about your husband."

"No, I'm not happy," she said, looking away from him.

Willie Lee held her in his arms. "Tell me what's going on, Nadine."

"Cyrus has a bad temper. One time, he beat me up pretty bad. Whenever I do something he doesn't like, I think he's going to do it again."

"Baby, I hate that you live in fear like this," said Willie Lee. "You deserve much better."

"Me, too, but I can't do anything about it. I'm stuck."

"There is a solution," he said, rubbing her back.

She looked up at him. "What?"

"Be my woman. I'll take care of you, love you, and make you happy."

Nadine threw up her hands. "You don't understand. We're not characters in a fairy tale. We can't live happily ever after. Cyrus will take my children if I leave him."

"We'll figure out something. Let's go to my place and talk it through. Please, Nadine."

"I don't see nothing to talk about. Let's just forget about it."

Willie Lee took a notepad and pencil, scribbled his address, and gave it to her. "This is where I live. Meet me there in half an hour," he said.

Nadine took the piece of paper. Her heart was saying yes, but her mind told her to pay for the groceries and go on home. When she got in her car, she berated herself for kissing Willie Lee.

Emotions were pulling her in both directions – to go to Willie Lee and to go home.

She decided to forget him and go home. Halfway to her house, she changed her mind.

Before she got to his apartment, she turned onto a side street and prayed. Meeting Willie Lee would be a sin, but she yearned to be loved and experience her first orgasm.

Nadine continued to Willie's apartment. As she sat in the car, all kinds of thoughts went through her mind. She worried that someone would see her and tell Miz Esther or Cyrus. She wouldn't be able to explain why she was on this street at this time of day.

A man pulling a wagon filled with tools walked past the car. She averted her eyes. A car driven by someone she vaguely recognized passed by, causing her to panic.

She had to make a decision quickly because Willie Lee's lunch break would be over soon. She took a deep breath, grabbed her purse, and got out of the car. She ran across the street and up the steps like a dog was chasing her.

Willie Lee opened the door before she rang the doorbell. She was weak in the knees and felt dizzy. Her feet wouldn't cross the threshold. Willie Lee reached for her hand and led her into the apartment.

"I've never been with another man," she said, searching his face for reassurance.

"It's all right, Nadine. We don't have to do anything if you don't want to."

"I do," she said, trembling. "It's just that I'm scared."

"We'll take it slow," he said.

Willie Lee kissed her on the neck and lips. Nadine surrendered to his passion, ready to fulfill her own desire. He guided her to the bedroom, never relinquishing her lips. He unbuttoned her dress and took it off. She removed her undergarments. He stroked her body, arousing Nadine with his electrifying touch.

"I'm going to love every inch of you," Willie Lee said. He kissed her on the forehead, neck, breasts, stomach, inside her thighs, and all the way to her toes. When he slipped his fingers inside Nadine, her body stiffened. "Baby, you okay?"

"Yeah, it's been such a long time since I—"

"Just relax. I won't hurt you. Tell me what you like."

"I don't know," Nadine said innocently.

"That's all right. Just let me know if you don't like what I'm doing."

"Okay."

Willie Lee fondled Nadine until she was wet. He eased on top of her and tickled her clitoris with the tip of his penis. She grabbed his butt and guided him inside her. Willie Lee pinned her hands to the bed, their fingers intertwined. They began moving slowly in a rhythmic motion.

"This feels so good," Nadine said.

"I want you to feel good, baby."

"Faster! Faster!" she demanded as their lovemaking intensified.

Unable to hold back any longer, Willie Lee thrust himself inside Nadine with all his strength.

"Oh, my God! Oh, my God!" Nadine cried as they came together.

Willie Lee thought the water on his chest was sweat from their frenzied lovemaking until he saw Nadine's eyes were wet. "What's the matter?"

"Nothing," she said. "That's the first time a man has ever made love to me like it's supposed to be, like they describe in the magazines."

"I'll always love you like that. Your body was made for loving. Cyrus is a fool for not recognizing that."

Willie Lee spread the sheet over Nadine as they lay nestled with her back against his chest. "In a few months, I'll be able to provide a home for you and the girls. Y'all can move in right away. When the time is right, we'll get married."

Nadine raised up on her elbows and stared at him. "You really mean that?"

"With all my heart."

"Willie Lee, we're just getting to know each other. I think it's too soon to be talking about getting married."

"If I had my way, you'd leave that house today. I hate that you have to go back there. If Cyrus lays a hand on you again, I don't know what I'll do," he said, punching the palm of his hand.

"Don't worry," she said. "I know how to protect myself. I got Daddy's gun under the mattress."

Willie Lee was aghast. "A gun? You want to go to prison?" He sat on the edge of the bed and touched her face. "Nadine, promise me you won't do anything that you'll regret. Just hang in there a little while longer. I'm going to get you out of that house."

Nadine gazed at him with admiration. "Willie Lee, there's no doubt in my mind that you're a good man. But I don't want us to jump into something that you're not ready for. Do you know what having a ready-made family is like? I have two children, and one of them is sick. That's three extra mouths to feed."

"Four extra mouths because my son is coming to live with us," he added.

"That's a lot for a man used to looking out for only two people."

"That won't be your worry," he said, holding her hands.

Nadine got up and picked up her clothes from the floor. "I can't help but worry about it. I've already had one bad marriage."

"I'm not Cyrus," Willie Lee said as he put on his pants. He went over to her and took her face into his hands. "When you leave Cyrus, you'll have everything you want and need. And you'll be a happy woman."

Nadine bit her lip. "I want to believe you. It's just that…"

"Trust me. I'm a man of my word," he said.

"Okay. I believe you."

After Nadine got dressed, Willie Lee asked, "When am I going to see you again?"

She blinked rapidly. "I, uh, don't know."

"Nadine, I want to hold you again and make love to you."

"What do you want me to say?" she asked. "I don't know if I can keep coming over here. It's too risky."

Willie Lee placed his forearms on her shoulders. "We can't just stop seeing each other after today."

"What if Cyrus found out? I don't want to be kicked out of the house and lose my children."

"I want to see you. We can meet anywhere you want. Hell, we can go over to West Memphis or down to Mississippi. We don't have to do nothing. We can go out to lunch. Just sit and talk. Spend some time with each other."

"I'll let you know."

Willie Lee held Nadine for the longest time. He kissed both cheeks and her lips. He got hard again and rubbed his body against hers. "We get our next produce shipment in three days," he said. "I'll put some aside for you in the back."

She laughed. "I don't know about going back there again. Seems like that room gets you all excited."

"Gets me excited? I tell you what, you can go back there by yourself since you're afraid that I might bite."

"Oh, no, I'm not going by myself. It's too scary."

"I'll have to go with you then," he said, running his hands along her backside.

"I guess you do," she said, heading for the door. "Bye, bye."

"Take care of yourself," he said. "Call me when you can."

For the rest of the day, Nadine wrestled with feelings of guilt. She didn't like the idea of sneaking around with Willie Lee, but she was tired of a loveless marriage. She felt giddy thinking about making love to him. Surprisingly, she wasn't sore like she was after having sex with Cyrus.

Nadine assumed that the dryness she experienced with Cyrus was the result of getting her tubes tied after Salena's birth. Now, she knew exactly what it took to get her juices flowing.

Chapter Thirty

~

Cyrus stood on the sidewalk, taking in both sides of Beale Street as far as his eyes could see. Everything looked run down in the daylight. Some storefronts were boarded up. Others still had gaping holes where marchers had thrown bricks through the windows. A handful of pawn shops, liquor stores, and retail shops were the only businesses still open on what was once the heart and soul of the Negro community.

He pushed the door of Sonny's bar too hard, knocking it against the wall. The loud clanging sent Sonny running from the back with a shotgun. "Freeze, muthafucka!"

"Hold up, Sonny, it's me," Cyrus yelled with his hands in the air.

"Man, I thought you was some of those hoodlums coming back here to start some shit like they did during the march," Sonny said, placing the shotgun on the counter. "I was about to bust a cap in your ass."

"Sorry, Sonny. I didn't mean to scare you," Cyrus said as he climbed on a stool. "How you been?"

"I'm all right. I closed up for three days, but I stayed right here. Me and Roscoe," he said, patting the shotgun.

"You probably scared the shit out of them. I wouldn't worry about them coming back."

"If they do, I'm ready. You want a drink?"

"Yeah, whatever you got."

"I'll be right back."

Sonny returned with a bottle of whiskey and filled two glasses. "To peace and quiet and the garbage workers, who finally got what they wanted." He clinked his glass against Cyrus's.

"It shouldn't have taken the mayor and City Council over two months to settle the strike. They would rather bring the city to its knees than give a colored man a decent salary," Cyrus said, swallowing a mouthful of whiskey. "It's a shame all the colored businesses down here closed. It looks like a ghost town."

"Yeah. It's just me and a couple of other fellas on the block now. It ain't like it used to be. Leave it to Mr. Charlie, it'll never be like that again."

"What do you mean?"

"You know Beale Street is on the National Register of Historic Places, which means it ain't ours no more. Some of them Jew boys that own those big stores on Main Street been buying up the property. One cracker came in here calling me 'Uncle' and asking if I was ready to sell this spot and retire. I told him I would be behind this counter 'til the day I die."

"This is good real estate. I can see why white folks want it."

"They ain't getting mine. I'm so sick of these goddamn peckerwoods that I could kill each and every one of them with my bare hands."

"That won't do any good. There are more of them than us. They're going to see to it that we don't have too much power. Look at what they did to Dr. King. They didn't like him marching around trying to tell them what to do. It wasn't no colored man who killed Dr. King. It was a cracker, and somebody put him up to it."

"Muthafuckas," said Sonny, wiping his eyes. "Every time I think about that poor man and how they shot him in the face, I get upset." He took one long gulp and emptied his glass.

"Sonny, I'm ready to get up out of Memphis. I'm fed up. I don't see this city getting any better, not after the strike. We're not making any progress down here. They took down the signs, but Jim Crow is still all around us."

"Son, it's like that everywhere. It ain't just Memphis."

"I've been to a lot of northern cities for conventions, and the colored people live way better than we do. They've got good jobs and make more money. The white people don't treat them like they're still on the plantation."

"I been up North, too. My cousin live in Chicago. It's big all right, but look how they got colored folks stacked on top of each other in the projects. The buildings so tall that if you go to the top floor and look down, everybody look like ants running 'round. I don't want to live like that. I need me some open space, grass, and trees. And man, you talking about cold. I ain't been so cold in my life. No thank you, you can have the North. I'm staying right here. If anything, I'm going back to Mississippi and build me a little house on the land my mama left me."

"Not me. I'm headed North as soon as I can get everything lined up."

"I hate to see you go, but I understand. What about Esther? She going to?"

"Yeah, her mind is getting bad. I can't leave her here. She needs somebody to keep an eye on her. I don't want to put that burden on anybody else."

"Well, the old girl is getting up there, but she ain't the only one. Some days, I don't know if I'm coming or going."

"You're doing fine, Sonny. There's nothing wrong with your mind, at least not today," he said chortling. "Thanks for the drink. I'll check you later."

"Come back anytime you feel like it. Tell Esther I said hello."

It no longer mattered what anybody else thought, Cyrus was determined that his daughters would live someplace where people wouldn't judge them by the color of their skin. That part of Dr. King's speech had struck a chord with him.

He didn't know how Nadine and the girls would feel about moving away from Memphis. Nadine hadn't traveled much but liked doing new things. She would enjoy picking out a house and decorating it. The girls would protest leaving their friends but would eventually get used to the idea.

At home that night, he waited until Nadine got into bed before bringing up the subject. "How would you feel about us moving?"

Nadine shrugged. "I don't know. Why?"

"I want to move. And I'm not talking about another house. I want to move to another city."

"Leave Memphis?" she asked alarmed. "Why would you want to do that? We've been here all our life. I don't see no reason to move."

"*I* need to move," he said, pounding his fist on the mattress. "I've got to go some place where I'm treated like a man. The people here are too small-minded. White folks are always going to try and keep colored folks down because they still own everything and run everything."

"What about your practice? You're just gonna leave it?" Nadine asked.

"I can start over," he assured her. "I'm thinking about New York because I have two colleagues from med school there. The city has got everything you could imagine - first-rate hospitals, fine department stores, and jazz clubs. And the people are more progressive."

"I don't know, Cyrus. This may not be the right time to move with Jocelyn's sickness. What about Miz Esther?"

"Mama is going to come with us. I know she'll fight me every step of the way. As for Jocelyn, New York has some of the best doctors in the country."

"There's nothing wrong with the doctors here. Why don't we just get a bigger house and stay put?"

"'Cause I can't live here anymore!" he shouted. Cyrus got out of bed and stood facing Nadine. "I'm suffocating. You have no idea of the red tape I have to go through to get privileges at the white hospitals, even at the new one. I know it's because I'm a Negro."

"Sounds like you got your mind made up."

"I was hoping that you'd be more supportive," he said, getting back into bed.

"Do whatever you want, Cyrus. You always do." Nadine got up and went to the bathroom.

Cyrus's decision to move the family to New York meant that he wouldn't be involved with raising the twins. He was determined that they would get to know him, especially his son. He just had to figure out how that would happen living far away.

Mamie was his other concern. A woman like her wouldn't wait long, even for a man of Cyrus's stature. The phone calls worked for now, but eventually she would issue an ultimatum. He expected it would come when she came for a visit next month. In the meantime, he would keep his voice inside her head. He called her the next day.

"Hey, there. What are you doing?"

"Hi, yourself. I'm looking at some photos from the gala."

"I'd like to see them," he said. "I bet you were the belle of the ball."

Mamie laughed. "I didn't look too shabby among the doctors' and lawyers' wives."

"You know, you could be a doctor's wife one day."

"From what I can tell, that's a pretty good job. I think it would suit me just fine, if it's the right doctor."

Cyrus jumped on the opportunity to persuade Mamie he was worth the wait. "*I* am. We're a perfect match. With your professional and social connections, we would be a power couple."

"Maybe," she said coyly. "But we can't be anything but friends until you're divorced."

"Soon, Mamie, real soon."

Chapter Thirty-One

To show his appreciation for her reporting on the King story, Bob asked Carrie out to dinner, but she turned him down out of fear that they wouldn't be welcomed in a white restaurant. She didn't want the waitress to spit or put something in her food.

When Bob suggested a picnic by the Mississippi River, Carrie had misgivings but agreed so that he would stop pestering her. On the day of the picnic, sunny weather bathed the city, replacing a spate of gloomy days. Carrie sat in the car, her eyes darting around Tom Lee Park looking for troublemakers, while Bob unloaded the trunk.

"Are you getting out?" he asked.

"I guess."

"Well, come on," he said, opening her door. "Let's get this picnic started."

Carrie followed him to a spot near the water, where he spread a blanket and laid out containers of food. "What did you get at the deli?" she asked.

"Pastrami, turkey, potato salad, pickles, sodas, and New York cheesecake."

"I've never had cheesecake."

"It's delicious," Bob said. "I can't get enough of it."

Carrie unwrapped her sandwich and took a bite. It tasted like cardboard. She added some mustard and mayonnaise, but that didn't help. The potato salad was bland, nothing but potatoes and a lot of mayonnaise. No boiled egg, mustard, onion, celery, relish, and seasoning. She broke off a piece of sandwich and hid it under her plate.

Bob was so busy talking about work that he didn't notice. After he finished his sandwich, the conversation turned serious. "Carrie, do you ever think about living anywhere else?"

"No, I like it here. It's close to home if I need to go check on Mama and my babies. Why?"

"I don't know," he said, stretching out on the blanket. "I was just thinking about my next job. I've been here almost four years. I'll give it another year, then I'll be ready to go someplace else."

"Like where?"

"I don't know. Chicago. Maybe back home."

"I thought you liked it here."

"It's okay, but I miss the hustle and bustle of the big city. I don't know what I'm going to do after the King story moves off page one. There's not a lot happening down here to hold my interest."

"I'm going to miss you. You been such a big help getting me a new job and all. It won't be the same without you."

"I've got an idea," he said excitedly. "Why don't you come with me?"

Carrie was flabbergasted. "Stop talking crazy, Bob. I can't go with you."

"Sure, you can. Up North, interracial couples are everywhere, and people don't stare or make nasty remarks."

She dipped her head and gave Bob the side-eye. "What are you talking about? We ain't no couple. We work together. That's all."

"You're going to sit there and tell me that you don't have feelings for me?"

"No, I don't," Carrie said, looking him straight in the eyes.

"I don't believe you."

"I don't care. It's the truth," she said, getting up to throw away her plate. When she came back, Bob's mood had turned somber. Carrie decided to ignore him. "I'm ready to try the cheesecake," she said.

Bob handed her a Styrofoam container with two slices of cheesecake topped with strawberries. "Carrie, listen to me," he said. "We *can* be together. I know another interracial couple, and they're living happily in New York. It's different up there. You wouldn't feel out of place. We'd blend in with everybody else."

"Bob, I can't be with you, plain and simple. Stop talking about this, and let me eat my cheesecake." She jabbed a fork in the cheesecake and let the creamy dessert sit on her tongue before chewing and swallowing.

He got up and walked over to the river. He stood with his back to Carrie, gazing at ribbons of yellow, orange, and pink that streaked the evening sky. After a few minutes, he went back to Carrie. "You know the only reason I'm not leaving now is because of you. I can go just about anywhere I want with the clips I got from the King story, but I want you to go with me Carrie. I'm in love with you."

"Bob, I can't keep going over this again and again. I can't be with you. You're white, and I'm colored. I don't want people pointing at me and talking behind my back. And what about your parents? I know they ain't ready to call no colored girl from Mississippi with two children their daughter-in-law."

"Don't worry about my folks. They're pretty liberal. If I love you, they'll love you."

"No, Bob," Carrie said, shaking her head. "You'll be better off with your own kind."

"I'm not going to pressure you, but I'm going to try my best to make you change your mind."

"You wasting your time. I ain't 'bout to run off with no white man.

I'm sorry if that hurts your feelings. That's just the way it is."

"Well, it does hurt my feelings, but I would feel better if you came home with me and let me cook dinner for you."

"We just finished eating."

"I ate, but you didn't. I saw you hiding the sandwich under your plate. Was it really that bad?"

She nodded. "Yeah."

"Let me make it up to you by cooking my specialty, steak and home fries."

"You can cook?"

"Sure, I can," he said, putting the leftovers in a bag. "They call me Chef Levine back home. We've got to stop by the store first."

"Okay, I'll help."

"No, thank you. I want to prove to you that I'm the perfect man for you despite how I appear on the outside."

"Okay, if that's what you want. Cook it all by yourself. I'll just sit in the living room with my feet propped up like Miss Ann."

"Miss Ann?" he said, looking confused.

"That's what we call the white lady."

"Well, Miss Ann, I got this covered." He bowed and extended his hand, allowing her to walk in front of him.

Carrie was amazed that Bob never gave up trying to get her to be his girlfriend. She had practically insulted him, and what did he do? Offer to cook dinner.

True to his word, he refused to let her set foot in the kitchen. After Bob stuck the steaks in the oven, he came back into the living room and put on an Otis Redding record.

"Let's dance," he said.

Carrie eyed him suspiciously. "What?"

"'Sittin' on the Dock of the Bay' is my favorite song. Come on, one little dance." He dragged her from the couch.

"Don't try anything funny," she warned.

"I won't. I promise," he said, giving her a peck on the cheek.

Carrie punched him in the chest. "See, you lying already."

She was rigid in his arms at first, but after a while she relaxed, resting her head on his chest. The light blue shirt he wore was unbuttoned at the top. She could see swirls of black hair on his chest. She detected the faint smell of Old Spice aftershave.

Bob held her waist with one hand and clasped her other hand. Halfway through the song, he put both hands around her waist. She placed her arms around his neck, and they danced face-to-face, their eyes fixed on each other.

"I want to make love to you," he breathed in her ear.

Carrie stopped dancing. She tried to break free, but Bob wouldn't let her go. "You want me, too. Admit it."

Before she had a chance to answer, Bob kissed her hard. He sucked her top lip, then her bottom one. She became aroused when she felt his erection. "Come with me," he said.

"Where are you taking me?" Carrie asked, playfully pulling back.

"Don't be a fraidy cat," Bob said. "Trust me, you'll enjoy this." He got behind Carrie and pushed her to his bedroom, where he had a mattress on the floor. He lay on the bed and pulled her on top of him.

"I don't know about this," Carrie said.

Bob stroked her hair. "Let go of your inhibitions. Surrender to the moment."

Carrie's mind told her to get her stuff and run out of his apartment as fast as she could, but she wanted to have sex. Needed to have sex. She was tired of punishing herself for succumbing to her sexual urges in the past.

"It was bound to happen sooner or later. There's a lot of chemistry between us. Haven't you felt it?"

"Bob, I don't think about stuff like that," she replied. When he lifted her arms to remove her blouse, Carrie balked and yanked it down. "No, I can't."

He took her face in the palms of his hands. "Don't worry, I've got a prophylactic."

"A what?"

"A rubber."

"That ain't the only thing I'm worried about."

"For once, forget what color we are. We're two people who want to make love. Relax." He took off her blouse and unhooked her bra. She wiggled out of her pants and panties. Bob's eyes grew big when he spotted the mound of black hair between her legs. "You're beautiful, so perfect. Like a brown angel."

Bob shed his clothes and faced her, his penis hard and slightly arched. His hands trembled as he explored her body. Pointy, black nipples emerged when he traced the dark circle that ringed them. He held a breast in each hand and buried his face in them. "Mmm," he moaned. "I can't wait to…"

The next thing Carrie knew, Bob lost his erection. There was an awkward moment of silence between them. "I'm sorry," he said, lacing their fingers. "I've been dreaming about this for the longest. Now, I'm nervous."

"Me, too," Carrie admitted. "I ain't been with a man in more than a year."

"I think we'll figure it out." He looked into her eyes as he played with her hair. "We're in sync more than you realize. If you'd just—"

"We ain't fixing to get into another long discussion right now, are we?"

"No, I got other plans." Bob was hard again. He opened her legs and began stroking her. "You are hairier than I am," he said.

"No, I ain't. It just look like it 'cause mine is bushy and yours is sticking straight up."

"I like it."

Carrie closed her eyes. One minute he was fingering her; the next, she felt something soft and wet inside her. She scooted up, but her head hit the wall, forcing her to lie still and enjoy it.

An overwhelming feeling of euphoria came over Carrie. She didn't know whether to scream or cry. It felt so good. At one point, she grabbed his head and pushed his face deeper. She had one orgasm after another one. "Bob, what are you trying to do to me? You driving me crazy."

A breathless Bob, lifted his head, his mouth glistening with her juices. "I want you to be crazy all right. Crazy about me." He flipped over on his back and positioned Carrie on top of him. "It's your turn now."

"My turn?" What do you mean?"

Bob tilted his head toward his penis. "You know."

"You want me to suck your thing? Unh-unh, colored people don't do that."

"You can't say you don't like it if you haven't tried it. Go ahead."

Bob nudged her toward his crotch. Carrie inched her way to his penis. This was the first time she had been on eye-level with a penis, and she studied it closely. His dick was pink and thick with blue veins. It smelled like cornstarch. It wasn't the size of a little finger like colored girls thought: His was the same size as a colored man's dick.

Carrie concluded that there was no way she could put his penis in her mouth. She slid up Bob's body and lay her head on his chest. "I can't do it."

"Chicken," he teased. "That's okay." He lifted Carrie by the arms and glided her down his penis. "I want to see your face while we make love."

Bob held her by the hips, moving them up and down his shaft. Although he was into it, Carrie held back, fearing she might get pregnant again. Just as she was about to remind him to use the rubber, he pulled out of her, ripped open the package with his teeth, and slipped it on.

He stuck his tongue in her ear and whispered, "Get on your hands and knees." He got behind her and thrust in and out of her rapidly.

"Yes, yes," Carrie squealed.

He gave a final push, and they came together. It had been such a long time since Carrie made love that she had forgotten how wonderful it felt. She wished that Bob had held on a few more minutes before he came.

"You can deny it all you want, Carrie, but your body just told me how you really feel about me," Bob said.

"What did my body say?"

"It said, 'Bob, I'm in love with you, but I don't want to admit it.'"

"I ain't heard all that."

"That's 'cause you won't listen."

Carrie sat up, sniffing the air. "I know one thing. The food is burning."

"Oh, no, the steaks!" Bob ran to the kitchen.

Carrie lay in bed, trying to sort out her feelings. Bob was right. They were pretty good together even though he was white and she was colored. But what kind of future would they have in the real world?

"So much for me cooking dinner tonight," Bob said when he came back. "The steaks are black and hard. I didn't realize that I had turned the oven too high."

"You done struck out twice today with food."

"Actually, my appetite has changed. I'd rather have some more of you." He grabbed Carrie by the waist as she playfully fought him off.

"It's getting late. I got to get home."

"Not yet," he said, nuzzling her neck. They made love again and would have done it a third time if Carrie hadn't run into the bathroom. "I ain't never seen no man like you. Ain't you wore out?" she said from the bathroom.

"This has been building up for some time. If I don't get it out, I'll go crazy."

"If we keep doing it, I'll go crazy," she chuckled.

"Okay, okay. I'll let you off the hook this time, but next time I want a third helping."

"Uh-uh-uh. Who would've thought?" she said, emerging from the bathroom. She stooped to pick up her panties. "They always said white boys didn't know how to do nothing but go down on a girl. You proved them wrong."

Bob picked up his shirt and turned to Carrie with a look of disappointment. "I wasn't trying to prove anything. I wish you'd forget about this race stuff and think of us as two people who are attracted to each other."

"Okay, you don't have to get all serious on me. I was just joking."

"I get sick of hearing all this stuff about what Negroes and Jews can and can't do."

"I won't bring it up again. You 'bout dressed?"

"Yeah, soon as I put my shoes on."

Neither one spoke as they walked to the car. That was fine with Carrie. She was sick of Bob getting worked up every time she mentioned race. They would never be compatible.

"Carrie, I know you're worried about people finding out about us but don't be," he said inside the car. "I won't tell anybody. As far as the folks at work know, we're just friends."

Carrie bit her lip. "That's all we can be, Bob."

"What do you mean?" he asked incredulously. "We just spent the whole evening making love. I'm sure you don't do that with all your male friends. Why are you still denying the fact that you have feelings for me?"

"Why are you making such a big deal out of this? We had sex, so what? That don't mean I'm committed to you and vice versa."

Bob leaned back against the headrest. "I thought things would be different after tonight."

"Ain't nothing changed. You still white, and I'm still colored. It'll be nothing but problems if we start seeing each other."

"We can be discreet."

"I don't think so, Bob," she said, putting her hands to her temples. "It won't work."

When they got out of the car, Bob said, "Just give me a chance. One chance. That's all I'm asking."

"You're wasting your time. I'll be your friend but not your girlfriend."

"We'll see about that," he said, leaning over to kiss her.

"No, not here!" she said. "Good night."

Chapter Thirty-Two

~

Nadine busied herself around the house while she waited for Cyrus to leave for the office. She was anxious to tell Willie Lee that she had to find a place soon because Cyrus was making plans to move the family to New York.

When she dialed his number, a woman answered the phone, prompting an apology from Nadine. She dialed the number again. The same woman picked up. Nadine was baffled. "Is this Willie Lee's apartment?"

"Who wants to know?"

"Who is this?"

"I'm his old lady. Who are you?"

"Never mind who I am," said Nadine, slamming down the phone. "His old lady, his old lady. He told me all that stuff about being his lady, and now he's got another woman."

Nadine was furious. She walked from one end of the house to the other, swearing and slapping herself upside the head. Finally, she grabbed her purse and drove frantically over to Greenberg's, leaving Miz Esther home alone.

She marched into Willie Lee's office, but he wasn't there. Nor was he in the stockroom. A cashier told her he was away on business.

Outraged because she couldn't find him, Nadine stomped out of the store, drove to Lydia's house, and rang the doorbell continuously until she answered. She rushed into the house like a tornado.

"Nadine, girl, what in the world? Are you all right?" Lydia asked. She closed the front door and ushered Nadine into the living room.

As they walked toward the sofa, Nadine started jabbering. "He lied to me. He took my money. Now he's got another woman."

"Cyrus took your money and ran off with another woman?" Lydia asked, trying to understand what happened. "Oh, Nadine, I can't—"

"Not Cyrus! Willie Lee!" Nadine shouted.

"Who is Willie Lee?"

"The man I was supposed to set up house with and marry," Nadine explained between sobs. "We were gonna run the store together and be one, big happy family. His boy and my girls, but he didn't mean it. He just used me. Why did he lie to me?" she cried, looking at Lydia for answers.

"I don't know, darling," she said sympathetically. "Some men are just dogs."

"This is what I get for being such a damn fool, thinking another man could rescue me from that hellhole," she said, wiping her eyes.

Lydia went to the bathroom for a box of tissues. When she came back, she lit a cigarette and took a long drag. "Nadine, you need to start from the beginning. How did you get mixed up with this Willie Lee person?"

Nadine blew her nose and told Lydia how she fell in love with her childhood friend. Lydia listened intently as Nadine recounted their meetings, how she gave him her life's savings, and the conversation she had with the woman at Willie Lee's apartment.

"I think you might as well kiss that money goodbye unless you want to lose your husband. If you go to the police, all the details about your relationship will come out. You know as well as I do that Cyrus wouldn't take you back after finding out you slept with another man. Your best bet is to forget about the whole thing."

"Forget about three thousand dollars?"

"Yes, ma'am, because you've got much more than that to lose. You can't be out on the street with two children if he lets you keep the girls. Forget about the man, Nadine. It's over and done with," Lydia said, taking the last puff of her cigarette.

"You're right," Nadine said. "I'll never forgive myself for being so stupid. Thanks for helping me get my head on straight."

"You'll get over him. I can tell you that from experience. Remind me to tell you about my little secrets one day," Lydia said, hugging Nadine at the door.

Forgetting about Willie Lee wasn't as easy as Lydia made it seem. The more Nadine thought about him, the angrier she got. She wasn't going to be satisfied until she gave Willie Lee a piece of her mind. She drove to the store again, but he still wasn't there. She got back into her car and went to his apartment. Nadine didn't know what she would do when she came face-to-face with his girlfriend, but she had to find out how long this woman had been with Willie Lee.

Nadine's hands shook as she took the key out of the ignition. She inhaled and exhaled three times, hoping that would relax her. With her jaw set and eyes thinned to slits, Nadine got out of the car, dashed up the steps, and banged on Willie Lee's door.

"Who in the hell is bamming on my door like a damn fool?" the woman said when she opened the door. She was a short, slanty-eyed woman, the color of sand. Her hair was rolled up in pink curlers, and she wore a black nightgown.

"Uh, my name is Nadine. I'm a friend of Willie Lee's."

"You the one who called here this morning?" She crossed her arms over her bosom.

"Yes, I am," Nadine said. "Who exactly are you?"

"Same as I told you this morning. His lady." The woman sucked her teeth. "You must be the woman been after him."

"After him? Is that what he told you? That's not what happened. We were supposed to get married."

The woman took a step toward Nadine. "Look, bitch, he don't want you. That's why he sent for me. You got a lot of fucking nerve coming 'round here. You better get the hell away from here before I beat the black off you."

Nadine backed up and ran to her car. She didn't know if the woman had a razor or gun. The last thing she wanted was to get hurt fighting over Willie Lee. She still wanted to confront him, look him in the eye, and ask how he could be so cruel.

She drove to the store again and parked close to the main entrance. After about fifteen minutes, she got tired of waiting, cranked up the engine, and drove away.

When Nadine got home, she felt mentally and physically drained. She went to see about Miz Esther, who was talking to the radio as if she were lecturing students. Nadine asked if she needed anything, but Miz Esther told her to sit down and stop disrupting class. She closed the door and sat in the den. When she dozed off, Aunt Bessie Mae came to her in a dream.

"Chile, stop pining for something that's long gone. Money ain't nothing but a piece of paper. If Willie Lee stole from you, he got to answer to God for that."

"How come this had to happen to me? Why can't I get what I want for once in my life?"

"God gives you what He wants you to have. I can't help but believe that He ain't through blessing you. You just got to trust and believe."

"I want to, Aunt Bessie Mae, but all these bad things keep happening to me. I feel like a prisoner in this marriage, in this house, everywhere I turn."

"You a prisoner if you let yourself be one. Ask the Lord to show you the

path to freedom and give you strength to overcome obstacles along the way."

Just as quickly as Aunt Bessie Mae appeared, she vanished before Nadine could ask more questions. She dismissed the dream and rested on the couch until Salena came bursting in the room holding a jar.

"Look, Mama. I caught a butterfly. Ain't it pretty?"

Nadine looked at the yellow and black butterfly flapping its wings inside the glass jar and felt sorry for it. "Let it go, Salena. Butterflies should be free to roam because they don't live too long. Turn it loose before it dies."

"But, Mama…"

"Give me the jar," Nadine said, gingerly taking it from her daughter. With Salena in tow, Nadine went to the backyard and unscrewed the top. "Okay, little butterfly, fly far away from here and don't come back if you know what's good for you." She watched it rise, dip, and soar over the hedges into the neighbor's yard. "One day, I'm going be like you, little butterfly. Free to come and go as I please," she mumbled.

"What you say, Mama?"

"Nothing, baby. I was just thinking out loud."

***

Nadine's eyes watered and her nose burned from the chlorine bleach she inhaled while scrubbing the white tile floor with a toothbrush. The fumes were so strong that they made her cough and gag.

"Don't you have sense enough to open the window?" Miz Esther yelled. "If you feel like you're going to vomit, do it upstairs in your own bathroom. That stench hangs in the air. I don't want to smell it."

Nadine removed her scarf and tied it over her nose and mouth. Just as she got back down on her hands and knees, Miz Esther said, "Make sure you get behind the commode. You did a half-ass job the last time."

She stopped scrubbing midstroke, threw the toothbrush in the bucket, and walked into Miz Esther's bedroom, where she was watching *The Edge of Night*. Seething inside, Nadine stood behind Miz Esther with her fists balled. She wanted to beat the hate out of her but couldn't bring herself to strike the crippled old woman.

Without a word to Miz Esther, she went back to the bathroom and poured the bucket of water in the toilet. She had no intention of finishing the floor today or ever. She hoped Miz Esther choked on her own funk.

Nadine went upstairs, took a bath, and put on a clean dress. When she looked in the mirror, she hardly recognized herself. The breakup with Willie Lee two weeks ago had taken a physical toll on her. Her skin was dry and ashy. Dark circles ringed her eyes. The tiny lines that used to be barely visible were now deep crevices in her forehead. Her hair was dull and brittle.

She couldn't believe that she had let Willie Lee make her look and feel wretched. Tired of being the victim, Nadine took Aunt Bessie Mae's words to heart. She decided it was time to leave Cyrus.

Excited and scared, Nadine sat at the kitchen table and mapped out a plan. First, she had to find a job. She got the Classified Ads and pored over the job listings. She circled three - a bakery, cleaners, and TV factory. The factory job paid the most, one dollar and eighty-five cents to work on an assembly line.

She submitted applications at all three places over the next few days but prayed for the factory job. With money from Cyrus, Nadine calculated that she could cover all the bills. All she wanted now was peace of mind and a place of her own.

Because of random phone calls in the middle of the day, Nadine had a hard time getting over Willie Lee. She hung up the first few times but decided to have it out with him today.

"What do you want?" she said angrily.

"I want to explain what happened."

"I don't want to hear it."

"The woman you saw at my apartment, it's not what you think. She doesn't mean anything to me."

"You could've fooled me," Nadine said. "I saw what was going on."

"Can you meet me at my place? We need to talk."

"No. I'm not interested in anything you have to say. You got what you wanted. Leave me alone."

Nadine hung up, satisfied that she had heard the last word from Willie Lee. She told herself to focus on the future. She looked forward to being on her own for the first time in her life, beholden to no one but God Almighty.

Chapter Thirty-Three

~

Cyrus had been making calls to New York all week, finalizing plans to join the practice of two classmates from medical school. He thought that would be easier than trying to start from scratch.

Checking his list, he saw the word "Mama" underlined. Cyrus hadn't told Miz Esther about the move yet, but it was time she knew so that she could get her affairs in order.

He could tell from the humming coming from her room that she was awake. "Mama, can I come in?" he asked.

"Yes, son." Miz Esther tugged at her hair, which she had braided into tiny plaits in the front and twisted little balls on the side.

Cyrus had never seen her hair in such disarray. He couldn't figure out what she was trying to do with it. He attributed her peculiar behavior to one of those memory loss spells that came over her periodically.

He sat in the chair next to her bed. "Mama, uh, I'm making some plans that involve you, and I want to tell you about them." He took a deep breath. "I've decided that we're going to move to New York City in a few months. It's a good move for me professionally. I'll be able to have a private practice, work in the teaching hospitals, and do some of the other things I've talked about since I got out of medical school. As for the house, you can rent it or sell it. That's really up to you."

Miz Esther's bared her teeth at him. She hauled off and threw her brush at Cyrus, striking him on the head.

"Mama! Why in the hell did you do that?" he asked, checking his head for blood.

"Somebody needs to knock some sense into you, boy," Miz Esther said. "Why are you always coming up with these cockamamie ideas? I'm not moving, and I'm not letting you take my granddaughters anywhere either. They were born here, and they're going to stay here."

"Look, Mama. Whether you like it or not, I'm really the head of the house now. I know it's hard for you to accept, but you haven't been able to take care of things like you did before the stroke. I've got to think about the future and make sure everybody is taken care of. I know it's going to be hard for you to leave, but you'll get used to New York."

"You look here, you ungrateful piss. You can make all the plans you want, but as long as I'm living, this is where our family stays."

"Mama, you—"

"Get out!"

Cyrus did as he was told. "Stubborn old woman. I'm going to have to put you in a straitjacket to get you out of here," he muttered in the hallway.

He went back to the living room to catch up on some paperwork. However, he couldn't concentrate. Cyrus kept thinking about Miz Esther and how he could persuade her that New York was a better place for the whole family. He heard someone coming down the stairs and turned to see Nadine with a basket of laundry. "Come here. I need your help."

"For what?"

"Here is a list of things that I need you to do this week. Get some estimates from three moving companies. Buy a "For Rent" sign and stick it in the front yard. Put a "House for Rent" notice on the bulletin board at church. I'm shooting for us to be in New York by Labor Day. That gives us four months to get everything together."

"Humph," Nadine said.

"Did I forget anything?"

Nadine read the list. "No, I don't think so," she said, placing the sheet of paper on top of the laundry. When Nadine was out of sight, she tore it up.

***

Cyrus and Miz Esther were sitting at the kitchen table eating breakfast when Nadine made an announcement. "Cyrus, I need to tell you something," she said, removing her apron.

"What?" he asked without looking up from the newspaper.

"I, I, uh, got a job."

He put the paper down and looked from Nadine to Miz Esther and back at Nadine.

"I got hired at the TV factory," she said. "I start next week."

"Why did you do that?"

"Because me and the girls aren't moving to New York. We're staying in Memphis."

"See, I'm not the only one who thinks you've gone stark-raving mad," Miz Esther said, pointing a finger at Cyrus. "You're crazier than a bed bug if you think we're going to move because you say so. I'm with you on this one, Nadine. I'm not moving either."

"Mama, this conversation is between me and Nadine, do you mind?" He turned to Nadine and said, "I've already told you what we're doing. That's final."

"No, it's not," she said unflinchingly. "You have told me what to do for the last sixteen years, and I went along with it. Not anymore. You can do whatever you want, but my home is here."

Cyrus brought his fist down on the table. "Your home is where your husband says it is. My family goes where I go."

"I ain't leaving Memphis no matter what you say."

"What are you going to live off of?" he asked, smirking. "That little money you'll make won't cover everything. Don't expect me to pay for two households."

"Plenty women make do on their own. You don't have to give me a dime, but I hope you do right by your children."

"You got it all figured out, huh?" he said, folding the newspaper. "This sounds like some garbage Lydia put in your head. Keep on listening to that dried up crow, and you're going to find yourself out on the street."

"You don't scare me, Cyrus. Those days are over," she said, scurrying from the room.

Cyrus sat quietly, mulling over what Nadine had just told him. He never imagined that she would refuse to go with him. "She'll come around," he told Miz Esther. "I'll just have to be forceful."

"What are you going to do, beat her, tie her up, and put her in the car? You'll have to do all of us like that because that's the only way we're leaving this house. That girl's got more gumption than I gave her credit for. All this time, I thought she was dumber than dirt. I guess she showed both of us."

"She has obviously forgotten who makes the rules," Cyrus said. "After I have a little talk with her, I guarantee that she'll change her mind."

"I don't think so, son. Her mind is made up, and mine is, too. Since we're not going, it doesn't make sense for you to keep talking about moving. Why don't you forget about this New York business and be happy where you are?"

"Because I'm not happy here!" he yelled. "How many times do I have to say it?"

"I don't see how you're going to drag four people out of this house kicking and screaming. You can't make me or Nadine go. Can't you get that through your thick skull?"

"I have to go, Mama. I'll see you later."

"Uh-huh," Miz Esther said as she twisted a section of her hair into a tiny ball. "Whatever you say."

***

Cyrus was looking forward to Mamie's visit to get his mind off his problems at home. He told Mamie that he would pick her up around seven o'clock. It was almost eight. Every traffic light turned red seconds before he hit the intersection.

As he waited for the light to change, Cyrus felt clammy though he had just changed shirts before he left the office. He realized that it was excitement over seeing Mamie.

Cyrus checked himself in the mirror before he exited the car. He smoothed down his hair, tightened his navy striped tie, and moistened his lips.

When he rang the bell, Mamie opened the door quickly. She stood with a hand on her hip, pointing to her watch. "It's about time. I thought you had stood me up," she said.

Cyrus walked into the foyer and took off his hat. "I'm sorry. I got held up. Do you still want to go?"

"Of course," she said. "Let me get my purse."

Mamie was more elegant and exotic than Cyrus remembered from their first meeting. She had an oval face, large greenish-brown eyes, and long, glossy black hair styled in a chignon.

Her olive complexion reminded him of women in Tahiti. She wore a candy-apple red tint on her luscious lips and an intoxicating fragrance that made Cyrus horny. Mamie's royal blue sheath caressed her body in all the places that excited him. He admired her long shapely legs as she walked across the hallway in black leather pumps.

"You okay?" Mamie asked when she came back. "You have the strangest look on your face."

"I'm fine," he said, discreetly covering an erection with his hat. "I was just thinking about something at work. Nothing serious."

On the way to the club, they talked about politics and their jobs. Mamie was unpretentious and spoke her mind. "When I told my cousin I was seeing you tonight, he told me that was a bad idea."

"Why would Doc Adams say something like that?"

"Because he doesn't want me to ruin my reputation by going out with a married man."

"Look, we're just going out for a friendly drink," Cyrus said, changing the radio station.

Mamie switched off the radio and turned to him. "Let's not play games," she said in a measured tone. "You told me that you were getting a divorce. Did you or didn't you?"

Cyrus clenched his teeth. "It's a little complicated, Mamie. You know what I've been dealing with this year – my mother's stroke and now her senility, the shooting incident with Salena, and Jocelyn's lupus. I couldn't abandon my family with all that going on. I'm in the process of relocating them up North so my daughters will have a better life. Once they're settled, I'll be free to do whatever I want."

He had hoped to garner sympathy from Mamie with the touching story about his family obligations. She listened stone-faced with her tongue planted inside her cheek. "In other words, you're still married."

"Yes, but not for long," he said.

Mamie lost her temper. "Take me back to my auntie's house," she said. "I'm not doing this again."

Cyrus ignored her request and kept driving. "What do you mean you're not doing this again?"

"Turn this car around!" she demanded.

"Okay, if that's what you want. I came all the way across town to see you for a little intelligent conversation. I don't see the harm in having one drink with a friend."

Mamie gave him the silent treatment, staring out the window. "So now you're not talking to me? Cat got your tongue? Lion got your tongue? I know, hippopotamus got your tongue," he quipped, dipping his head with each question.

She couldn't hold back the laughter. "Okay, Cyrus, we can go to the lounge for one drink, maybe two, but that's where it ends," she said firmly. "I will not be your mistress."

"Don't worry," he said. "That was never my intention."

In the parking lot of the Nite Owl Lounge, Cyrus didn't immediately turn off the ignition. "Are you absolutely, positively sure you want to go in? This is your last chance to bail. I don't want Doc Adams to think I held you against your will," he said.

"I'm too old to play games, Cyrus. We're either going to do this the right way or not at all."

"Understood," he responded. "All I ask is that you be patient until I work things out."

"I'm not going to wait on you forever. Life is too short for that," she said bluntly.

Cyrus wanted to take her in his arms and kiss her but doubted she would let him. Instead, he traced her jawline with his finger. Her skin was smooth as velvet. "It'll be worth the wait. I promise you."

Chapter Thirty-Four

～

The image of Bob between her legs kept flashing in Carrie's head, making it hard to concentrate on work. Every time she saw him, she blushed. Bob, on the other hand, didn't seem fazed at all.

Carrie didn't understand how he could be laid-back about what happened, and she was so conflicted. She chastised herself for sleeping with him, vowing it would never happen again.

In her weak moments, she fantasized about them living as a normal family in New York. Inevitably, reality brought her back down to earth. He was white. She was colored. There was no way they could exist happily ever after.

She stuffed her notes in a folder and went to get a soft drink. On the way to the cafeteria, she bumped into Cleary.

"Hi, Carrie, where you headed?"

"Hi, Cleary," she said flatly. "I'm going to the cafeteria."

"I'll ride with you," he said, pressing the elevator button. "What's up?"

"Nothing, why?" she asked defensively.

"You look a little funny."

"Ain't nothing wrong," she said, forcing a smile. "I'm just trying to figure out what to write about a new art program for kids at the YWCA. I been stuck on one sentence for the last hour."

"Relax, it'll come to you. I'm glad I ran into you. I was gonna call and ask if you wanted to go to the drive-in tonight?"

"No, I got something to do," she said, brushing him off.

"How 'bout tomorrow?"

"I'm going to be busy."

"Okay, so we back to that," he said, staring at the ceiling.

"What?"

The elevator door opened, but Cleary didn't move. "You know what, Carrie. Bye."

"Bye," she said, avoiding eye contact.

At the end of her shift, Carrie stopped by the security office to apologize for being standoffish earlier in the day. His face lit up when he saw her. "You changed your mind about tonight?" he asked.

"No, we need to talk," Carrie said.

"Just a minute." Cleary got up and closed the door. "This look like some bad news," he said, sitting behind his desk. "I don't know if I want to hear it."

"I'm sorry if you thought I was mean this morning. I would never hurt your feelings on purpose. I hope you know that," she said.

"Don't worry 'bout it."

Carrie cleared her throat and kept her eyes glued to the floor. "I appreciate you being my friend, but we can't see each other anymore. You know, like in a romantic way."

"I see," he said, leaning back in his chair. "You got somebody else? I hope you ain't fooling 'round with that cracker you always talking to."

Carrie squirmed in her chair and gave Cleary a dirty look. "You don't need to be concerned about who I'm seeing. I just don't want you wasting no more time on me. There are plenty women out there looking for a man like you."

"I told you a thousand times, I ain't interested in no other woman. I cut them loose when we starting going out."

"I don't know why you did that. I said in the beginning that we should just be friends."

"Yeah, that's what you said, but that ain't how you been acting. Don't worry, I got your message loud and clear." He got up and opened the door. "You have a good evening, Carrie."

"Take care," she said. Deep down, Carrie knew she was doing the right thing for both of them.

***

When Carrie got ready to leave for work, Miz Lula was bubbling over with excitement. "Ida Mae called me last night and said she is retiring and moving back to Mississippi. I think that white lady done got on her last nerve. We'll have to make a big celebration dinner for her before she go."

"That's a good idea, Miz Lula," Carrie said. "We can talk about it some more when I get home. I need to hurry before I miss my bus."

"Oh, yes, chile. I'm standing here running my mouth, and you need to be going. Have a good day now."

As it turned out, that wasn't the only bit of news that Carrie got that day. Bob strolled over to her desk after lunch, tossing a baseball in the air. "Guess what?" he said.

"What?"

"My folks are coming to town, and I want you to meet them."

Carrie looked around to see if anyone had heard him. "Why?" she whispered.

"Because you're my lady friend."

"I'm your *friend*," she reiterated. "We ain't about to get married. What's the point?"

"Since they'll be here, I thought it was a good idea." Bob tossed the ball high in the air and caught it. "If your mother came to town, I'd want to meet her."

"That's different," she said matter-of-factly.

"How?"

Carrie gave him a sideways look. She didn't feel like getting into a long discussion about the difference between white people and colored people. "You just don't get it, do you?"

"Nope. How does Sunday sound? You got any plans in the afternoon?"

"No, I don't. I'm telling you now this is a bad idea. I hope I don't regret letting you talk me into this."

"I'll pick you up at three and bring you back to my place to meet them."

"That's fine."

"It's a date. They get in tomorrow night. We've got some running around to do Friday and Saturday, but I'll call you."

"I can't wait to meet them," Carrie said sarcastically.

After Bob left, she came up with a long list of reasons to back out. What if they didn't think she was good enough for their son? What if they were rude to her? She reminded herself that she could always leave if they made her feel uncomfortable.

***

Carrie spent most of Saturday primping for her big introduction. Bob called shortly after six o'clock. Carrie noticed right away that something was wrong. He wasn't his usual easygoing self. His voice was strained.

"What's the matter?" Carrie asked.

"Something's come up. My parents won't be able to meet you tomorrow," he said in a taut voice.

"Are they leaving?"

"No, they'll be here until Tuesday."

"Well, I can meet them some other time."

Bob didn't assure her right away that was a possibility, making her suspicious. "What is it, Bob?"

Finally, he said, "Uh, uh, I don't know how to say this but..."

Carrie got angry. "They don't want to meet me, do they?"

"No," Bob said in a barely audible voice. "I didn't tell them that you were a Negro until last night."

"I thought you told them all about me before they came."

"I didn't think your race was important, but I didn't want them to be shocked so I decided to say something. I'm really sorry, Carrie. I had no idea my folks were against interracial dating. I never heard them say a bad word about Negroes in my life, honest."

"They just don't want their son dating a colored girl," Carrie snapped. "It's all right if we wipe your ass, but we ain't good enough for nothing else."

"You know how I feel. That's all that should matter. My folks will be gone in a few days. It'll be just you and me again."

Carrie tore into him. "You must be crazy if you think I'm going to sit around waiting for you," she said, pacing the living room. "You should have told your folks they had to accept me since you're so in love with me."

"I didn't see the point of forcing the issue," he said. "I can't help the way my parents feel, Carrie. They're from a different generation. What they think shouldn't affect our relationship at all."

"And just how you figure that? If your folks don't like me, they'll constantly be coming between us."

"I think we still have a future. I…"

"Bob, you a coward. And you stupid. I don't want to talk to you again." Carrie hung up the phone so hard that it fell off the table.

She went into her room and closed the door. Carrie felt like marching over to Bob's apartment and slapping the shit out of him and his parents. The only thing that stood in the way was her pride. "What makes them think they better than me?" she said. "They ain't."

A knock on the door made her realize that she was still talking loudly. Carrie owed Miz Lula and Miz Ida Mae an explanation because they heard the whole conversation from the kitchen. They never pried into her personal life, but her argument with Bob had become very public.

"Carrie, can we come in?" asked Miz Ida Mae.

"I'll be out in a minute," Carrie replied.

She stayed in her bedroom until she had calmed down. When she went into the kitchen, the ladies were talking quietly and drinking tea.

"Is everything all right, baby?" Miz Lula asked with a raised eyebrow.

"Yes, ma'am," Carrie said. "I'm just having a problem with somebody at work, but I can handle it."

"Don't you let anybody take advantage of you," Miz Lula said. "You stand firm, you hear me?" She nodded at Miz Ida Mae, who pressed her lips together and nodded back.

"Yes, ma'am."

"Anyway, we have come up with a wonderful plan that we know you're going to love."

"Since I'm leaving, my bedroom will be available," Miz Ida Mae said.

"Why would I need another bedroom? Mine is okay."

The two women exchanged looks. "Ida Mae, Carrie ain't thinking straight today," Miz Lula said. She turned to Carrie and said, "To bring your children up here."

"And stay here?" Carrie asked.

"Of course. I'll look after them while you're working. I always wanted a daughter, but God gave me a son instead, rest his soul. Now, I'll have a boy and girl to fuss over," Miz Lula said.

Carrie sat with her hands over her mouth, letting the news sink in. "I don't know what to say. I didn't think I would ever save enough money to get my babies and move into my own place. Miz Lula, I can't thank you enough." She gave her a hug.

"Lula, they look just like doll babies, but they sho got some energy. You better start taking your tonic now," Miz Ida Mae said.

Miz Lula smiled. "You know I get up early. I'm looking forward to having some company."

"You'll have more help than you know what to do with when Vicki and Victor come. I can't believe this really happening." Carrie stamped her feet in the chair. "My babies are coming!"

"Honey, I don't mind helping young people when I see they're trying. It's about time you had something good happen to you. Lord knows, you've had your share of trouble, but I feel that's 'bout to change. Just stay on your knees, and trust in the Lord."

"I am, Miz Lula. Believe me, I am. Let me go write Mama and tell her I'll be down at the end of summer to pick up my babies. That'll give me some time to get everything ready. Thank you again, Miz Lula." She gave her another hug.

***

Carrie threw herself into her work to forget about Bob and their last conversation. She ignored him when he came into the newsroom and gave one-word answers when he asked questions. She cut him off when he tried to apologize.

He sent her a beautiful bouquet of red roses - the first flowers she had ever received - but she refused to accept them. One Saturday morning, he followed Carrie as she walked to the bus stop. "Carrie," he called out.

When she saw who it was, she sped up. Bob parked the car and ran after her. "Please, listen to me just for a minute."

Carrie stopped and confronted him. "What do you want?"

"How long are you going to be mad at me?"

"How long you gonna be white?"

"That's not fair. Let's not fight. I thought we had something special. What happened?"

"Your people came to town, and I found out what kind of man you really are."

"Look, you know how much I care about you. Nothing's going to change that. I can't stand you being mad at me another day. Let's just put this behind us, please. I'll get everything straight with my folks, I promise. Just say you'll take me back. Look, I brought you something," he said, fumbling in his pocket. Bob brought out a little black box. Carrie didn't touch it so he opened the box. "It's an engagement ring, but we can call it a commitment ring or whatever you want to call it." He tried to slip the ring on her finger, but she snatched her hand away.

"Get your hands off me!" Carrie yelled. "Go away!"

At that moment, a big, burly colored man stepped from between the houses with a baseball bat.

"Miss, this man bothering you?" He was talking to Carrie but looking at Bob as he walked toward them.

Bob dropped the ring box on the sidewalk.

"No, sir, he's leaving right now. Thank you, very much." She turned to Bob and said, "You ain't got no business here. Go home."

Bob started walking backward down the street, still keeping an eye on the man. He turned around after a few steps, walked to his car, and drove off.

Carrie was unnerved by the whole incident and walked quickly to the bus stop. When she reached the corner, the bus was leaving. She dug inside her purse for a schedule and saw that the next bus to Nee Mama's apartment would arrive in thirty minutes. Carrie sat on a bench, angry with Bob for making her miss the bus.

Every few seconds, she looked over her shoulder to see if he had sneaked up behind her. She fanned herself with the bus schedule, but that didn't cool her off or lessen her agitation.

Carrie walked to the edge of the sidewalk and looked down the street. There was no bus coming. She plopped down on the bench again. She didn't want to admit it, but she had feelings for Bob. She was punishing him for his parents' refusal to meet her. However, being angry with Bob was eating away at her, too. She had to forgive him. That was the right thing to do.

She headed home to call Bob. Before she reached her house, she saw his bug-shaped car parked at the end of the street.

Bob saw her coming and got out of the car. Before he could speak, Carrie said, "Let's walk over by the pumping station." They stopped under a big sycamore tree, and Carrie leaned against the trunk.

"Carrie, I didn't handle the situation with my parents very well. It won't happen again, I promise. Just give me another chance," he pleaded.

"Bob, it won't be a next time. We can't see each other no more. It just cause too many problems. I told you that from the beginning, remember?"

"Yeah, but I also remember the night we made love. I know you care about me, Carrie," he said, reaching for her hand.

Although it was broad daylight, Carrie let him hold her hand and didn't worry about who might see them. "It just wasn't meant to be. We're from two different worlds. It's not going to work," she said.

Bob was overcome with emotions. "If that's the way you want it, I don't have a choice, do I? And if that's the way it's going to be, there's no reason for me to stay in Memphis. You were the only thing keeping me here."

She looked away.

In a quivering voice, Bob said, "I'll stay if you ask me to."

Carrie knew that she had to choose her words carefully to keep Bob from getting his hopes up. "I don't want you to leave, Bob, but I can't be the reason you stay either." As Carrie blinked away the tears, she spotted a mama bird feeding baby birds huddled in a nest.

"Know anybody who wants to buy a two-carat diamond ring real cheap?" he joked.

"How much is it?"

"The price is negotiable."

"Can I see it again?"

He took the ring out of his pocket and placed it in the palm of Carrie's hand. "I did have a box but dropped it when this big, scary guy came after me," he said smiling.

The emerald-cut diamond sparkled in the midday sun. She slid the ring onto her finger and held out her hand to admire it. "I ain't never seen a diamond ring this big. What are these red stones on the side?"

"Rubies. They were my grandmother's favorite. She left me the ring in her will. She told me to make sure that the girl I gave it to is worthy of being a member of our family. Being the obedient grandson that I am, I followed her advice."

Carrie took off the ring and handed it back to Bob. "You'll find some-body else. Just don't forget me."

"I could never forget you, my brown angel. I'll always love you." He kissed her full on the mouth.

She wrapped her arms around his neck. After the kiss, they stayed locked in each other's arms. Bob kissed her again, but this time on the forehead. They walked hand-in-hand back to his car.

"Take care of yourself," Bob said as he drove away.

Carrie watched the car disappear around the corner before she went inside the house. She would never forget Bob either. He was the man who unlocked her heart and helped her feel alive again.

Chapter Thirty-Five

~

Nadine was so anxious about her first day on the job that she barely slept. She stared at the clock off and on until it was five o'clock and time to get up. Her shift started at seven. She slipped out of bed quietly. She hadn't told Cyrus she was starting work today, but the girls knew. Nadine gave them the new house rules last night. Stay inside. No friends in the house. Obey Vera.

After Nadine washed up, she tiptoed back into the bedroom and put on her green uniform. She was sitting in a chair tying her shoes when Cyrus turned over and raised his head.

"Why are you up at this hour?" he asked, rubbing the sleep out of his eyes. "And what are you wearing?"

"My work uniform," she said proudly.

Cyrus heaved himself out of bed and stood over her. "Don't push me, Nadine," he said in a menacing tone. "You're not going to that factory."

Nadine walked around him and over to the dresser. She expected him to start a fight and remained unperturbed as she brushed her hair. "How are you going to stop me, Cyrus?"

"You can't leave Mama and the girls home alone while you go off to that stupid job," Cyrus ranted.

"Vera will be here at eight. She'll fix Miz Esther's breakfast. If the girls get hungry before then, they can eat cereal."

Exasperated, Cyrus walked over to the door, blocking her way. "What are you trying to prove, that you're capable of getting a job? If that's the case, you've shown me. Now, you can stop this little game. It's gone too far."

Nadine looked at him smugly. "I'm not playing. This is for real." She got her purse and stood in front of Cyrus, waiting for him to move. When he didn't, Nadine tried forcing him out of the way. "You can't keep me from going!" she bellowed.

"If you leave this house, you'll pay dearly."

They struggled briefly, and Cyrus flung her onto the floor. When he lunged at Nadine, he stepped on one of his shoes, causing him to fall.

Nadine scrambled out of the room, ran down the stairs, and out the front door. When she looked in the rearview mirror, Cyrus was standing on the sidewalk. "I guess you believe me now," she said.

The rest of the day would have been just as horrible had it not been for two women who took Nadine under their wing. After a supervisor gave Nadine a ten-minute lesson, she was on her own.

Nadine's frustration grew by the minute because she couldn't fit the cardboard securely around the TVs. They were coming down the line faster than she could wrap them. Mattie, who was in her twenties, came to her rescue and demonstrated her quick-pack method. She was tall, skinny, and witty.

"Take a deep breath," Mattie told Nadine. "You ain't a machine. They know you're new and can't go fast yet."

Bea, a motherly type in her forties, checked Nadine's work before it left her station.

"We have to stick together," Bea said on their lunch break. "We'll help you make your quota until you get the hang of it."

"I appreciate it," Nadine said.

"Where did you work before?" asked Mattie, chewing on a bologna sandwich.

"Around the house, cooking and cleaning for my mother-in-law."

"Chile, please," Bea said. "I've had a couple of them but not no more. I know you glad to be here."

"You don't know the half of it," she joked.

Nadine had left her lunch in the refrigerator, but she was so glad to be away from Miz Esther's house that she didn't feel hungry at all.

***

The smell of the colonel's fried chicken filled the car and made Nadine's stomach growl. Too tired to cook, she bought take-out food for dinner. All she had to do now was open a can of vegetables and heat leftovers for Miz Esther.

When Nadine unlocked the front door, Jocelyn was on the phone and saw her mother's hands were full but didn't budge from the chair. Salena, who was watching TV in the den, saw her mother loaded down with bags and got up to help Nadine.

"Who set the table?"

"Me," Salena said. "Are the knives and forks in the right place?"

"Yes, they are," Nadine replied.

"I tried to remember where everything went. I don't want Grandma to yell at me like she did the last time."

"What did Jocelyn do?"

"Nothing," Salena said. "She's been on the phone all day."

After Nadine had fixed everyone's plate, she walked over to Jocelyn and snatched the phone. "She has to get off the phone now, bye."

"Mama, you had no right to do that," Jocelyn yelled, jumping to her feet.

Nadine pushed her down. "Don't you dare raise your voice at me.

Who do you think you're talking to? I'm not one of your friends."

"You didn't have to hang up like that. All you had to do was ask me to get off the phone," she said in a surly voice. "Why do you always have to embarrass me in front of my friends? I see why Grandma can't stand you. You ruin everything."

Nadine grabbed Jocelyn's chin in her hand. "First of all, I don't care how Miz Esther feels about me. Don't you ever throw that up in my face again. Second, I don't have to ask you to do anything. I'm your mama. I tell you what to do." She let go of Jocelyn's face and continued fussing. "I told you to put the dishes up, and they're still in the drying rack. This is the second time this week I told you to do something, and you haven't done it. I expect you to help out around the house now that I'm working, and I don't want to hear your smart remarks."

"I ain't said nothing," Jocelyn shot back.

"You've said too much. I've been trying to ignore you, but I see that ain't working. I know exactly what you need." Nadine pushed Jocelyn into the hall and up the stairs to the girls' bedroom where she pulled the extension cord from an outlet. She grabbed Jocelyn by the shoulder and whacked her across the butt and legs.

"You think you can do what you want and talk to me any kind of way? You ain't grown!"

"I'm sorry, Mama," Jocelyn cried. She nearly knocked down Nadine trying to scramble out of her reach.

"You're not going to run over me," Nadine shouted as she pushed Jocelyn onto the bed. "You will respect me just like you do your daddy and grandma. Do you hear me?"

"Yes, Mama. I won't do it again. Stop, Mama, please," she begged.

"I know you won't because I'm going to give you something to help you remember." Nadine gave Jocelyn a few more licks. "And don't come out of this room. No dinner for you tonight."

She went downstairs to check on Salena, who had eaten half her dinner.

"Mama, why did you whip Jocelyn?" she asked.

"She sassed me and disobeyed me. And the same will happen to you if you do that."

"I'm never gonna make you mad at me. Are you gonna tell Daddy so he can whip her again?"

"No, I took care of it. One whipping is enough."

***

To avoid Willie Lee, Nadine had been driving to another grocery store that was farther from the house. She was rushed for time today and had to make a difficult decision. Since Vera had to leave in an hour, Nadine steered the car toward Greenberg's.

She hadn't been there since she and Willie Lee broke up a month ago. Nadine worried about bumping into him around every corner, but she managed to get out without seeing him. She rolled the cart to her car, where she found Willie Lee leaning on the trunk.

"Hi, Nadine," he said, twisting a cap in his hands.

She stepped in front of him and opened the trunk. Willie Lee reached into the cart to grab some bags, but she stopped him. "I don't need your help," Nadine spat.

"Will you let me explain?"

"I told you there's nothing to say. It's pretty clear you got somebody else."

"No, that's not true," Willie Lee said, shaking his head. He touched her arm, but she brushed his hand away. "I used to go with her when I was in East St. Louis, but I broke it off when we got serious. I didn't see no need to tell you about something that happened in the past."

Nadine stopped putting the groceries in the trunk and faced Willie Lee. "Her timing was pretty good," she said. "She came down here right after I gave you the money."

Willie Lee raised his hand. "I swear on my mama's grave that I didn't tell her to come. My big mouth cousin told her I bought a store, and she came on her own, thinking we would get back together. Didn't nothing happen between us while she was here. I told her to go back home because I had somebody else. She pitched a bitch but left after she saw I wasn't playing."

Nadine rolled her eyes. "You must think I'm stupid. What woman would just up and visit a man in another state without being asked, especially since y'all supposedly broke up?"

"Honest to God that's what happened," Willie Lee said. "She just showed up on my doorstep one day. I was just as shocked as you."

"Why didn't you tell me that she was here? Or send her to a hotel?"

Willie Lee stuttered, "I, I don't know," he said. "I figured I'd just put her on the next bus before you found out. Things were going so good between us. I didn't want to upset you."

Nadine finished loading the car and closed the trunk. She stepped over Willie Lee and walked to the driver's side. Willie Lee grabbed her arm. "Nadine, don't shut me out."

"It's over," Nadine said as she opened the door.

"Just like that?"

"Uh-huh," she said, refusing to look at him.

"Can we at least talk about it some more?"

"It's too late for that. I've got to get home. Do you mind?"

He stood in front of her, his eyes imploring her to stay with him. "Think about all the plans we made. You gave me all that money. For us. For our future together."

"Don't remind me," Nadine said, shoving him out of the way. "I ain't got nothing else to say, Willie Lee."

"I love you, Nadine. I want to spend the rest of my life with you."

Nadine stood motionless with one leg in the car and the other on the ground. No man had ever professed his love to her. She turned and looked at him, like she was seeing him for the very first time.

"I need time to think," she said, getting into her car.

Her problems with Willie Lee were soon forgotten. When Nadine got home, Vera was waiting in the hallway with her purse. She was red in the face and angry.

"What's the matter?" Nadine asked.

"Miz Esther hit me with her cane," Vera screeched. "That woman is out of her mind. She was acting crazy, and when I tried to calm her down, she hit me on the shoulder. She kept talking about I stole her boyfriend. I ain't got the mind or the strength to be fighting with no old lady. You'll have to find somebody else."

"Vera, I'm sorry. Are you all right?"

"My shoulder hurts, and it will probably be worse tomorrow," Vera said, massaging her arm.

"Do you think you can stay on a few more days until I find a replacement?"

"I have my health to think about. I appreciate the opportunity to work for you and Dr. Mitchell, but I have to quit."

"We'll miss you, Vera. Thank you for your service." Nadine paid Vera, and she stormed out of the house.

Nadine panicked because she didn't have a backup caretaker. She decided that Jocelyn would have to look after Miz Esther for the time being. She didn't care if Cyrus liked it or not.

Later that night when the girls were in bed, and Miz Esther was having a conversation with invisible friends, Nadine dragged herself upstairs and drew a bath. Her mind more so than her body was weary. Seeing

Willie Lee made her realize that she still cared for him.

Nadine undressed and slowly descended into the hot water. She could feel her hair drawing up without the scarf but didn't bother to get one. The scalding water made little bumps pop out on her skin. It burned and felt good at the same time.

She thought about everything Willie Lee had said earlier in the day. Was he telling the truth about the woman she saw at his apartment? Although it wasn't her nature, Nadine knew that some women chased men. She had seen church women pounce on a widower at the repast.

As Nadine sat in the tub, she spread her legs and let the water rush between them. She remembered how Willie Lee touched her in bed. She began stroking herself until she had an orgasm. Nadine closed her eyes and let her body sink lower in the water until it reached her neck. She felt lighter, like her body could float out of the tub and up to the sky. Everything was peaceful.

The moment reminded her of the words to "Silent Night." All is calm, all is bright. In the stillness, Aunt Bessie Mae spoke to her again. *"Chile, why you making a mountain out of a molehill? That man told you the truth. What more you want? If he wanted that woman, she'd still be here. Don't be foolish."*

Nadine sat up in the tub, covered her breasts, and looked around the bathroom. She was alone but could feel Aunt Bessie Mae's presence. Her words gave Nadine clarity.

She got dressed and went downstairs to call Willie Lee for a heart-to-heart talk. Before he could answer, Nadine heard someone walking down the hallway. She hung up. The phone call to Willie Lee would have to wait until tomorrow.

Chapter Thirty-Six

~

Every time Cyrus thought about his predicament, he got depressed. Loveless marriage. Sick daughter. Dead city. Senile mother. Racism. He had no solutions to any of these problems, and that plunged him deeper into despair.

Cyrus hated Miz Esther for ruining his life. And he felt guilty about that because she was the reason for his success as well. He hadn't seen his mother in several nights because he had been coming home, downing two glasses of brandy, and falling asleep in the living room. He decided to pay her a visit tonight.

He knocked on her bedroom door, but she didn't answer. He opened it slightly to see if she was asleep. Miz Esther was propped up in bed. "Mama," he said heading toward her bed. Her eyes were open, but she didn't respond. He walked to the side of her bed and leaned over Miz Esther. The look of death stared back at him.

"Mama! Mama!" He shook her. She didn't move. He felt for a pulse. Nothing. He lay her flat and blew into her mouth. When that didn't work, he pressed on her chest, trying to get a heartbeat.

For ten minutes, Cyrus tried everything he had learned in medical school, but nothing brought her back. Miz Esther was dead. He placed her head on the pillow and pulled the cover up to her chest. He fell across her body, wailing uncontrollably. "I'm sorry, Mama. I'm sorry," he said.

"Cyrus, what's wrong?" Nadine asked from the doorway.

"Mama's gone," he cried.

"Gone? What do you mean gone?"

"She's dead."

"Oh, my God," she gasped, moving closer to get a better look. In death, Miz Esther looked just as mean as she did in life. Nadine didn't know what to feel for the woman who had tormented her for almost half her life.

"Call Dr. Adams and the funeral home," Cyrus said between sobs.

***

Cyrus and Sonny sat at a card table in a back room of his bar, downing shots of whiskey and exchanging stories about Miz Esther.

"The first time I met Esther, she was coming out of the Daisy Theater with my classmate, Clara. You should've seen them all dolled up, looking fine. I invited them in for a drink. When Esther went to the restroom, Clara told me to forget about her 'cause Esther was high class. I didn't pay that no mind. I just wanted to get to know her as a friend. We hit if off right away. Me and that gal had some good times together." Sonny wiped his eyes with a dish towel. "One by one, they all leaving. If they ain't closing up shop, they dying."

"You ought to close up too, Sonny. Beale Street is dead," Cyrus said.

"It ain't dead, son. It's hibernating, like bears do in the winter. You see, I know what's gonna happen. When the crackers done bought up everything, the city will come back down here and build something nice. You know, something white folks can come to on a Sunday afternoon with their children."

"If I were you, I'd take the money and run."

"See, your generation want everything quick, fast, and in a hurry.

Y'all don't believe in waiting for nothing 'cept the bus."

"I don't believe in waiting for something that ain't coming no time soon. That's why I want to get the hell out of Memphis. Things move too slow. I couldn't get Mama to see that."

"Esther knew what she was doing. She didn't want to spend her last days in a strange city. Now that she's gone, you can do what you please." He finished his drink and poured another one.

"I should've made this move a long time ago, before she got sick. It would've been a lot easier," he said, disappointed in himself.

"Who's to say she would've felt any different. Esther had her own way of thinking and doing things."

Cyrus thought about it for a moment. "You're right about that. And she stayed that way until the very end."

"She was true to herself. Rest in peace, Esther," he said, looking heavenward.

Cyrus stood and shook out his legs. His whole body felt tight as a rubber band. He rotated his shoulders and tilted his head from side to side. He grabbed his jacket off the chair and stumbled to the door. "You coming to the wake?"

"I'll be there," Sonny said. "If you need anything, just holler."

What Cyrus craved most was a good night's sleep. He thought about taking a sleeping pill when he got home but worried that he might become dependent on them. Tonight, he was counting on liquor to do the job.

By the time Cyrus reached his bedroom, he was drunk with sleep. He took off his clothes and huddled under the covers. He drifted off only to wake up two hours later. He couldn't fall asleep again and went to check on the girls. They were resting peacefully.

He lingered over Jocelyn for a few minutes, trying to imagine what the future held for her. She was a young lady now, soon headed to college.

He prayed that she would remain healthy and lead a normal life.

Cyrus saw in Jocelyn not only a physical resemblance but a younger version of himself. She was a strong-willed girl who would probably do what she wanted in life even if that meant going against her parents. That was something that he could never do. He admired and envied her sense of independence.

He would lose Jocelyn if he tried to break her spirit. He had to find a way to control it without taking over her life, which is what Miz Esther had done to him. He patted Jocelyn's hair like he used to when she was a little girl.

She opened her eyes. "Hi, Daddy. Is it time to get up?"

"No, baby, it's still night. I was just checking on you. How have you been feeling?"

"Okay," she said.

"Have you been taking your medicine?"

"Most of the time."

"You've got to take it on schedule if you want to feel better. Promise me you will."

"Okay, Daddy."

"Okay, Daddy, what?"

"I'll take it."

"Night, night, precious. Sleep tight. Don't let the bedbugs bite." Cyrus couldn't remember the last time he had recited that rhyme. It was their special little saying when she was a toddler. He wandered through the house for the rest of the night, reminiscing about the good times with Miz Esther.

***

On the day of the funeral, the family arrived at the church thirty minutes early because Miz Esther's sorority was holding a special ceremony for her. About fifty women dressed in white occupied pews in the middle of the church. One woman read a poem, and they sang in a circle around Miz Esther's casket. After their service, the organist and pianist began playing as four hundred people filled the sanctuary.

For nearly two hours, mourners praised Miz Esther for her dedication to family, students, community, and church. A soloist sang Miz Esther's favorite song, "Precious Lord Take My Hand," in such an angelic voice that people in the audience stood and clapped when she finished.

The family held up well until Reverend Tyson started preaching. Aunt Lillian and the girls wept. Cyrus wiped his eyes with a handkerchief and stared at Miz Esther's coffin. He broke down when he viewed her body.

Aunt Lillian's knees buckled as she looked down on her sister, but Uncle Mack and one of the attendants caught her before she hit the floor. Nadine and the girls walked arm in arm to the casket, but Salena didn't want to look and buried her face in Nadine's chest. Jocelyn cried as they walked back to the pew.

The attendants closed Miz Esther's casket, and the family lined up for the recessional and trip to the cemetery. Aunt Lillian and Uncle Mack rode in one limousine. Cyrus, Nadine, and the girls were in the second one.

"I'm hungry," Salena said.

"You're always eating. That's why you're fat," Jocelyn said.

"I ain't fat," she replied, elbowing Jocelyn. "At least I don't look like Olive Oil."

"That's enough," said Nadine, who was glad to see the girls were back to normal. "There will be plenty to eat at Aunt Lillian's house."

"Just don't let Porky eat it all," Jocelyn said.

Salena made a face at Jocelyn and muttered, "Olive Oil."

While the girls pestered each other, Cyrus looked out the window.

He felt lost, bereaved, and orphaned. He dreaded the final goodbye at the cemetery.

The long line of cars snaked its way through Memorial Gardens and stopped at the top of a hill. Miz Esther's plot was near a magnolia tree that formed a leafy canopy for family members, who sat in a row of white chairs facing the casket.

Reverend Tyson prayed and delivered a few words of comfort to the family. As the cemetery workers lowered Miz Esther's casket into the ground, Aunt Lillian cried out her sister's name. She was inconsolable. Cyrus and Uncle Mack walked her back to the limo.

Nadine and the girls gathered ribbons from the floral arrangements to save as mementos. When they finished, Cyrus told them to wait for him in the limo.

He went over to his mother's grave and spoke from his heart. "Miz Esther, you were the best mother I could have ever asked for. I hope that I made you proud. I'll never forget the things you taught me. I'll pass them on to my children. You'll always be in my heart, Mama. I love you."

Chapter Thirty-Seven

~

Carrie saw Miz Esther's death notice in the newspaper and immediately called Miz Lillian to offer her condolences. Miz Lillian broke down during their conversation, and Carrie got teary, too. She felt sorry for her and was tempted to stop by the house after the funeral but knew that would be a mistake.

After Carrie finished washing clothes, she fixed a lunch meat sandwich and watched TV. A talent show featuring local bands put her in a dancing mood. Desperate for company and fun, Carrie phoned Cleary. She got a busy signal. She waited five minutes and called again.

"Hello."

"Hey, this is Carrie," she said cheerfully. "What you doing?"

"Ain't this a surprise. I'm just sitting here. What you got going on?"

Carrie sat in a chair next to the phone and propped her feet up against the wall. "Nothing much. What you planning to do tonight? I know you ain't staying in."

"My partner just called a few minutes ago. We're meeting up at this club called The Velvet Room about ten. You welcome to join us."

"It ain't no juke joint, is it?"

"There you go always thinking I'm gonna take you to some hole-in-the-wall. This is supposed to be a real nice club in South Memphis. And the band is pretty good. I heard them play at another spot."

"I'd like to check them out," she said. "What time can you pick me up?"

"How 'bout nine?"

"Okay, it's a date." Carrie hung up and ran to the closet to pick out something to wear. She felt like dressing up tonight and doing something fancy with her hair. She chose a black, clingy dress that Miz Ida Mae had retrieved from a bag of clothes her boss was donating to the Goodwill.

Carrie laid the dress on the bed and went to the mirror to work on her hair. She combed her hair back and folded it into a French roll. Next, she brushed some hair forward and curled it with her fingers, making a row of tendrils that framed her face. "Don't tell me I don't know how to fix hair," she said to her reflection.

She took her time getting dressed, checking her hair in the mirror every few minutes to make sure that not a curl was out of place. Carrie usually didn't like to show off her shape, but tonight she wanted to make heads turn.

Fully dressed, she walked to the bathroom to get a look at herself in the mirror on the back of the door. Everything looked fine except her makeup. She got the red sponge, dipped it in powder and wiped her face. Afterward, she applied orange frosted lipstick. "Perfect," she said, pressing her lips together. "I look like Leslie Uggams's twin." She put some tissues, lipstick, and the powder sponge in her purse, and went in the living room to wait for Cleary. Ten minutes later, he rang the doorbell.

"Check you out," he said grinning. "I need to hire some bodyguards to keep the niggas off you."

"Thank you," Carrie said. "Let's go."

"Yes, sir. I got the prettiest girl in town with me tonight. We'll have to hit a couple of clubs so I can show you off. You ain't got to be up early tomorrow, I hope."

"Nope, I can stay out 'til the cows come home."

"Well, let's get this show on the road," he said, offering his arm.

They stayed at The Velvet Room with Cleary's friend, Ray, for a couple of hours before they moved on to the Kit Kat Club. Carrie had never danced so much in her life. She was having a good time. Cleary was attentive and entertaining. He knew people everywhere they went. They got the best table in the house, and the manager always came over to greet them.

"Cleary, you have a lot of nice friends," Carrie said as she sipped a glass of rum and coke. "They treat you like a star."

He waved off the compliment. "They're people I met when I was a bouncer."

"Why did you quit?"

"The hours were bad, and I got sick of drunks throwing up on me, and trying to fight."

"They threw up on your good clothes? I know you busted some heads."

"No, girl, I had on a uniform," he said. "I see you got some new threads. I really like that dress. It looks classy, like you." His eyes roamed her body.

They exchanged looks. Carrie's stomach fluttered. It caught her by surprise. She smiled to herself as they sat listening to a local singer belt out "Since You've Been Gone." After the song ended, Cleary checked his watch and said, "Why don't we dance a couple more times and head on home. They 'bout ready to close up anyway."

Cleary led her to the dance floor, where Carrie cut up. "Watch out there now, girl. You gonna rip that dress shaking your booty like that."

She stuck out her tongue and wiggled her butt even more. She could feel Cleary's eyes on her. When they slow danced on the next song, he got a hard-on. His body was rigid as he held her close. Carrie pictured his sinewy body wrapped around hers. She kissed him on the ear.

Cleary drew back. "What did you just do?"

"Hush, I ain't done nothing. Dance."

"You a little tipsy, huh?"

"Shush!" she said, brushing her lips across his mouth.

Cleary grunted. "Is that your liquor talking?"

"No, it's me wanting to kiss you."

"Since when?"

"Since now," Carrie said.

After she kissed him again, Cleary said, "Come on, you're drunk. Time to take you home." He grabbed their belongings.

"What's the matter? You don't like me anymore?" she asked, stopping in the middle of the doorway.

"Come on, Carrie, people trying to get out. We'll discuss this when you're sober."

Carrie snuggled up to Cleary in the car. "I had a really good time tonight, Cleary. We should do it again."

"Uh-huh," Cleary said.

At her front door, Cleary spun Carrie around to face him. "Don't play with me, Carrie," he said in a serious voice. "I ain't no child."

Carrie wrinkled her nose. "What you talking 'bout?"

"You know exactly what I mean. You told me you wasn't interested not too long ago. Tonight, you acting like I'm your man. How long will this last? You think all you got to do is snap your fingers and I'll come running like a dog? Well, that ain't the way it work."

Carrie put a hand on her hip. "If you didn't want to go out, all you had to do was say so."

"I ain't talking 'bout that Carrie, and you know it," Cleary said angrily. "I'm not gonna let you play me for no fool. When you decide you ready for me, call me. Until then, lose my number. Good night." He left Carrie on the front porch with her mouth open.

Chapter Thirty-Eight

~

Nadine staggered to the bathroom, feeling like she had a hangover. She had slept for ten hours but still felt weary. There was a piece of paper stuck to the bathroom mirror.

Nadine,
I went to the hospital. Aunt Lillian is coming over after church to go through Mama's things. After she takes what she wants, pack up the rest and drop the bags off at the Goodwill.
Cyrus

Nadine threw the note in the trash. She had planned to spend the day resting, not cleaning out a musty old wardrobe and dresser. She was even going to let the girls skip church. She couldn't remember the last Sunday they had stayed home. Miz Esther insisted everyone go to church unless you were burning up with fever.

Now that Miz Esther was gone, Nadine decided that she would periodically declare Sunday a lazy day, and everybody could do as she pleased. She found the girls in their room. Jocelyn was reading, and Salena was working a puzzle.

"Good morning," Nadine said.

"Hi, Mama. We going to church?" asked Salena.

"You know we are," Jocelyn replied. "Why do you always ask dumb questions?"

"No, not today. We're going to stay home and do absolutely nothing. Aunt Lillian's coming over later to help me clean out Miz Esther's room. Why don't y'all get dressed, and I'll fix some breakfast. Let me take my bath first. Maybe that will wake me up."

Nadine sat in the bathtub until the water turned cold. Even that didn't get her going. It was like sixteen years worth of fatigue came down on her all at once. She didn't have the strength to get out of the tub.

"Mama, you okay in there?" Jocelyn asked.

"I'll be out in a minute." Nadine got out of the tub and dried off, still feeling sluggish. She needed another eight hours of sleep. She threw on a housecoat and fixed some rice, scrambled eggs, and bacon. Usually, Nadine was famished in the morning but not today. She just wanted to crawl back into bed. It was Jocelyn's turn to clean up the kitchen so she went back upstairs and lay down.

The next thing she knew, Miz Lillian was ringing the doorbell. Nadine threw on a dress and brushed her hair. Miz Lillian looked at her strangely when she came downstairs. "Were you sleep this time of day?"

"I was just lying across the bed."

"You feeling okay?"

"Yes, ma'am, I'm fine. Would you like something to eat or drink before we get started?"

"I'll have some iced tea. Here, let me help you." Miz Lillian followed Nadine into the kitchen and got two glasses from the cabinet. "Pastor had a lovely service for Esther, didn't he?"

"Yes, ma'am. Everything was nice. Where's Mr. Mack?"

"He had to drop something off at his frat brother's house. He'll be back in about an hour. Why don't we take our tea to Esther's room and start sorting through her things."

Nadine wanted to get it over quickly but knew that Miz Lillian would have a story about every item and slow them down. It took them more than three hours to go through Miz Esther's clothes and jewelry. Miz Lillian claimed her mink coat, pearl earrings and necklace, and diamond earrings. She gave the gold wristwatch to Jocelyn and the charm bracelet to Salena.

Miz Lillian looked at all the things she had decided to keep and realized there was nothing but costume jewelry left for Nadine. She offered her the pearl earrings, but Nadine told her Miz Esther would want her to have all the pearl jewelry. Nadine lied and said there were some things on the what-not shelf that she would keep in memory of Miz Esther.

After everything was packed, Mr. Mack conveniently showed up and helped Nadine load her car. They said their goodbyes, and Nadine trudged back into the house and went into Miz Esther's room. She sprayed Lysol to get rid of the sickly, old lady smell. Next, she stripped the bed and rearranged the furniture.

"What are you doing, Mama?" Jocelyn asked as she and Salena entered the room.

"Turning this into your new bedroom."

Jocelyn looked horrified. "No, Mama. It's spooky in here."

"It won't even look like the same room after I finish painting and decorating."

"Grandma's ghost is going to get in the bed with you at night," Salena teased.

"Shut up, ain't no such things as ghosts."

"Stop it. When y'all get hungry, fix some sandwiches. We got enough food in there to last a week. I'll be upstairs."

When Nadine walked into her bedroom, she saw the clothes they had worn over the last two days on a chair. She made a pile for laundry and another one for the dry cleaners. She went to Cyrus's closet and saw two dirty suits rolled up on the floor. When she stooped to pick them up, she discovered a manila envelope stuck between two shoeboxes.

Nadine opened it and read the documents. The first page was a bunch of legal mumbo jumbo about a petition for custody. She kept reading, flipping pages until she got to the last one. She sank to the floor. It felt like someone had knocked the wind out of her.

The papers said that Cyrus was seeking joint custody of the twins, Vicki and Victor Boyd, whom he fathered with Carrie Boyd last year. The shock of learning that the sad, young woman from the food bank had twins with her husband sent Nadine into a tailspin.

Nadine's pity for Carrie turned into hatred. She imagined Carrie and Cyrus playing house at out-of-the-way motels. Who else knew about the babies? Miz Esther? Miz Lillian? Did Cyrus plan to tell her about them?

She put the papers back where she found them, hoping they would still be there if she needed to get her hands on them again. Nadine sat on the bed so deep into her feelings that she didn't hear Cyrus coming up the stairs. It startled her when he opened the door.

"Why are you jumpy?" he asked, shutting the door.

"I didn't know anybody else was up here."

"Listen up." He rested his elbow on the chest of drawers and stuck a hand in his pocket. "I'm going to file for divorce."

That didn't surprise Nadine, considering Miz Esther was no longer there to stop him. Nor did she care because she was planning to leave him when she got her first paycheck.

"I've found a job in New York, and I'll be moving in a few weeks." He paused. "I plan to take Jocelyn with me."

"What?" Nadine jumped up. "You can't take Jocelyn. Do whatever you like, but she's staying here."

"I'm going to enroll her in a boarding school in upstate New York. I want to be near her to monitor the lupus. You and Salena can stay in the house. I'll take care of everything so you don't have to work."

Nadine was livid. She got close to Cyrus and pointed her finger in his face. "You think you can just come in here and proclaim that you're taking my child? You must be out of your mind."

"She's better off with me. You either do as I say or else."

"Or else what?"

"Go live in the projects, I guess," he said shrugging. "I'm not going to give you any money, and you can't stay in this house unless Jocelyn goes with me."

"You don't have the right to take Jocelyn. I'm her mama," she cried. She grabbed his arm and pleaded, "Don't do this, please, Cyrus. Even Miz Esther wouldn't agree with you breaking us up."

"Don't bring Mama into this," he yelled. "I'm Jocelyn's father. I know what's best for her."

"You're not getting away with this," she said.

"What are you going to do, Nadine?" He eyed her with disdain. "Just what I thought. Nothing. Take the money and house, and go on with your life. I'm trying to do right by you."

"Do right by me?" she screamed hysterically. "How's that doing right by me? You're the reason my life has been hell for sixteen years. First, you rape me and get me pregnant. Then, I was forced to be a slave to you and your mammy. You didn't give a damn about what I felt or what I needed, and now you're stealing my child. You never did right by me. You call yourself a father. What kind of man separates his children? All you think about is what you want. Well, you ain't getting my child. Now, get out!"

"This is still my house. You can't tell me when to leave. I'll stay as long as I please."

"No, you won't. Both of us ain't sleeping under the same roof another night." Nadine was in a rage. She walked toward him and began pushing him toward the door.

He shoved back.

Nadine ran over to the bed and grabbed the gun under the mattress. She walked toward him with it aimed at his head. She wanted to blow him to smithereens.

This time, he backed up. "Put down that gun, Nadine, before somebody gets hurt."

"I'll shoot if you don't get out," she said. "Don't make me do it."

"I don't know what's gotten into you, but you better put that gun away. I bet this is some more of Lydia's influence. She's got you acting common."

"No, Cyrus, Lydia ain't to blame. You are. I'm sick and tired of you treating me like a dog. You want everybody to think you're such a good husband and father, but people know about you. Your college degrees haven't made you no better than nobody else. You ain't nothing but a low-class nigga in a silk suit, trying to act like a white man. Too bad Miz Esther didn't let you get a divorce the first time you asked her. Me and the girls would've been better off."

"I'm leaving, but I'll be back later to get my clothes," Cyrus said.

"No, you ain't coming back here. Take what you want now because I'm changing the locks first thing tomorrow morning. You ain't welcome here."

Nadine went to the kitchen to think about what she was going to do next. She needed to talk to Carrie Boyd. She remembered seeing the address of where Carrie worked on the legal papers. That would be her first stop when she got off work tomorrow.

Chapter Thirty-Nine

~

Aretha Franklin's new single "Think" blared on the radio as Cyrus pressed the accelerator to the floor of his Thunderbird. He gripped the steering wheel, driving fast and furiously down dark, deserted Highway 51, daring a state trooper to stop him. He would slice the throat of any cracker who crossed him tonight with one of his surgical instruments.

The fight with Nadine had been worse than he anticipated. The crazed look in her eye when she pulled out the gun convinced him that she would use it if she felt threatened. He thought about wrestling it away from her but didn't want to get shot or shoot her by accident. She wasn't worth the humiliation of being hauled down to the police station, fingerprinted, and thrown into a cell with a bunch of degenerates.

He didn't have to worry about his reputation and social standing now that he was leaving Memphis. He lamented the fact that things were never the same with the Commodores after he lost the election. The members were polite, but it was obvious that he was no longer part of the inner circle. He still had some unfinished business with Judge Jacobs though.

Cyrus couldn't wait to get away from the backward people and their plantation mentality. Colored and whites alike. He was finally free to divorce Nadine and put this hick town in the rearview mirror.

He would wait until Nadine cooled off before bringing up the subject of taking Jocelyn with him. The next time, he would offer Nadine more money and promise visits from Jocelyn on holidays and in the summer. Satisfied with his plan, Cyrus relaxed his grip on the steering wheel, checked his rearview mirror, and made a U-turn.

***

Cyrus sat in Aunt Lillian's living room talking about his plans for a new life in New York City. She listened, nodding occasionally. When she failed to play devil's advocate as she often did with him, he realized something was wrong. "Auntie, are you okay?"

"I'm feeling a little down," she said. "I've lost my sister and best friend. And now you're telling me that you're moving away."

Cyrus walked over to Aunt Lillian and put an arm around her. "Auntie, I'm sorry. I didn't mean to upset you."

She raised her hand. "Don't worry about me," she said. "Time will take care of everything. I know you young people have to live your own life."

"And that's the whole point. I can't live a full life here because Jim Crow is always on my back."

"Cyrus, I don't doubt things have been hard on you, but if you don't stay here and fight for your rights, who'll do it? Look at the young people coming behind you. You're paving the way for them."

"I can't be worried about them. I've got to think about what's best for me. They've got to fight their own battles."

Aunt Lillian threw up her hands. "I'm glad Esther isn't here to hear you talk like this," she said. "All that Dr. King and the civil rights workers went through, and you just want to turn tail and run when the going gets a little tough."

"No, no, Auntie," he said. "It's more than that. I've got plans that

Memphis isn't ready for because Negroes and whites are divided."

"You've got to be patient, son. Things are going to change."

"I don't have time," he said.

Aunt Lillian tapped the arm of the sofa, trying to keep from losing her temper. "Tell me why you're separating your daughters. Divorcing Nadine is one thing, but taking Jocelyn with you is just plain wrong."

"Here's the thing, Auntie. She'll have better medical care up there. And she'll be going to one of the best private schools in the country."

"She'll be growing up without her family, surrounded by white people," Aunt Lillian pointed out. "That's going to be hard on her."

"It will make her stronger. Trust me, Jocelyn will be fine."

"I bet Esther is turning over in her grave listening to you talk like this," Aunt Lillian said sadly. "I'm going to turn in. Good night."

"Good night, Auntie. We'll talk some more in the morning."

***

Cyrus had rehearsed what he was going to say to Mamie all day. He fumbled with his key ring waiting for her sultry voice to come on the line. He checked his watch. It was a little after seven o'clock.

After several rings, he hung up and turned on the radio. He returned journals to the bookcase and looked at his calendar for the next few days. Half an hour later, he switched off the radio and called Mamie again. She picked up this time.

"Hello, beautiful," he said.

"Hi."

Cyrus removed his lab coat and leaned back in the chair. "It's good to hear your voice. These last few days have been rough with Mama's funeral and all. I wish you had been here."

"I can't imagine what you're going through," Mamie said softly. "It'll get better each day. The best thing to do is allow yourself time to mourn. If you feel like crying, do it."

"I'll remember that. I called earlier but didn't get an answer. Were you out with friends?"

"I was out with *a* friend tonight."

"Anybody I know?"

"I doubt it."

Cyrus walked over to the bookcase. He was nervous about Mamie's reaction to what he was about to say. "Mamie, I know that you were expecting things to move a little faster than they have…"

"Cyrus, let's not talk about that tonight. We can discuss it some other time when you're up to it."

"It's done," Cyrus blurted out. "I'm getting a divorce. There's nothing standing in the way of me ending my marriage now. I've already told Nadine." He switched the phone to his other ear. "I'm planning to move to New York, and I'd like for you to come with me."

"I really didn't want to discuss this now but since you insist." She paused. "Cyrus, hearing you say, 'I'm getting a divorce' isn't the same as 'I'm a free man.' As far as I'm concerned, you're still married until the judge signs the divorce papers."

"I've moved out, Mamie," he said. "The divorce will be quick. I promise."

"I can't build my life on promises. Besides, I can't move now anyway. Daddy has given me more responsibility at the funeral home. I'm finally getting a chance to run part of the business."

"Is that what you want to do for the rest of our life? That's no kind of life for a woman like you."

"Are you kidding?" Mamie asked. "There's a lot of potential here. I have all these ideas for bringing in more business."

"You gave me the impression that you wanted to be a doctor's wife.

My wife. You can't do both if you're staying there."

"How long did you expect me to wait for you, Cyrus? We've been talking almost a year. I'm sick and tired of hearing about what you're *going* to do. So, let me tell you what I *am* doing. And that's moving on with my life."

"Just be patient a little while longer, Mamie," he begged. "I'll send you a copy of the divorce papers."

"That doesn't mean anything to me at this point. I'm sorry, but I'm no longer interested in pursuing a relationship with you."

"You don't really mean that. How——"

"I'm going to say goodbye now."

"Mamie, don't hang up."

But she did.

***

After the Commodores meeting, Cyrus stayed for the social hour so that he could talk to Judge Jacobs. He finally got a chance when Jacobs stepped out on the balcony to smoke a cigar.

"Your Honor, the candidate you brought in tonight was excellent," Cyrus said with a pat on the back. "I'm sure the body will endorse him for City Council."

The judge took two puffs and removed the cigar from his mouth. "He's just what Memphis needs, someone who is young, forward-thinking, and not afraid to roll around in the dirt if necessary."

Cyrus had no intention of listening to Jacobs get on his soapbox about politics. He cut the small talk short and got straight to the point.

"Judge, I need your help."

Jacobs gave Cyrus his attention. "What can I do for you?"

"My wife and I are getting a divorce. I want full custody of my oldest daughter, but my wife is fighting me. Can you pull some strings and get me in front of a judge who will rule in my favor?"

Jacobs took a puff and blew the pungent smoke over his shoulder. "I'm sorry to hear that your marriage is breaking up, but I'm in Juvenile Court not Family Court."

"But you know some judges over there, don't you?" Cyrus asked.

"I don't know any of those white boys well enough to ask for a favor like that. If I go to the wrong one, and someone reports me, then I'm in trouble."

"I'd be willing to make a sizable donation, like the one I gave you for the election that you didn't help me win," he said with a piercing gaze.

"I wouldn't go throwing my money around if I were you. That could land you in jail on bribery charges," Jacobs warned.

"You're telling me there's nothing you can do," Cyrus said, raising his voice.

"I'm afraid not," Jacobs said. "Do you have a good lawyer?"

"I do, but I need a sure win."

Jacobs stubbed out his cigar and flicked it over the balcony. "I wish I could do more, but I can't risk my career over your divorce. Good night, son. Good luck."

The judge offered his hand, but Cyrus considered the gesture meaningless and turned his back. After Jacobs left, Cyrus stayed on the balcony, looking at the bright city lights, which never seem to shine on him.

Chapter Forty

~

C arrie had a terrible hangover the morning after her date with Cleary.
It felt like a hundred woodpeckers were inside her head, drilling
to the core of her brain. "God, how much did I drink last night? I don't
want to see any more liquor for a long time." She pushed herself up in
bed, checking the clock as her feet touched the floor. "Twelve-thirty? This
clock ain't right."

Carrie searched the nightstand for her watch before realizing it was
still on her wrist. It *was* twelve-thirty. Too late for church.

She caught a glimpse of herself on the way to the bathroom. She
looked like a two-dollar whore with makeup smeared and hair matted.
She shook her head in disgust. After she relieved herself, she took two
aspirin and some Pepto-Bismol. She was glad Miz Lula and Miz Ida Mae
weren't home to see her looking like this.

Carrie curled up in bed and waited for the medicine to take effect but
couldn't get comfortable because the room was hot. She turned off the
fan and plugged in the air conditioner. She was so sweaty that her nylon
slip clung to her body. When she got up to change clothes, she felt sick
and ran to the bathroom to throw up.

Afterward, Carrie washed her face, brushed her teeth, and got back in
the bed. As she rested her head on the pillow, she remembered what happened last night. The club hopping. The slow dancing. Cleary's erection.

Kissing. His angry words.

She didn't blame him for being mad at her. She was upset with herself, not to mention confused about her feelings. True, she had used Cleary to get out of the house and have some fun, but she wasn't pretending when she kissed him.

Carrie felt warm and secure in Cleary's arms. With Bob, she was always jittery and scared. She trusted Cleary but not Bob. Cleary made her feel like she was on cloud nine, which is how she felt with Cyrus.

That thought made her shoot upright, further aggravating her headache. Carrie lined them up side by side, making comparisons. Finally, she lay down, confident that her attraction to Cleary had nothing to do with Cyrus.

She thought about everything that had happened between them from the day they met. Whenever she ran into a problem, got homesick, or felt insecure, she turned to Cleary for comfort.

It hadn't occurred to her until now that he was the solid rock Ruth said she needed in her life. She liked Cleary a lot. It was time to stop running from him. She gave Cleary a call.

"Hello."

"It's me, Carrie. You busy?"

"What you need now?" he said impatiently.

"About last night, I know you think I was using you, but that wasn't the case."

"Could've fool me. I thought maybe you went out with me to make Jew Bob or somebody else jealous."

"Like I told you before, Bob and me just friends. That's all. Besides, he won't be at the paper much longer 'cause he looking for another job."

"What you want from me?"

"I know I messed up. I'm sorry for being wishy-washy. I was wondering if it's too late for us."

"You mean us being in a romantic relationship?" Cleary asked.

"Yeah, I think I'm ready."

"Think? I want you to be sure 'cause I don't want to be wasting my time with you if you're not."

"I'm sure," she said.

"It took you long enough, woman," Cleary joked. "Let's go celebrate. I'll come and pick you up."

"Not right now, Cleary. I woke up with a bad hangover. What did you put in my glass?"

"I had the root lady whip me up some stuff that I snuck in your drink when you went to the restroom."

"Ah-ha! That's why I was acting like that last night."

"No, baby, you acted that way 'cause you wanted me but was too scared to accept what I had to offer. Ain't no reason to be scared. I won't hurt you."

"I believe you, Cleary."

"Get some sleep and call me when you wake up. If you don't want to go out, I can pick up some food, and you can come over here and watch TV."

"That sounds good. I'll call you when I wake up."

"Okay, see you later."

Carrie laughed out loud after she hung up. Finally, she had found the right man. Things were looking up all the way around.

***

Carrie hated Mondays. There was a ton of mail to open, and the phones rang constantly. Today was no exception. She was playing catch-up from the minute she punched in. The phone on her desk rang again. It was the receptionist.

"There's a lady in the lobby who has an envelope for you," she told Carrie.

"I'll be right down." Carrie thought it was someone with a news release. When she got to the lobby, she found Nadine waiting for her. By the scowl on her face, this wasn't a social visit. Carrie panicked but looked poised. "Hello, Nadine," she said in her professional voice. "I'm surprised to see you here. How can I help you?"

"Is there some place we can talk in private?" Nadine said in a businesslike tone.

"What is this about?"

"I don't think you want me discussing it right here," she said, looking at the receptionist.

Carrie glanced at her watch. "I can take my break now. Let's go to the cafeteria." They got on the elevator with three other people and rode in silence. Carrie felt queasy, and her cheeks were flushed. She wiped the perspiration off her forehead with the back of her hand.

When they got to the cafeteria, Carrie led Nadine to a table in the corner. As soon as they sat down, Nadine blurted out, "I know about you, Cyrus, and the babies."

"I don't know what you're talking about," Carrie said with a straight face, even though her heart was beating rapidly.

Nadine opened her purse and took out the documents she found in the closet. She placed them in front of Carrie. "I guess these papers are a lie."

"I don't know nothing about those papers," Carrie insisted, refusing to look at them. "You got me confused with somebody else."

Nadine moved closer to Carrie. "Look, I don't give a damn if you're whoring around with Cyrus. You can have him, but you can't take my daughter to New York."

"What? I ain't moving nowhere with him," Carrie said.

"Stop playing dumb. It's all right here," Nadine said, tapping the papers. "Cyrus wants his name on their birth certificate and joint custody. And he told me that he's leaving Memphis."

Carrie slowly opened the papers and read them. "I don't know anything about this custody business," she said angrily. "He ain't got no right to be asking for nothing."

"Why doesn't he? Aren't they his children?"

Carrie looked down at her shaky hands. She never expected to have this conversation with Nadine. She couldn't look her in the face and lie.

"Nadine, this happened a long time ago. I was young, had just moved up here from Mississippi, and Cyrus took advantage of me."

"Yeah, right," Nadine snorted. "You saw doctor in front of his name and thought you had hit the jackpot. Did you honestly think he would leave me and marry you?"

Carrie shook her head. "I don't know what I was thinking. I made a big mistake. When I realized it, I stopped fooling with him."

Nadine was skeptical. "So, you're saying that he's not moving to New York with you?"

"No, I swear to God. I have a boyfriend who works in this building. You can go to the security desk at the side entrance and ask him. His name is Cleary Pollard. I'm planning to bring my son and daughter up here at the end of the summer, but Cyrus don't know anything about that. I don't even talk to him."

"If what you're saying is true, then you've got a problem, too."

"I don't know why he's interested in the babies all of sudden," Carrie sighed.

"Who knew about them?"

Carrie lowered her head in shame. "Miz Lillian did, but I don't know about Miz Esther."

"So, I *am* the last one to know?" When Nadine snatched the papers from the table, Carrie's hands flew up to shield her face. "Stupid girl, I wasn't going to hit you, but you need your yella tail whipped for taking up with a married man," Nadine said as she stuffed the papers in her handbag.

Nadine glowered at Carrie, trying to determine whether she was telling the truth. Carrie seemed genuinely sorry and apparently detested Cyrus as much as she did. Nadine gave Carrie the benefit of the doubt, hoping that her instincts were right.

"Look, you got twice as much to lose as I have." She put her purse on the table and scooted closer. "I'm going to get a lawyer to keep Cyrus from taking my daughter to New York. Would you be willing to tell the judge all about you and him, and the twins?"

Carrie blinked several times. "You want me to testify?"

"Yeah," Nadine said. "I've got to prove that Cyrus is a lowdown dirty dog who ain't fit to take care of a child."

"I don't know," Carrie said. "How will that help me?"

Nadine wasn't sure how bright Carrie was and slowly explained the plan. "It's simple. You stand up for me, and my lawyer will handle your case."

"But I can't afford a lawyer. I've been saving up to bring my children here."

"Don't worry about that. I'll take care of it."

Carrie was silent for several seconds and finally said, "Okay, I'll do it."

"Good," Nadine said.

They exchanged phone numbers.

"I'm really sorry, Nadine. I hope you'll find it in your heart to forgive me."

"Really?" Nadine said, glaring at her. "Right now, the only thing I'm concerned about is keeping Cyrus from taking my daughter."

Chapter Forty-One

~

After she left the cafeteria, Nadine felt sick to her stomach for conspiring with Cyrus's mistress but realized there was no other way to stop him. Finally, he would get his comeuppance and know how it felt to lose something precious.

The thought of Jocelyn being taken from her had unleashed a fierceness in Nadine that she didn't know existed. She was like a lion protecting its cubs.

Nadine was willing to do anything to keep Jocelyn from experiencing what she felt growing up without a mother. There was no one there when she came home from school. No one to share girl stuff. No one to fuss over her prom night. Aunt Bessie Mae was a good substitute, but it wasn't the same as having a mother.

Her biggest fear was losing control over Jocelyn if Cyrus took her away. She would come back a stranger, an independent young woman used to making her own decisions Without her around, Nadine worried that Cyrus would mold Jocelyn into another Miz Esther.

***

Nadine did a little dance after she dropped off Miz Esther's clothes at the Goodwill. She looked forward to taking down the dark green drapes and hanging a bright pair of curtains at the window. Every day, she came home and did a little more work in Miz Esther's room.

By Friday, she had almost finished turning Miz Esther's sick room into Jocelyn's new bedroom. It had a fresh coat of greenish-yellow paint, new curtains, and matching bedspread. Miz Esther's old bed, dresser, and wardrobe were on the back porch waiting to be hauled away.

Nadine took the girls out for hamburgers to celebrate the end of the first week on their own. They stopped by the drugstore to buy magazines and nail polish. Nadine was in a good mood until she came home and found Cyrus sitting on the front porch with a manila envelope. He walked to the curb to greet them.

"Where have y'all been this time of night?"

Nadine ignored him.

"Hi, Daddy," Salena said.

"Hey, Daddy," Jocelyn said. "We went to get some hamburgers."

"And I got a double chocolate milkshake," Salena added.

Cyrus followed them into the house and spent a few minutes talking to the girls in the living room before telling Salena to get her mother. Nadine didn't know what Cyrus was up to, but she wasn't in the mood to fight with him. He led the way into the kitchen and motioned for her to sit.

"I need you to sign the divorce papers," he said, passing her several sheets of paper. "I'm giving you child support and twice as much as required in alimony. I'll have sole custody of Jocelyn, and she'll come home for holidays and the summer."

Nadine didn't touch the papers. Instead, she got a sheet of paper and an ink pen from the cabinet drawer.

"What are you doing?" Cyrus asked.

After she finished writing, she gave the paper to Cyrus. "This is the name, address, and phone number of my lawyer. He'll be glad to look over whatever you're proposing."

"You got a lawyer? How can you afford one, you don't have any money?"

Nadine crossed her arms. "He said that since you are the breadwinner that you'll pay his fees."

"That's ridiculous. I know all the colored lawyers in town, and none of them would accept this case. If you think I'm going to pay your legal bills, you're crazy."

"Who said he was colored?" Nadine said smugly. "He's Jewish. The first thing I asked him was if he knew you, and he said no."

"So what, you got a Jewish lawyer. You still can't win."

Nadine poured herself a glass of cherry Kool-Aid and sat at the table. She was amazingly calm and enjoyed this exchange with Cyrus. "He seems to think so. You know what he told me? He said you can't take our child out of state without my permission. And he said that since Jocelyn is a teenager that the judge will probably ask her who she wants to live with. If I had to guess, I'd say Jocelyn would rather stay here with me and Salena than go to New York. My lawyer said if there was a history of abuse that the judge would definitely rule in my favor. You do remember that incident when you slapped Jocelyn, busted my eardrum, and Miz Esther had to call the doctor?"

Cyrus began breathing heavily. He clenched the table. "I make all the money. I'd be the better parent. Any judge would see that she would be better off living with me."

Nadine got up from the table and stood in front of Cyrus. "You're a whore, Cyrus. You were never a good father. You treated the girls like they were your possessions, the same way you treated me. No judge in his right mind would give custody to a grown man who had babies by a teenage girl and abandoned her."

Cyrus was startled when Nadine mentioned Carrie and the twins.

"Where did you hear that? Gossip from the beauty salon? Oh, I know. Lydia."

"It doesn't matter. The fact remains that I know all about Carrie Boyd and your babies. She'd be willing to tell the judge all about your little affair. After a judge hears her story, you'll look like a fool for making any demands. My lawyer described me as, what did he say? Oh yes, 'the long suffering wife.' If you don't want your private life to come out in court, you'd better not mention anything about taking Jocelyn to New York in the divorce."

Cyrus put the papers back in the envelope. "You think you got the upper hand because you hired a lawyer?" he snorted. "Don't start celebrating yet."

"In due time, Dr. Mitchell. And my lawyer said you can't just show up here anytime you want since you moved out. Next time, call before coming over here."

"I'll see you in court," he said on his way out of the kitchen.

"I'm looking forward to it," Nadine responded. "By the way, I got that Jewish lawyer's name from Lydia. She said he did a real good job for her when she divorced her last husband."

"Bitch," he uttered.

Nadine didn't know if that was meant for her or Lydia. After Cyrus left, Jocelyn and Salena came into the kitchen, both distraught.

"Mama, please don't let Daddy take me to New York," Jocelyn said. "I don't want to leave all my friends and have to go to a new school."

"Jocelyn, were you eavesdropping on grown folks' conversation? You know better."

Her lip quivered as she spoke to her mother. "You treat me like a baby and won't tell me anything."

"What's going to happen to me?" Salena asked tearfully.

Nadine motioned for them to sit at the table. "Girls, I'm sorry you had to hear us going back and forth like that, but like I told you when your daddy left, we're going to work things out. Don't worry."

"I don't understand why he wants to take me away," Jocelyn said.

Nadine saw the fear in Jocelyn's eyes and tried to reassure her. "Honey, your daddy thinks the schools and the doctors are better in New York, but he's wrong." Nadine reached for their hands. "Nobody's going anywhere. We're all staying right here."

"You promise, Mama?" Jocelyn asked.

"Cross my heart," she said, making a sign on her chest.

After the girls went to bed, Nadine decided it was time she made up with Willie Lee. She hadn't spoken to him since they argued in the parking lot two weeks ago. She was ready to tell him how she wanted their life to move forward.

He answered the phone in his crisp business tone but softened up when he found out it was Nadine. "I've been praying you would call," he said.

"You've been on my mind, too. I thought about everything you said, and I believe you really didn't know she was coming. I just wish you had told me up front. We've got to be honest with each other," she said.

"I know that now."

"There's something else I need to tell you. We can't see each other for a while. I don't want to risk Cyrus finding out about us and using that against me in court."

"How long will the divorce take?" he asked, his voice full of emotion.

"About three months."

"I'll wait as long as it takes," he said. "Just promise that you'll come back to me."

Tears welled in her eyes. "I will."

Chapter Forty-Two

~

Cyrus woke up a little after six o'clock, made himself a pot of coffee, and sat at Aunt Lillian's kitchen table, making a list of things he needed to do before moving to New York. It turned out to be a short list because he wasn't packing up a house and moving the entire family. He estimated that it would take another week to put the rest of his affairs in order.

His practice would be taken over by a young doctor he had interviewed for partner. He was from Birmingham and knew the ways of the South. Cyrus was confident that his patients would be in good hands.

Cyrus looked around the kitchen and remembered all the good times he and Miz Esther had in this house. It was his second home. Cyrus's departure would leave a void in Aunt Lillian's and Uncle Mack's life because he was like a son to them.

Aunt Lillian would be happy to know that he had decided to leave Jocelyn behind. His lawyer advised him that it would be a long, bitter fight that he would probably lose in the end. Cyrus would have taken his chances and fought for Jocelyn if he hadn't been pressed for time.

Confident that he had resolved those issues, Cyrus focused on his problems with Carrie. He set the coffee cup down and rubbed the stubble on his chin. He wanted to meet his son and daughter before he left for New York but knew that wasn't going to happen. All the pleadings and threats hadn't softened her one bit. He also worried that Nadine's lawyer might have advised Carrie not to talk to him.

If he had more time, Cyrus was sure that he could make Carrie come around. The only way to get what he wanted was to somehow gain Carrie's trust again. Dropping the petition for custody and voluntarily giving her child support with no strings attached might persuade her that he was a changed man.

He walked over to the buffet and retrieved Aunt Lillian's fancy stationery. Cyrus spent a few minutes thinking about what to say in the letter. He didn't want to sound too sappy or too terse. He jotted down a few sentences and slipped the letter and money into an envelope.

***

Cyrus made one last trip to Beale Street to say goodbye to Sonny. When he pushed the door handle, the glass rattled, jarring Sonny from a nap in one of the booths. "Are you sleeping on the job, man?"

Sonny closed the centerfold of *Jet* and broke into a wide smile. "I'm guilty. I was catching a few winks before it got busy."

Cyrus strolled over to the bar. Sonny got a bottle and filled two glasses with whiskey. "Things back to normal down here?" Cyrus asked.

Sonny took a swig. "It won't be normal 'til all these stores open back up," he said. He took a toothpick from a ceramic cornstalk figurine and stuck it in his mouth. "How you keeping?"

"Okay," Cyrus said, swirling the glass of liquor. "I'm heading up to New York next week."

Sonny raised an eyebrow. "Oh, yeah?"

"I got a job lined up and everything."

"I'm sorry to see you go, son."

"With Miz Esther gone, I don't see any reason to stick around."

"You got your wife and girls with you, you'll be all right up there."

"They're not going."

Sonny removed the toothpick. "What you mean? They're coming later?"

"They're not going at all. I'm getting a divorce, starting fresh." Cyrus raised his glass. "Here's to a new beginning." He touched his glass with Sonny's, and they downed their drinks.

Sonny put his glass on the counter and stuck the toothpick back in his mouth. "I didn't see that one coming. A divorce? And y'all got them two pretty girls."

"It's all for the better," Cyrus assured him. "My family will be taken care of. Don't worry."

"I know you'll make sure they got everything they need. It's just that I hate seeing a beautiful family fall apart. Y'all reminded me of those white families in *Life* magazine."

Cyrus pshawed, refusing to let Sonny make him feel guilty. "Yeah, but it wasn't anything like that. We had a lot of problems from day one."

"Everybody got problems. Ain't nothing perfect."

"Don't even try talking me into staying with her," Cyrus said. "It's over."

"No, I ain't trying to do that."

"Good," Cyrus said, slapping the counter.

Sonny spread his arms and gripped the edge of the bar. "But does it make sense to leave your family and move way up there?"

"I got to do it, Sonny. It's the only way I'm going to get ahead. Besides, they don't want to go."

"Just remember what I told you: The grass ain't always greener on the other side."

"I know," Cyrus said, "but it's got to be better than here."

"The colored newspaper say things are gonna get better for us. You may want to stick around and see what happens."

"Don't hold your breath," Cyrus said. He opened his wallet, peeled off five twenty-dollar bills, and laid them on the counter. "Sonny, thanks for being you. I appreciate everything you've done."

"It's 'bout time you paid for a drink," Sonny said. "By my calculation, you owe a lot more than that. I'll keep your tab running." He scooped up the glasses and put them in a pail under the bar.

Sonny didn't like goodbyes so Cyrus made it quick. "I'll see you when I see you," he said.

Sonny walked from behind the bar, and the two men embraced. "Take care of yourself, son. Give 'em hell in New York."

"I plan to," Cyrus said. When he got to the door, he looked back at Sonny, who pointed gun-like fingers at him. Cyrus returned the gesture. That had been their way of saying goodbye when he was a little boy.

Cyrus walked out into the night and took a last look at Beale Street. Despite what Sonny said, Cyrus knew change would be a long time coming. He spotted a pay phone on the corner and walked over to make a call.

"Hey, baby," he said. "It's me."

"You coming by tonight?" she asked.

"No, I need to turn in early." He switched ears with the receiver and continued, "What did you decide?"

"W-e-l-l," she said slowly.

"Well what?"

"I'm going with you. My manager said it wouldn't be a problem getting a week off, and my mother is going to look after my son."

Cyrus leaned against the phone booth, happy that he wouldn't have to make the trip alone. He needed a woman to help him get settled. Cozette would handle his business like a top-notch executive secretary. "New York, here we come," he said.

"I can't wait to see the fine stores and elegant restaurants you talk about."

"And I'm taking you to a supper club and the theater."

"My, my, you're going to spoil me," Cozette said.

"You'll earn your keep. In fact, I just might not let you come back to Memphis."

Chapter Forty-Three

~

Cleary rearranged the packages in the trunk and peered over the lid to see if Carrie was coming out of the house. He walked to the front door and yelled, "Carrie, come on. We're gonna be late getting on the road if you don't hurry up. I don't think you need to take all the toys. Why don't you leave some behind so they can be surprised when they get here."

Carrie walked onto the front porch holding an armful of toys. "You're right. I'll just take a doll and a truck. Or should I take the teddy bears? Aren't they cute?"

"Okay, bring them, too, but let's go." Carrie ran back into the house and got the bears. She threw them on the backseat with the other packages. Carrie had bought everyone in her family a gift with the money that she would have spent on a bus ticket to Hattiesburg.

Cleary volunteered to drive her home to pick up her children and refused to accept gas money. Instead, he told her to spend it on her family. Carrie blew fifty dollars at Shainberg's department store. She was so excited about going home that she could hardly contain herself.

Miz Lula had packed them a big lunch, and she took the bag out to the car.

"Young man, don't drive too fast 'cause you know the state troopers looking to stop colored folks for any little thing," she warned. "Y'all don't need to stop for nothing but gas and the restroom 'cause I fixed plenty food."

"Yes, ma'am. I'll be careful," Cleary said.

"Carrie, call me when you get there. Remember, let the phone ring twice and hang up. I'll know it's you calling."

"Yes, ma'am," Carrie said smiling. "We'll be back day after tomorrow."

When Cleary drove off, Carrie said, "I can't believe I'm finally going home to pick up my babies. I can't wait to see everybody. You'll love Vicki and Victor. They're the sweetest babies, and I'd say that even if they weren't mine."

"If they take after their mama, I know they're sweet," Cleary said.

Carrie opened her purse and took out some mail that she didn't have time to open at work. There were two announcements about meetings coming up next month. The third letter had a return address and handwriting that she recognized right away.

August 26, 1968

Dear Carrie,

I just wanted to let you know that I'm moving to New York soon, and I've decided not to ask a judge for joint custody. I'm really sorry for the way I've treated you and the twins. I hope that you'll be able to forgive me one day. Enclosed, you will find forty dollars, which I will send you each month to help take care of them. I would like a picture, which you can send to the address on the front of this envelope.

Sincerely,

Cyrus

Carrie read the letter again, thinking she had missed something. It was short and to the point. No demands or threats. "Humph." She put the letter in her purse.

"Who is that from?"

"My babies' daddy."

"What did he say?"

"He said that he was going to send me some money every month."

"That's all?"

"Yup, that's all."

"That's cool. He's supposed to take care of his children. He ain't trying to get back with you, is he?"

"No, ain't nothing like that. It's been over."

"Good, 'cause you know I'll crack a nigga over the head for messing with my woman."

"Stop being jealous," she said, slapping him on the arm.

Cleary pecked her on the cheek. "Now that I finally got you, I want to keep you all to myself."

"You always think somebody else want me. Well, I got news for you. Don't nobody want me but you."

"That suits me just fine. Now, tell me what your mama said when you told her I was driving you down."

"She said she was glad to be finally meeting you."

"Finally?" he asked surprised. "You told her 'bout me before?"

"Yeah, I wrote her a while back and told her I had met somebody nice at work."

"I'll be damned. All that time I thought you liked that white boy."

"No, I liked you all along, Cleary," Carrie said. "I was just afraid to admit it."

"Like me? Is that all?"

Carrie grinned. "It's more than just like."

"How much more?"

"Like a whole lot more."

"How much is a whole lot? Huh?"

"Drive, Cleary, and stop giving me the third-degree."

"I'm gonna have to drag it out of you, Carrie Boyd. You're a stubborn woman."

"I ain't."

"Oh, yes, you are."

Carrie kissed him on the cheek. "You're a good man, Cleary Pollard."

"And don't you forget it," he said, rubbing her thigh.

"I won't," Carrie said. "You're stuck with me."

Chapter Forty-Four

Nadine was in the front yard weeding the flower bed when she saw the mailman. She had expected the letter to come earlier in the week, but all she got was bills. She tried not to get too excited in case it didn't arrive today. There were five letters in the mailbox. Slowly, she read the name on each letter. The first two were for Cyrus. Then, she saw it.

She tore open the envelope and carefully read each page. She was officially divorced from Dr. Cyrus Mitchell. They would share custody of their daughters. Nadine closed her eyes and let the warm sunshine bathe her body, inhaling and exhaling deeply. She felt born again with a clean slate to control her own destiny.

She went inside and changed clothes. The girls were at the movies with Lydia and wouldn't be back until later in the day. Nadine called to make sure Willie Lee would be in his office.

As she stepped off the sidewalk, something in the air caught her eye. It was a black and orange striped butterfly. "Well, little butterfly, you came on a good day. I told the other one that I would be free one day. Today is the day."

Nadine sped over to Greenberg's, parked the car, and ran to Willie Lee's office. When he looked through the glass window and saw Nadine, he tripped over a cardboard box trying to get to the door.

"Willie Lee, my divorce is final. I'm free!" Nadine shouted as she embraced him.

"Welcome back, baby," he said, kissing her. "I've missed you so much. It's been torture seeing you come in here, and the only thing I could do was wave."

"I missed you, too," she said, tears dampening her cheeks. "I didn't think this day would ever come."

"I never gave up hope. We were meant to be together."

"I got a question for you?"

"Shoot."

"You got any fresh greens in the back?"

"Huh?"

"I'm fixing a special dinner for my business partner tomorrow. I want to impress him."

"I'm sure he'll be satisfied with anything you cook. He's easy to please."

Nadine cocked her head to the side. "I'm going to like that. It'll be a nice change."

Later that night, Nadine sat down at the kitchen table and wrote Frannie a letter.

September 15, 1968

Dear Frannie,

How are you doing? I am fine. It's been a long time since I wrote you a letter. I have so much to tell you. First, I got a divorce from Cyrus. Miz Esther passed away. Me and the girls are still living in the house but plan to move when I get married to Willie Lee Griffin. He went to high school with us and worked at Daddy's store. He was on the track team, and you had a crush on him. I know you're shocked, so let me start from the beginning and tell you how we met again...

Made in the USA
Columbia, SC
12 February 2018